Praise for the no

ALSO BY JACKIE LAU

The Stand-Up Groomsman
Donut Fall in Love

Love, Lies, and Cherry Pie

A Novel

JACKIE LAU

EMILY BESTLER BOOKS

ATRIA

NEW YORK LONDON TORONTO SYDNEY NEW DELHI

EMILY
BESTLER
BOOKS

ATRIA

An Imprint of Simon & Schuster, LLC
1230 Avenue of the Americas
New York, NY 10020

First Emily Bestler Books/Atria Paperback edition May 2024

EMILY BESTLER BOOKS/ATRIA PAPERBACK and colophon are trademarks of Simon & Schuster, LLC

Simon & Schuster: Celebrating 100 Years of Publishing in 2024

For information about special discounts for bulk purchases, please contact Simon & Schuster Special Sales at 1-866-506-1949 or business@simonandschuster.com.

The Simon & Schuster Speakers Bureau can bring authors to your live event. For more information or to book an event, contact the Simon & Schuster Speakers Bureau at 1-866-248-3049 or visit our website at www.simonspeakers.com.

Interior design by Esther Paradelo

Manufactured in the United States of America

1   3   5   7   9   10   8   6   4   2

Library of Congress Cataloging-in-Publication Data has been applied for.

ISBN 978-1-6680-3076-9
ISBN 978-1-6680-3077-6 (ebook)

For Mom

The Great
Mark Chan

1

—♡—

*"It is a truth universally acknowledged that a single woman
in her thirties—especially one with four married sisters—
must be in want of a wedding of her own, even if she claims
otherwise. And her family should do everything
in their power to secure a match for her."*

—My mother, probably

H ow old are you, Auntie Emily?" my little niece Scarlett demands.

I take a healthy swallow of my drink and crouch down in
my bridesmaid dress to get closer to her. Cocktail hour is in full
swing, and it's a bit loud in this small room at the banquet hall.
"I'm thirty-three."

"Thirty-three? That's so old!" She sounds positively horrified.
I guess being over thirty is incomprehensible to her. "You're not
married, are you?"

"No."

"You should get married so I can be a flower girl at your
wedding."

My littlest sister, Hannah, got married today, and Scarlett was
a flower girl, a role she enjoyed very much.

"I'll be sure to keep that in mind," I say.

I totally expected to get hassled about my marital status at

Hannah's wedding, seeing as I'm now the last single Hung sister; I just didn't expect it to come from a five-year-old.

Not only am I the last single one in the family, but I'm also the second oldest, which makes it even worse in everyone's eyes. I have three younger sisters who have now tied the knot. I'm *way* behind.

It's fine with me. It really is. Not because I'm against marriage, but because I have different priorities in my life. Dreams that are finally coming to fruition.

It is not, however, fine with my mother.

Mom and Allison—Scarlett's mother and my older sister—head toward us, glasses of wine in hand.

"Mommy," Scarlett says, "Auntie Emily is *thirty-three!*"

Allison chuckles. "And do you know what? I'm thirty-five."

Scarlett's mouth falls open.

Allison seems amused by this whole interaction. My big sister is often annoyed with me for one reason or another, but not today.

Mom is less amused. She takes my arm and leads me away, probably to meet some eligible bachelor.

"Can't you just enjoy the reception, rather than attempting more matchmaking?" I ask.

Mom clucks her tongue. "What would be the fun in that?"

Inwardly, I groan.

"A wedding is the perfect place to meet men," she says, steering us with ease through the crowds of people at the reception. "Ah, I see Mark Chan."

I stop walking. "Tell me you didn't."

"Didn't what?" Mom asks innocently.

"Invite Mark Chan to the wedding. It's not like he even knows Hannah."

"Why shouldn't I have invited Mark?" Mom asks. "His parents are friends of ours and he's an engineer who—"

"What does his profession have to do with why he should be at Hannah's wedding?"

It's a foolish question, of course. I know *exactly* what she's doing: she's extoling the virtues of the great Mark Chan because she wants me to date him and marry him and have his babies. He's here only so she can introduce the two of us.

My mother's matchmaking tendencies have hit a critical level since Hannah got engaged a year and a half ago. She's tried to throw me at many men, but Mark—oh, Mark is her favorite. Though she met his parents only a few years ago, they now play mahjong together on a regular basis. I think she's seen Mark once or twice, but from those brief encounters, she's somehow decided he's perfect for me.

I, on the other hand, am convinced that Mark is *not* perfect for me.

First of all, there's my previous experience with Mom's matchmaking. A few years ago, when I turned thirty and had no prospects for marriage, as she put it, she tried to set me up with a man named Alvin. Let me tell you, that's an experience I do not want to repeat. So, I'm more than a little suspicious of her judgment in this area.

Second, whenever Mom talks about Mark, her voice is full of excitement, but the words she says are another matter.

This is what I know about Mark Chan: he's a thirty-two-year-old computer engineer. (*He's so smart, Emily, and he makes plenty of money!*) He owns a condo. (*Once you get pregnant, he can sell it and you can buy a house together!*) He won an award for getting the highest mark in first-year calculus in university. (*And you were always so good at calculus too!*) He likes reading. (*Isn't that so perfect for you?*) He went to an all-boys private school. He won a big chess tournament when he was twelve.

Okay, fine. None of those things is completely terrible, but I'm sick of hearing about him, and I can't say he intrigues me at all.

And seeing him for the first time doesn't change my opinion.

Mom points to a man standing at the edge of the crowd, drink in one hand. With his other hand, he's reaching for a canapé. He looks utterly ordinary.

I suppose this is what I expected, even if my mother acts like he single-handedly stopped the polar ice caps from melting or ended child poverty in Canada. I . . .

OMG! Food!

It's been a very long day, and I haven't had enough to eat. By midnight—after the ten-course banquet and wedding cake—I'm sure I will have consumed eight thousand calories, give or take. But the banquet hasn't started yet, and I'm more than a little hungry. I saw a waiter walking by with canapés ten minutes ago, but by the time I hurried over, my uncle had claimed the last one.

Fortunately, this platter is full. I scurry over, grab two shrimp something-or-others and a napkin, murmur my thanks to the server, and begin stuffing food into my mouth.

"Hi. Emily, is it?" Mark says.

Ugh, I hate when people talk to me when my mouth is full of food. I feel pressured to chew as fast as possible.

"Yes," I say as soon as I swallow.

"You two seem to be getting along *so* well," Mom says. "I'll leave you to it."

Before I can comment on the ridiculousness of her statement—I've said a grand total of one word to Mark—she disappears into the crowd, and I hear her accepting congratulations that yet another of her daughters is married. Mom had nothing to do with this match, though; Hannah met her now husband when she was away at university.

As I finish eating my food, I examine Mark Chan. He's about five ten, and he has short black hair. Now that I see him up close, I concede he's better-looking than I initially thought, much to my annoyance. Not that I, personally, find him attractive, but I can see why someone would, even if his smile is rather bland.

"Hi," I say, since I haven't actually said that yet.

I shove the next canapé in my mouth, and in my rush to placate my growling stomach, I swallow it before I've finished chewing. A too-large piece of food scrapes my esophagus. (Is that the right word? I'm not the medical professional in my family.)

My eyes water.

"You okay?" Mark asks.

"Yep," I croak.

God, I can't believe I'm being such an idiot in front of Mark fucking Chan. Not because I have any interest in dating someone my mother thinks is suitable, but just the principle of it. When you meet a new person, you don't want to make a terrible impression, you know?

I gulp half my cocktail to wash down the food, but that proves to be a mistake. The drink is strong, and it makes me cough all the more. Tears blurring my vision, I manage to grab a glass of water from a server, and by some miracle, I don't choke and require Mark to perform the Heimlich maneuver. If he saved me, I would *definitely* have to go out with him, and Mom would never stop talking about how he rescued me, a fate in which I have exactly zero interest.

I look around the room, at all the people in their suits and dresses, here to celebrate my baby sister, then turn my attention back to Mark.

"So, uh." He scratches the back of his neck. "I hear you wrote a novel?"

Yes, I did. It's called *All Those Little Secrets*, and you can buy it at Indigo. It's my greatest accomplishment.

And I hate talking about it.

Not because I'm excessively humble, but for some reason, I find it weird to discuss, especially with people I don't know, *especially* sweater-vest-wearing men my mother wants me to date.

Okay, fine, he's not actually wearing a sweater-vest—he's decked out in a dark suit, appropriate for a wedding—but I imagine he'd wear one on a regular Saturday.

"What's it about?" he asks.

In theory, I know the answer to that question. I mean, I wrote the damn book. But in this moment, a succinct-yet-compelling answer escapes my mind.

"It's women's fiction. About secrets in immigrant families and . . . stuff."

Yep, I'm a writer. I'm great with words.

"Interesting," he says. "I've always wanted to . . ."

Oh God. He's going to tell me he's always wanted to write a novel but never found the time, and would I like to hear his brilliant idea? Then he might generously offer to split the royalties if I write the book, i.e., do all the hard work.

"Look," I say, "many people have told me—"

"Read more. I've always wanted to have time to read more fiction."

Oh.

"What did you think I was going to say?" he asks.

I shrug, and we stand there awkwardly in silence.

Of course, it isn't actually silent in this room. We're surrounded by crowds of people imbibing alcohol, and there's music in the background. But despite the noise, it's still uncomfortable that Mark and I aren't saying anything to each other.

See, Mom? Mark Chan and I have no chemistry.

I scramble to think of another topic, figuring I should make a few more minutes of polite conversation. Mom is probably watching us, and if I don't spend enough time talking to Mark, she'll come over and drag me back.

But Mark beats me to it. "I hear you like calculus?"

I don't *like* it, but I vaguely remember being *good* at it once upon a time. I've forgotten most of what I learned, though.

And why are we talking about calculus at a wedding?

"I haven't had to do calculus in years, thankfully," I say. "It's one of those things you learn in school, but who actually uses it in their work?"

"Well," he says, "one example—"

"It was a rhetorical question, Mark."

Of course I know some people use calculus at their jobs. Calculus teachers, for example. Just not baristas-slash-novelists. Though I do tutor a few hours a week, and I suppose it would be useful if I wanted to tutor more advanced math students, but I just do grades nine and ten now.

"I believe my parents said you have a degree in mathematics?" he says.

Did he really have to bring that up? It sounds like he's judging me for not putting my degree to good use, for no longer being a woman in STEM.

When I graduated, I worked for a software company for five years, and I'm certainly not getting into that whole story with him.

"Yes," I say shortly, in a tone suggesting the conversation should end here.

"What made you want to be a novelist instead?"

Ugh, what's with all the questions and that judgmental look on his face?

When I don't immediately provide an answer, he moves on to a more benign topic.

"It was a lovely ceremony," he says.

"Yes, it was."

Another awkward gap in the conversation.

I wonder if I've spent enough time with Mark to satisfy my mother, then shake my head at that foolish thought. Mom is *never* satisfied with me, and she won't be even a little satisfied with this situation until Mark has put a ring on my finger, which isn't happening.

I glance around the room to see if she's watching, but to my surprise, she's not—she's in conversation with Auntie Janie, who's probably relaying some juicy gossip.

Excellent. Time to make my escape.

"It was great to meet you," I lie, "after hearing so much about you." I try not to sound too sarcastic, even though this man has managed to hit on the worst conversational topics and is the opposite of my type.

"I've heard a lot about you too," he says.

Huh. I wonder whether his parents have made me sound amazing or merely desperate. I'm not sure I want to know the answer. I figure there's at least a 63.2 percent chance of it being the latter.

I give him a nod and a smile. "I see someone over there that I've got to, um, talk to. Later!"

Ugh, that sounded weird. Oh well.

As soon as I take a step back, he pulls out his phone. I bet he was eager for me to leave.

Turning away from Mark, I scan the room. My cousin is standing by a server holding more canapés. Perfect. I head in her direction, but before I can get there, Uncle Wayne and Auntie Sharon—old friends of my parents'—appear in front of me.

Oh no. I know exactly where this conversation is heading.

"Emily!" Uncle Wayne says. "So great to see Hannah married. Are you next?"

"Uh . . ."

"You didn't bring a date today, did you?" He makes a show of looking around.

"Nope, it's just me," I say with a smile, followed by a gulp of my drink.

"Been on any dates lately? You know, time only moves in

one direction. You're not going to get younger." He chuckles as though he's said something funny. "There are so many ways to meet people that didn't exist in my day. Apps, is that what they're called?"

The thing about Uncle Wayne is that he can carry on a conversation by himself with minimal response from anyone else.

Auntie Sharon puts a hand on his shoulder. "Don't rub it in," she says quietly to her husband. "It's probably tough for her." She shoots me a sympathetic look.

That's even worse than Wayne's questions. I don't need pity just because I'm a single woman in my thirties whose sisters are all married. I've got a decent life, and it's better to be single than have a crappy husband. It's the twenty-first century; it's not like I need a man to take care of me.

"Did you talk to that guy your mother wanted you to meet?" Uncle Wayne asks. "Mark Chan, I think?"

"I did." I try not to sound frustrated that I'm hearing about the great Mark Chan yet again. I've now met the man; he doesn't live up to his reputation.

After a few more minutes of conversation, I manage to escape. I head toward my father, who's eating a canapé. I grab some food for myself, and this time, I don't swallow wrong and choke, which I consider an improvement.

Seriously, I feel like I need to go back to toddler day care and learn how to eat properly.

"You doing okay?" he asks. "You look a little . . ." He gestures with his wineglass.

"I'm happy for Hannah." That isn't a lie. "And I'm hungry. I thought those pictures would never end." It was like they had to take photos with every combination of people in the family.

"Me too."

I've always been able to relax more around my father than around my mother. He doesn't comment on my single status or drag me off to meet eligible bachelors. Dealing with my mom just requires so much energy.

"Auntie Emily! Auntie Emily!" Scarlett runs over to me.

"What's up?" I crouch down to talk to her, hoping for some conversation about the food, rather than about my age.

"I found you a husband."

Oh God. My niece has already started matchmaking? She's only in kindergarten! Couldn't she at least wait until, I don't know, high school?

"Yeah?" I say. "Who?"

"That man over there."

It takes me a moment to figure out who she's pointing at. It's a man with gray hair who, if I remember correctly, is Hannah's father-in-law's older brother.

"Uh, he's too old for me."

Scarlett frowns. "But you're old, Auntie Emily. You're thirty-three."

And the man in question is, oh, I don't know, maybe sixty-three.

"I'll consider it," I say, hoping to put an end to this train of thought, and then we can talk about picture books or PAW *Patrol* or . . . something like that.

"Can you burp the alphabet?" she asks me earnestly. "This boy in my class, he can burp the alphabet."

Well, I suppose that's one way to change the conversation.

Scarlett scurries toward her father, and I head over to check the seating chart, seeing as we'll be heading to the dining area any minute now.

Oh, you've got to be fucking kidding me.

2

———♡———

"It is a truth universally acknowledged that a single young man who can actually afford to buy property in Toronto probably had help from his parents, even if he claims to be self-made . . . and he will look down upon those who haven't had his good fortune."

—My friend Paige, while drunk one night last year
(well, she didn't put it quite so eloquently,
but that was the general gist)

It's my baby sister's wedding, but I'm not sitting with the rest of my family.

I stand at the edge of the room as people take their seats in chairs covered in white fabric. My table is off to the back left, where Mark Chan is seated.

That's right. My mother has arranged for me to sit beside Mark fucking Chan, and since this banquet won't be short, we'll have lots of time to get acquainted with each other.

Just shoot me now.

Why can't I be allowed to enjoy my sister's wedding? Why does today also have to be about finding a husband for me?

"You're not sitting with your sisters?" Auntie Carmen—my mother's younger sister—comes up to me as I'm glaring at the back corner of the room.

"No. I'm supposed to sit beside the man my mother desperately wants me to date."

Auntie Carmen, more than anyone else, will understand my situation.

When I was a kid, I thought she was the coolest of my relatives. I had no idea what she did for a living, but she was single and traveled a lot and brought us gifts from around the world.

I also remember my grandmother harping on her single status and trying to set her up with men. Though at some point, Po Po decided it was a lost cause and stopped bothering.

I figure I have several more years before my mom gets to that point with me, and who knows? Maybe I'll actually get married in that time.

But if I do get married, it will *not* be to a man of my mother's choosing.

It will not be to a man who sets an alarm even on his days off, and who wears dress shirts and sweater-vests for fun. My last boyfriend was literally in a circus troupe, so no, Mark Chan really isn't the sort of man I usually date. I'm sure he'll make some person sufficiently happy, but that person isn't me, the family rebel. My sisters' professions are, in order: optometrist, pharmacist, pharmacist again, and engineer. I'm the thing that doesn't belong. Sure, Hannah was a little "wild" in high school—if you have a generous definition of that word—but now she's married at twenty-seven and has a good job.

"You know," Auntie Carmen says, "we could switch seats? I don't mind."

I nearly throw my arms around her—yes, I tend toward the dramatic at times—before approaching the table where she's supposed to sit. I don't think changing seats will cause too many complications. At these wedding banquets, guests aren't served individual meals chosen in advance; rather, for each of the many courses, a big platter of food is brought to each table and efficiently portioned out by the server.

But before I can sit down, I see my mother barreling toward me.

Yeah, I should have known I couldn't pull this off. My mom has five kids; she's used to keeping an eye on multiple situations at once, and she's not afraid of making a scene.

Sighing, I take my assigned seat.

I try to count my blessings. I really do.

For example: the food is delicious. The duck? Perfection.

Another example: although I'm seated next to Mark Chan, fortunately, I've been spared the indignity of also being at the same table as his parents. That's the only thing that would make this situation worse. But his parents are seated with other friends of my mother and father's—Mom insisted they all be invited to Hannah's wedding.

And lastly: the emcee is doing so much talking that I don't have a chance to make forced conversation with Mark.

Actually, I'm not sure that's really a blessing. The emcee isn't an entertaining stand-up comedian or some quasi-amusing uncle. No, it's one of Hannah's new husband's friends, who's drunk.

It's painful. Like off-pitch, loud singing that makes you cringe and cover your ears . . . except I can't do that because, you know, it's my littlest sister's wedding, and I have to behave myself. I'm an adult, after all.

Even though I've been an adult for fifteen years, sometimes it's still hard to believe.

As the servers begin bringing out the soup, the emcee finally decides he's tired of hearing his own voice, and I find myself looking at Mark and sharing a smile with him.

A strange quivery feeling passes through my body. How odd.

It's probably hunger.

He immediately looks away, takes out his phone, and starts texting, like he thinks he's too good to make conversation with me now. But he's the one who's texting at a wedding banquet! How rude. Private School Boy doesn't have great manners after all.

As his thumbs move over the screen, a notch appears between his eyebrows. I admit I'm curious to know who he's texting and what he's saying—I hope it isn't about me—but at least I'm not rude enough to look over his shoulder.

It takes two more courses before he deigns to speak to me.

"Which part of the city do you live in?" he asks as he slides his phone into his pocket.

"My roommate and I share an apartment in the west end."

Mark makes a face. He quickly papers it over with another one of his bland smiles, but I didn't miss it.

More judgment from Mark Chan. How wonderful.

And you know what? That fucking does it for me.

"Are you going to criticize me for having a roommate?" I snap. "Not everyone is lucky enough to buy a place in such an expensive city. I bet you're going to say you were able to afford it all on your own, and that anybody could do it if they just worked hard enough and only ate home-cooked meals and drank home-brewed coffee—"

"Emily." He holds up his hands. "That's not what I was planning to say."

I snort in disbelief. "Right."

I'm quite familiar with his attitude. It doesn't usually come from people who are a full nine months younger than me—for some reason, my mother felt the need to tell me Mark's birthday the other week—but those who are my parents' age.

Now, my parents are immigrants and didn't come to Canada until their midtwenties, when they'd been married a couple of years, so some of the "back in my day" conversations aren't really the same with them as with people who grew up here. But still.

There's also a group of young people who boast similar attitudes. Ones who are unaware of how all their advantages in life led to their success. My friend and roommate, Paige Lo, briefly dated one of these men last year. I told her at the beginning that he was an intolerable asshole, but she didn't listen, alas. Went on three whole dates with him.

"Really," Mark says. "I . . ."

He trails off when I give him a look and mutters something under his breath.

We're saved from any further conversation when the emcee takes the stage again. His emceeing skills might be lacking, but listening to him is still better than talking to Mark, who's probably fantasizing about going home and putting on a sweater-vest.

A moment later, he pulls out his phone again.

At midnight, some people are on the dance floor, but I'm not one of them. I'm sitting at a table, Scarlett leaning against me.

Mark Chan, I note, is also not dancing—and not because he has a small child sleeping on him—but I can't blame him. The music leaves something to be desired.

I'm rather surprised he's still here. If I were him, I would have left the minute we'd finished eating, but for some mysterious reason, he didn't. Hmm. He's also not on his phone anymore.

In the corner, a friend of Hannah's is necking one of my cousins, and I'm going to assume that sex will probably happen once they leave.

Honestly, the last thing I want to do after a Chinese wedding banquet is get naked with someone. I don't understand people who hook up after weddings. Now, not every wedding is a ten-course banquet, but at least half the weddings I go to fall into that category. And even at the others? There's a pretty decent amount of food. At the wedding I attended last October, they served a "snack" of poutine and pizza at eleven, and I couldn't restrain myself, despite dinner having ended only an hour and a half earlier.

Let me tell you, I was not feeling particularly frisky after that.

"Emily."

I startle at my mother's voice. I guess I was lost in my thoughts about hookups and weddings.

"Mark has offered to drive you home," Mom says.

The brief look of surprise on Mark's face—once again quickly covered by a small smile—indicates that he has done nothing of the sort, and while I'm not particularly fond of him, I do feel a little sympathy for anyone who gets stuck in my mother's traps.

"I'm not ready to leave yet," I say, even though I'm definitely ready to leave.

My mother glares at me, then turns to Mark, as though expecting him to offer to wait.

He does not.

"I should be heading out," he says politely. "Goodbye, Emily."

I nod at him. "See you around."

I don't actually intend to "see him around," but it seems like a decent thing to say.

Well, at least that's over.

3

— ♡ —

"Even if you don't feel like it, it's important to write every day at the same time. Set a routine. The only time in the past twenty-one years that I missed my 7 a.m. writing session? The day my first son was born."

—Randy Cooperson, *New York Times* bestselling science fiction writer

It's my morning off from Coffee on College, which moved a few months ago and isn't actually on College Street anymore. Maybe I ought to be doing something better with my time than curling up in bed with my phone, but whatever. I'm still recovering from yesterday's seventeen-hour wedding extravaganza.

Yes, seventeen hours. I'm not joking. With hair and makeup, followed by the tea ceremony, church ceremony, photos, cocktails, ten-course banquet, etc., I was away from home for seventeen hours.

But it's not just the fact that yesterday was a particularly long day that has me in bed at a time when I'd usually be serving coffee or writing. It's also the emotional toll of spending so many hours around my family.

I love my family. Of course, I don't actually *say* those words out loud, God no, but I do. Still, my family is . . . just a bit much. Especially my mother.

And then there was Mark.

I got the distinct impression that he thought he was too good for me, even if he didn't actually say as much.

There's a knock on my bedroom door.

"I made coffee," Paige says. "You want some?"

"How did you know I was awake?" I ask.

"It's after eight. You're always awake by now. Plus, a few minutes ago, there was a thump and I heard you swear."

Paige is a great roommate with one flaw: she has amazing hearing.

I'm serious! She's like a—well, in truth, I have no idea which animals are known for their great sense of hearing. Zoology isn't my strong suit. But she's one of those.

It's not without its benefits. When we watch a movie and the dialogue is barely audible over the music and unnecessarily loud sound effects, she always knows what's being said.

But if I bring a guy back to the apartment, she'll hear, even if I do my best to be quiet. That's a little unnerving, although it's been quite a while since I brought anyone home with me.

"I'll be out in a few minutes," I tell her.

I finish looking at my social media, then do a search for animals with great hearing. Elephants, bats, and moths are a few. Hmm. Of those, I think Paige would most like to be compared to an elephant.

I finally stumble out of my room in sweatpants, an old T-shirt, and probably a third of last night's makeup. I did my best to remove it when I got home, but there was more than I usually wear, and I don't think I got it all off. After I drink my coffee, I'll have a nice long shower.

"You hungover?" Paige asks as we sit down at our small, barely functional table.

I shake my head. I had a few drinks, but I didn't get drunk. Though I'm not in peak physical condition at present, that has more to do with the long day, the heels that pinched my feet, and the large quantity of food I consumed.

"How was the wedding?"

It takes me one and a half mugs of coffee to tell Paige about Hannah's wedding, including the fact that I finally met the great Mark Chan.

"And?" She gestures for me to continue.

"I can't say I was impressed. He's not my type, and he reminds me of that lawyer you dated last year. Besides, he seemed to find his phone more interesting than me."

Paige makes a face. "Do you think your mother will stop talking about him now?"

I snort. "Ha."

As if on cue, my phone rings. It's my mother.

Paige can tell who it is by the special ringtone I have set for my mom, and she heads to the washroom as I answer the call.

"Hi, Mom," I say with a cheerfulness I don't feel.

Chance of Mom bringing up Mark Chan in this conversation? One hundred percent.

"Ah, Emily, what's wrong with your voice?" she asks.

"Nothing." I try to bring down the level of fake cheer without sounding like Eeyore.

I don't think I succeed.

"Are you sure you're okay?" she presses. "I understand it's hard to see Hannah get married first and—"

"Mom, no! I'm fine. I'm not upset that I'm unmarried."

"If only you'd allowed Mark to drive you home yesterday . . ."

"Can you please stop trying to throw him at me?" I'm not sure why I bother. "My dating life is none of your business."

I swear she cackles at that.

"What are you talking about?" she says. "You're an unmarried thirty-three-year-old."

"Thanks for reminding me. I'd forgotten."

"And I'm your mother! It's very much my business. For many years, I let you deal with it yourself."

That's stretching the truth, though she was less involved than she is now.

"Have you forgotten about Alvin?" I ask.

"No, I didn't. I've been practicing my matchmaking skills so that won't happen again."

I'm not quite sure what she means by "practicing." Am a little scared to ask.

"Mark is a much better match for you than Alvin," Mom continues. "I would like to arrange a date for you two."

"That's really not necessary."

"He told me he wanted to see you again."

For some stupid reason, there's the tiniest of flutters in my chest at her words. I don't understand.

"I highly doubt he said that," I say before downing the cold coffee in my mug.

"When are you free next weekend? Perhaps you could go out for dinner together. I know just the place. I'll make a reservation in his name."

"Mom, no." I need to change the topic. "How long do you think it'll be before Hannah gets the pictures for her wedding?"

"I think it was a month for May's wedding—or was it six weeks? I can't remember. Didn't Hannah look so beautiful yesterday? Still, I think she should have gone with the first dress."

I disagree—Hannah definitely chose the right one—but instead of saying so, I let Mom voice her opinions for a few minutes. It's about 147 percent better than listening to her talk about Mark.

Just when I think I might be able to get out of this conversation without her mentioning him again, she says, "So, I'll make a reservation for next Sunday?"

"No."

She huffs. "Fine. Here, talk to your father."

There's a bunch of yelling on the other end of the phone, and then my dad says, "Hi, Emily. Did you enjoy the wedding? Were you inspired to plan your own?"

"Dad . . ."

"You know I'm kidding. Look, I'll do my best to stop your mother from throwing Mark in your direction."

"Thank you."

"Though he is quite a nice young man."

"Dad!"

"I'm just saying. You could do worse."

Well, obviously. Things could always be worse; it's just a fact of life. There are natural disasters, for starters. If you're already dealing with one of those, a second natural disaster is still a possibility, right? Especially given, you know, climate change.

And when it comes to dating, Mark has things to recommend him. He didn't try anything inappropriate. His breath didn't reek. He didn't brag about himself for twenty minutes straight. He isn't already married.

Yep, could be worse.

But that doesn't matter, because he clearly didn't think much of *me*.

For a split second, I wonder if I'm wrong about this, then push the thought aside. Nah, I'm pretty sure I'm right.

By the time I get off the phone with my father, Paige is ready to leave for the gym. I have a shower and consider doing some writing. I feel guilty that I haven't written in a few days.

Last night, while I was waiting for an Uber—I almost always take public transit because it's cheaper, but I was too tired for the bus—I saw a post from Randy Cooperson. He was bragging about how he's still writing every day, even though his mother is dying.

Because apparently that's what serious writers do. He's not the only person who says you're supposed to write every day; I've seen this advice over and over.

Randy Cooperson also, apparently, continued to write when his wife was in labor with their second and third sons, as well as when he had a terrible bout of food poisoning, proudly proclaiming that he'd gotten vomit on his notebook.

And, look. If that's what works for him, cool. Some people take comfort in having a routine or schedule. You do you, buddy.

But you know what? There's not one way to be a writer, and I'm not going to let some guy I don't know make me feel guilty when I've had an exhausting few days.

I might not have had three books on the *New York Times* bestseller list, but I have a published novel. I've completed and trunked two other books. I have another one that'll be heading to copyedits soon. At least, I hope it will.

Writing every day isn't the only way to finish things.

I sigh as I look at the desk in my room, tucked against the small window that faces another apartment building. Maybe I would feel like working now if I had a better writing space. My own home office, rather than a tiny corner in my bedroom.

Instead of sitting down at my laptop, I decide to run a few errands downtown. Once those are complete, I reward myself by going to the bookstore and looking at my book on the shelf.

There it is, my debut novel about two families and their web of lies. One mother's shocking not-so-little secret? Her daughter's biological father isn't who everyone thinks it is—and that's just the tip of the iceberg.

Seeing my book in the store makes me feel like I've made it, even if I really haven't.

In fact, when I slide out a copy of *All Those Little Secrets*, I see a "signed by author" sticker on the front. I signed four copies here, one week after the book was released five months ago, and there are now three copies, all with that sticker.

It appears the bookstore has sold a grand total of one copy of my book.

Yep, it's flying off the shelves.

I glance at a different novel, which I know is doing very well. I'm counting the copies—twenty-two—when a man picks one up and walks toward the cash register. I try not to be jealous of that book's author, knowing that won't get me anywhere. Jealousy can eat you alive in the publishing business if you're not careful.

When I get home, Paige is watching something on TV.

"The bathroom sink is leaking again," she says.

Well, that's great. We'll tell the super, and he'll get around to fixing it . . . never.

Even better, when I try to start a load of laundry, every washing machine in the basement laundry room is in use. Every machine that isn't broken, that is—half of them have Out of Order signs on them. I return to my unit.

I bet Mark Chan doesn't have to deal with nonsense like this.

This is my impossible dream: having my own washing machine and proper home office, and writing a book that actually sells well and earns out the advance in a few months.

A boyfriend or husband?

Meh. No matter what my mother says, there are more important things in life.

Since I can't do laundry, I sit down at my laptop and start typing.

4

"I like being productive."

—Tess Donovan, seven-figure
indie-romance author

"Emily! Wake up!"

"Go away," I mutter.

"Emily! We're meeting Ashley in an hour."

Reluctantly, I open my eyes and peer at Paige, then the alarm clock on my bedside table.

Shit!

I usually work a Saturday shift at Coffee on College, but I asked for the last one off because of the wedding.

Today, though, I was working. When I got home after my shift, I stripped down and figured a nap would be in order, though I didn't bother setting an alarm, because I'm usually pretty bad at napping unless I'm in a moving vehicle. I figured I wouldn't be able to fall asleep, or I'd have a light, fitful sleep and get out of bed an hour later, at five o'clock.

But now it's seven fifteen.

The reason I was tired? I stayed up late last night being "productive."

I wasn't tapping away at my computer. Some people might consider a writer productive only when they have their butt in a chair, but you can dictate while on a treadmill or out for a walk, for example.

Not that I was doing those things either.

But reading a novel or bingeing a show on Netflix can also count as productivity in my mind. At least, that's what I told myself when I stayed up past midnight yesterday to watch a K-drama. I was learning about story and compelling characters!

That's the great thing about being a writer. It's easy to rationalize what you do as being "for your writing," either for inspiration or for research.

But maybe staying up late was a mistake.

Once Paige is assured that I'm awake, I wash my face and get ready for a night out, i.e., another night of productivity. Trying a new cocktail bar and socializing with my friends is a great way to get inspired, isn't it? Plus, I'm the rare breed of writer known as an extrovert.

Yes, really. We exist.

Some writers would much prefer a night alone in their pajamas, but going out and seeing people normally energizes me . . . when I haven't just woken up from a nap, and when I'm not resenting the idea of wearing proper clothes.

But by the time I've put on my favorite pair of jeans—which make my ass look amazing—as well as black stilettos and a gorgeous pink shirt that I found on sale last weekend, I'm feeling good, even if I've yawned ten times in the past twenty minutes. After spending far too long debating which jacket to wear, I head out with Paige.

In March, the weather in Toronto is such that you might see some people wearing parkas and others wearing shorts and T-shirts . . . all on the same day. And it's rarely photogenic outside. I cannot imagine anyone waxing poetic about the crusty, shrinking snowbanks—which are now more dirt than snow— lining the roads.

As we head down the street, I decide the parka was the right call. The wind is brutal tonight.

A four-hundred-meter walk takes us to the falafel joint where I have spent more than a little of my money over the years. Usually, we'd try something more exciting on a Saturday night, but we're saving our money for the fancy bar. Besides, Ashley isn't eating with us—she's on a dinner date with Frank, her boyfriend of two years who recently moved in with her. He's meeting up with some friends after their meal, and she's meeting up with us.

The man working behind the counter knows exactly what I like on my falafel sandwich, so I don't have to tell him. Once Paige and I have our food in hand, we sit by the window to eat.

I've just finished wiping off my hands when my phone rings. My mother, of course.

"Allison!" she says.

"Uh, wrong daughter," I tell her. This happens approximately 37 percent of the time.

"Oh yes. I decided to call you before her, and I got confused." She's talking loudly, as though we're at opposite ends of a long hallway, but she'll quiet down in a few minutes, so I don't bother saying anything. "I was wondering if you'd like to go out for brunch tomorrow? I made reservations."

"Where?" I ask.

"Lily's Kitchen."

Oh.

The truth is, I've wanted to eat there for a while. It's in the east end, though, so I'm not usually in the area.

But it's supposed to be very good, and if I'm with my mother, she'll pay.

"We can go shopping afterward," she says.

"Where? What did you have in mind?"

"Oh, I don't know," she says airily, "but I can drive."

One of the many things that makes me feel like I'm not a

"proper" adult: my lack of car. The only vehicle I own is a twenty-year-old bicycle. I claim it's because I'm an environmentalist, but it's mostly because I'm broke. And I don't have kids and I live a ten-minute walk from the subway, so a car's not strictly necessary.

I don't love the idea of shopping with my mother, but I do like the idea of brunch. While Sundays are usually reserved for writing, after I had a brain wave in the shower on Wednesday, I finished my first round of revisions on my third novel. My third novel that will see the light of day, I mean; I have a three-book deal with my publisher, and the second book is currently being reviewed by my editor.

Besides, people-watching at a nice brunch restaurant is productive, isn't it?

"Sure," I tell my mom. "What time?"

"Eleven. I made the reservations under your name."

Slightly odd that she used my name rather than hers, but whatever. I'm going to Lily's Kitchen for brunch tomorrow!

I end the call, and once Paige finishes her falafel sandwich, we head in the direction of the cocktail bar, which has the rather minimalist name of "suave" (all lowercase). However, I'm distracted when we pass a new place called the Shakerie (capitalized in the normal way).

"Holy shit! Fifteen bucks for a milkshake!" I exclaim, looking at the poster for the special of the month: cherry pie milkshake. I, personally, consider fifteen bucks to be too much for a drink that doesn't have alcohol.

But as I study the photo, the price point starts to make sense. The milkshake is literally topped with a slice of cherry pie, which is then topped with vanilla ice cream. And it's, like, a full slice of cherry pie, not some itty-bitty version.

"It's two desserts in one," Paige says. "Really stretching the definition of a milkshake."

"Yeah. I think you have to share it with someone else."

"Don't look at me! I'm lactose intolerant."

When we arrive at the cocktail bar, it's not very busy for a Saturday night. Huh. I thought this was the hot place to go. Still, despite the lack of customers, it takes us a few minutes to locate Ashley Tanner, as the lighting isn't terribly bright. But as soon as we see the white woman with wavy brown hair in the corner, we head over.

"Sorry, we're late," Paige says.

"It's all my fault," I say. "I woke up from my nap after seven o'clock, and then my mother called just as I finished my falafel, and then I got distracted by a fifteen-dollar milkshake."

Still, we're barely ten minutes late.

"Why is it so empty here?" Paige asks.

"Because it's early," Ashley replies.

"What?" I cry. "It's well after eight."

"As I said." Ashley sips her blue drink. "Early. Remember, we're old now."

I realize in horror that she's right. Once upon a time, back in Ye Olden Days, I would never have gone out for drinks this early. In fact, I probably wouldn't have considered going out before ten, though I might have done some pre-drinking.

But it's just so much more *pleasant* to go out early. To never worry about what time last call is—I think it's two?—because you're always in bed by then, your white-noise machine and humidifier at just the perfect settings.

Oh God. A dozen years ago, I didn't even know what a white-noise machine was, and I would have been able to consume that entire cherry pie milkshake without feeling gross, as I'm sure I would feel now.

"In fact," Ashley says, "you should order soon because happy hour ends at nine."

"Wait, are you serious?" I ask. "Happy hour ends that late?"

Ashley seems amused by my shock, her lips curving up in a slight smirk. "They don't call it 'happy hour,' but yeah, they have a list of drinks that are fifty percent off until nine."

I scan the QR code for the menu—all in lowercase because apparently this place is allergic to capital letters—and quickly decide on something with cardamom. In my opinion, cardamom is one of the greatest things ever. Particularly with coffee or tea . . . or ice cream. At work, we have a cardamom latte, and it's pretty awesome, especially with the employee discount.

Once we've placed our orders with a waitress wearing all black, Ashley turns to Paige. "How was your date last night?"

OMG! I totally forgot that Paige had a date. Damn, I should have asked her about it earlier, though on the plus side, she won't have to recount it twice now.

"He was intimidated by me." Paige rolls her eyes. "Specifically, my workout schedule and how much I can bench-press."

Paige's workout schedule *is* a little scary, I admit, but I say this as someone who doesn't go to the gym. I'd never be able to handle her workouts, though I do think it's pretty awesome that she has big arm muscles and could pick me up with ease. For her, working out is a way of clearing her mind and destressing after dealing with her frustrating colleagues at her office job. Like the colleague who periodically steals her lunch, which she's just supposed to accept, as a "good team player."

"Your date saw it as a threat to his masculinity?" Ashley asks.

Paige shrugs. "Apparently, but 'forgetting his wallet' and not being able to pay wasn't a threat to his masculinity? I'm not sure why I bother with dating. I wish I was off the market. Like you." She looks at Ashley, who groans.

"What?" I ask.

"I think living together might be a mistake," Ashley says. "He's just always . . . there. I don't have any time alone, and yesterday, his mother stopped by in the evening and I had no warning."

I make a face. "Yikes." I can't imagine subjecting a significant other to my mother without notice.

"But he was very apologetic. Told me he forgot because he wasn't used to living with someone, and it would never happen again, and would I like breakfast in bed?"

"What did you say?" Paige asks.

"I said yes, and today, he made me waffles and did all the dishes afterward."

"Well, that's not so bad," I say, though I feel a bit out of my depth. I've never lived with a romantic partner before, though I suspect most people have by the time they're my age.

Ashley sighs. "I don't know. Cohabitation is exhausting."

To be honest, this is a bit depressing. Frank has always seemed like a sweetheart to me, and if it's hard to live with a man like him, what hope do the rest of us have of finding someone we can tolerate? Once again, it seems like a smart choice not to devote my precious energy and time to dating.

My drink arrives, and I take a sip. Mmm, yep, that hits the spot.

"I think it'll just take a while to get used to it," Paige says. "It's been, what, two weeks? Give it a few more months."

After responding with her you're-being-sensible-but-I-don't-like-it expression, Ashley, who's a high school teacher, tells us about her plans for March break.

By eleven o'clock, suave is getting busier, and Paige is recounting her horror story of setting up her mother's Wi-Fi. It's a horror story not because setting up the Wi-Fi was particularly difficult but because explaining technology to her mother is always painful.

We head out around eleven thirty, when things are really getting going at suave. Ashley takes the subway north to the apartment she now shares with Frank, while Paige and I head west. Once I get home, I decide to do the responsible thing and go to bed within half an hour.

But getting into bed and turning out the lights does not, alas, mean that I fall asleep.

I used to fall asleep easily, but now it appears my body is more sensitive to shit like having a late-afternoon/early-evening nap.

All right, next time I nap, I'm definitely setting an alarm, even if I'm convinced it'll "just" be twenty minutes. Ah, the joys of getting old.

Sunday morning, I make a few posts on social media, something I'm supposed to do as an author to promote myself, but I'm rather unconvinced of the efficacy of posting things like cherry pie milkshake pictures to sell a book that's partially about generational trauma.

Not that I have a photo of that milkshake, but it did sound delicious. I can't justify the cost, though if I'd ordered it, I would definitely have posted the picture. Just like I posted a picture of the "chocolate cake" donut I bought a few weeks ago. It wasn't a cake donut but a yeast donut, dipped in chocolate ganache and chocolate cake crumbs, then topped with an actual piece of chocolate cake.

Anyway, I suppose that's why foods like this exist: because people like me will post pictures of them on social media, in the hopes that they'll somehow make readers buy my book.

As I'm wasting time on my phone, I find a video of Tess Donovan, a prolific romance author, talking about how she likes being productive. Admittedly, I don't think she uses that word in the same way that I do. She puts out six full-length novels a year, totaling half a million words. Her business is more like an empire, and she says she doesn't have an assistant because she's a control freak.

I'm surprised she hasn't burned out yet, but everyone has a different brain. While I can't sustainably write six novels a year—hahaha—that doesn't mean other people can't.

At nine thirty, I decide it's time to get dressed to meet my mother. She'll probably judge my outfit no matter what I wear, so I shouldn't overthink this too much. I settle on a blue sweater, jeans, and black boots. A little light makeup and I'm ready to go.

I listen to music as I take transit to the other end of the city. When I get off the streetcar, I take all of three steps before I hit some hidden ice and fall flat on my ass.

"You okay?" a middle-aged woman asks me.

"Yeah, yeah, I'm fine." I wave her off as I suppress a groan.

It's several seconds before I'm able to sit up, and it hurts more than expected. I'm not like my little nieces, who fall down all the time and get up a split second later as though nothing happened. To be fair, they're much closer to the ground than I am. Still, I used to be better at falling on my ass, even once I achieved my full height at the age of twelve.

I heave myself up with the help of a pole that supports a No Parking sign and walk toward Lily's Kitchen with a limp. By the time I arrive, I'm doing a bit better. I'll probably have a bruise tomorrow, but I don't think anything is twisted or sprained. And thankfully, no one I know was around to witness the not-so-fine moment of me landing on my ass.

God, I hate March weather.

I also don't appreciate some of the ways that my body has changed with age. I can't sleep as well, I can't get up quite as fast when I fall on the ice, I can't party until 3 a.m., and the rare times I do get drunk (rather than just a bit tipsy), my hangovers are waaaay worse than they used to be.

I remind myself that overall, my thirties are better than my twenties. Even if I'm starting to feel old, despite still lacking some of the traditional signposts of adulthood, I'm now a published author.

Yes, I should try my best to look on the bright side. Today is going to be fun. I'll have a nice brunch with my mother, who hopefully won't criticize my single status too much or mention Mark more than five times. Later, maybe I'll pop into my favorite east-end stationery shop.

When I enter the restaurant, the hostess greets me and asks if I have a reservation.

"Yes," I say. "Under Emily."

"Right this way." She leads me to the back of the cozy restaurant and gestures to a table for two, where someone else is already seated.

Except it's not my mom. Rather, it's just who I need to make me feel better about myself.

Not.

It's Mark fucking Chan.

5

"It was the worst of times."

—Me, upon seeing Mark Chan at Lily's Kitchen

I t's *you*." I barely restrain myself from pointing my finger in his face. I'm definitely not looking on the bright side anymore.

"Who were you expecting?" Mark asks, unruffled by my accusatory tone.

"My mother. I was supposed to meet her for brunch. At least, that's what she told me. I should have known she had something up her sleeve. Did you know you were meeting me here?"

"Yes."

"And you still came?"

He shrugs. "I was told you wanted to see me again."

My eyes widen. "You believed that nonsense? After our not-so-spectacular encounters at my sister's wedding?"

"Your mother was very . . ." He hesitates.

"Persuasive?" I suggest as I reluctantly sit down across from him.

"I was going to say 'scary,' actually."

I bark out a laugh before I can stop myself. "Yes, she can be, even if she's barely five feet tall. You figured it was best to be obedient and do what she said?"

"I suppose she was persuasive too. She claimed you tend to get rather, uh, flustered in large gatherings. She convinced me that we'd get along better when it's just the two of us."

Does my mother actually believe the garbage she's peddling? Or is she just super desperate to marry me off?

"She made a point of listing your many fine qualities," he says, and it bugs me that I can't tell if there's a hint of sarcasm in his voice. He speaks calmly, no matter what he's saying.

"Such as?" I gesture for him to continue. I really wish I could have listened in on that conversation. It would have been entertaining.

"Ah, she said you were very intelligent and kind."

Right. I'm the "intelligent" daughter who doesn't have a proper profession, unlike my sisters.

"And . . ." Mark looks slightly uncomfortable. "Beautiful."

"Do you think I'm beautiful?"

He declines to answer, probably assuming I'll get pissed at whatever response he gives. "She also said you're a brilliant writer."

"How would she know? She's never read my work, thankfully."

"I think she has. She started describing, in detail—"

"No!"

Maybe it's good I didn't have the opportunity to hear their conversation. I can't bear to know any more.

Yes, I wrote a novel, and I want thousands of people to read it; I just didn't expect my mother to be one of them. Although I gave her one of my free copies—proof that I was indeed published—I didn't think she'd actually open the book. She doesn't read novels and was never enthused about my writing dreams. In retrospect, I wish I'd marked the sex scene using a sticky note that said "Do Not Read."

Except that probably would have made her curious, and she would have read it first.

The very idea of my mother reading that scene is nearly enough to make me expire on the spot, but instead, I look around for a server who might bring me a vat of alcohol. When I can't find one, I sigh and turn my attention to the menu.

I don't want to have brunch with Mark, but since I trekked to the other end of the city and I do want to try the food here, I might as well eat something. Then I'll reward myself with a trip to the stationery store.

The problem is that everything on the menu looks good, but I eventually settle on the apple-crumble French toast, which undoubtably will be pretty enough to serve as "content" for my author social media accounts.

The server comes around and pours our coffee. I order the French toast and restrain myself from ordering a mimosa or three. I hope to get some work done later, so I better stay sober. Mark orders smoked salmon eggs Benedict, which comes with home fries and fruit salad. Not a bad choice, I must admit.

"Why wouldn't you want your mother to read your book?" he asks after the server walks away.

Not wanting to mention the sex scene, I say, "I'm afraid she'll be convinced that every female character over the age of forty is based on her. I'm afraid she'll ask questions. I'm afraid she'll be able to see the deep secrets of my mind from my written words. I'm afraid she'll hate it." I'm not lying; I'm worried about these things too.

"But she said you're brill—"

"She'll say anything; she just wants you to go out with me. She seems to think that having a single daughter in her thirties is the worst possible fate, and she aims to put an end to this catastrophe as soon as possible."

"Has she tried to set you up with other men before me?"

"Yes, but she's keener about you than she's been about anyone else." I sip my coffee. "Do your parents give you grief for being single?"

"Sometimes, which is why I couldn't say no to today, even if your mother hadn't been . . ."

"Scary," I finish.

"Exactly. They would have guilted me into coming."

I know all about guilt. I suppose we have something in common after all.

A tray of two small biscuits is set on our table, along with whipped butter and jam. The biscuits are a specialty at Lily's Kitchen, part of the reason I wanted to come here, but I totally forgot about them when I saw Mark. This meal is going to be a bit of a carb overload, but I don't care. I reach for a biscuit. It's still warm, and I break off a piece and moan around the flaky goodness.

Mark gives me an odd look. I think he's judging my choices, but he doesn't say anything, just proceeds to ignore the second biscuit.

"Are you seriously not going to eat that?" I ask. "Too indulgent for you?"

He raises an eyebrow and reaches for the biscuit.

Hmph. Perhaps I should have asked if I could eat it instead. My biscuit really is delicious, especially slathered with butter and jam, and I would have happily eaten two.

"Do you have any siblings?" I ask. My mother hasn't mentioned any, but maybe that's because she's so focused on setting me up with Mark.

"A younger sister who lives in Ottawa and works for the government. She and her husband have been married for two years."

"Any nieces or nephews?"

He shakes his head. "Much to my parents' disappointment."

"My parents already have a few grandkids, so they can't complain. I mean, they can and they do, but it's not as if they don't have any grandchildren." I shake my head. "When I was a teenager, I wasn't supposed to be distracted by boys, and now all my mom can talk about is marrying me off."

"My parents were the same. They didn't want me to be dis-

tracted by girls—which perhaps explains the all-boys school—
though at one point, my mom acknowledged that she didn't want
me to be distracted by boys either." He pauses. "Do you want to
get married one day?"

"If I meet the right person, sure. But if I don't, I don't. And
I'm positive my *mother* isn't going to help me find the right
person—no offense."

"None taken."

I suppose we're getting along well enough, and at least he
isn't ignoring me in favor of his phone today. It's not going to be
a hardship to survive a meal with him, but I'm still pissed at my
mom for lying to me.

"Do *you* want to get married?" I ask.

"Yes, I hope to," he says.

The server sets a plate of thick French toast in front of me.
It's garnished with baked spiced apples, whipped cream, and
crumble topping, and there's a little pitcher of maple syrup.

"Thank you," I say to the server. "Could we have more coffee
when you get a chance?"

"Of course. Anything else?"

"No, I think we're set." Mark smiles at her. One thing I can
say for him: he's not rude to the waitstaff, which is an improvement over Alvin.

Although he *is* wearing a sweater-vest. Ha! I knew he was a
sweater-vest kind of guy. He looks good, in a starchy, preppy sort
of way—if you're into that kind of thing. Which I am not. Obviously.

Before digging into my food, I take a couple of pictures.
Mark's lips thin, but he says nothing.

Ah. There's the judgment I expected from him.

"Am I allowed to eat?" he asks when I'm on my third photo—
the lighting here is tricky.

"Go ahead. I'm just taking pictures of my own meal."

There. I think I've got it. I put my phone away—I'll post later—then dig into my French toast, which is as heavenly as I'd hoped. It's more like dessert than a proper meal, but I'm not complaining.

I've just stuck my second bite—mostly whipped cream—into my mouth when I have a brain wave. "You know what we should do? We should pretend we hit it off today."

Mark frowns. "What are you saying?"

I set down my fork and lean forward. "We pretend it went well and we're interested in each other. Then in the coming weeks, we'll tell occasional lies about our dates, and they'll back off about our single status."

If my mom can lie to me about brunch today, then I can lie right back. I'll give her what she wants, and she can stop going on about how Mark Chan is so good at calculus and won a chess tournament when he was twelve.

"Um." That's the extent of his response.

Hmph. Perhaps he's too much of a Goody Two-shoes and this is a step too far for him. Or maybe my plan is ludicrous.

But my mother isn't great with words like "no." She's aware that I'm tired of hearing about Mark, but putting my foot down never works.

Instead, I can make up stories. *Yes, Mark and I had a lovely date at that new pulled-noodle restaurant on Dundas . . . No, I can't go shopping with you tomorrow because Mark and I are seeing the new Michelle Yeoh movie. Isn't that a coincidence?*

I'm a novelist. This is totally in my wheelhouse, and I think it has a better chance of success than honesty.

"Come on," I say. "I'll take care of the schedule."

"The schedule?" he says.

"Yeah, the schedule of our fake dates. Which nights we're having dinner and all that jazz. Since our parents are friends, they'll talk, so we have to make sure our stories are consistent."

"Right." He sounds skeptical of everything I've suggested in the past five minutes.

While I wait for him to say more, I drink my coffee. I've got a bit of a sugar/caffeine high—this coffee is particularly strong. And tasty.

"Could I think about it?" he asks. "If you give me your number, I'll text you."

"Sure." I'd prefer to get this sorted out now, but if he needs a day or two to think it over, he can have it. At least he hasn't already rejected my plan.

For the time being, I figure I ought to get to know him. You know, to make our ruse more believable if he says yes. My mother has told me many things about Mark, but she isn't the most reliable source.

"So, Mr. Potential Fake Boyfriend," I say, "what do you do for fun?"

For a split second, I'm afraid he's going to say that he doesn't do "fun," but fortunately, he proves me wrong.

"Reading," he says.

"Yes, you mentioned at the wedding that you'd like to read more fiction."

"Because I've spent a bit too much time—"

"Binge-watching reality dating shows?"

He grimaces, which is what I'd been hoping for; I enjoy getting a reaction out of him.

"Reading nonfiction," he says. "It's been a while since I picked up a novel. What about you?"

"I read a fair bit, but there aren't enough hours in the week for all the books that interest me."

I slide a small piece of French toast through the maple syrup on my plate before eating it, and for a split second, I swear Mark is laser-focused on my lips.

No. I must be imagining it.

"Have you given more thought to my proposal?" I ask.

"It's barely been five minutes, Emily. I'll need more time."

When the waitress comes to clear our plates, I ask for separate bills. I don't want to do a dance over who's going to pay.

At least I got to eat at Lily's Kitchen, even if my mother lied to me. Mark was tolerable company, and with any luck, he'll agree to my plan.

"I drove," he says as we exit the restaurant. "I can take you to the subway, if you like?"

I shake my head. "I have other things to do around here. I—"

I slip on the exact same piece of ice that hurt me earlier.

Mark holds out his gloved hand and pulls me up. "Are you okay?"

"I'm fine," I say. "Thanks." I let go of his hand. "Anyway, I've got some shopping to do. Time to buy a notebook or two that's too pretty to actually write in."

His brow furrows. "Why would you do that?"

I'm not in the mood to explain myself. "Goodbye, Mark."

As I'm walking to the stationery store, my phone rings. I switch it to vibrate and don't answer, since I'm not in the mood to talk to my mother.

Hmm. Mom might become insufferable if she thinks she made a successful match. She'll go on about how she always knew we'd be perfect together.

Still, I think my plan has its benefits.

I reach the store, and as soon as I step inside, a sense of calm seeps into my pores. I've always enjoyed stores like this. The saleslady asks if I need any help, and I tell her no, I'm just browsing.

I pick up some adorable baby seal washi tape, which is utterly frivolous—I'm sure Mark would not approve—and decide I need to have it. I'm just scoping out the notebooks when my phone vibrates with a call. It stops for five seconds, then starts up once more.

I suppose I have to pick up. "What is it, Mom?"

"Ah, good! You answered. I was afraid you'd been kidnapped."

My mom worries about kidnapping more than is normal. Given that she has five daughters, I don't know how she ever managed the anxiety.

"Are you still on your date?" she asks.

"Right. My *date*, which you tricked me into." I pause. "It went better than expected, I suppose." I'm hoping he'll agree to my proposal, so I have to start laying the groundwork now.

"Oh?"

"But please don't do that again."

"It was for your own good."

"I know you think that," I mutter. "Look, I'm still out. I'll talk to you when I get home, okay?"

I end the call and purchase the washi tape, plus a notebook whose cover looks like an enchanted forest. The store also sells an array of greeting cards, and for a split second, I wish I had a boyfriend. We'd rub noses and share a cherry pie milkshake with two straws and exchange cards with sappy words. It would be painfully cute.

But for now I'm on my own, and it's fine. It really is.

My phone buzzes—a text from Mark.

Okay, let's do it.

6

— ♡ —

"The publishing industry makes precisely zero sense."

—Oz Delgado, debut fantasy author

The Sunday following my brunch with Mark Chan, I find myself in a loud restaurant, seated between Meghan (my middle sister) and Scarlett (my elder niece). Family dim sum—which happens about once a month—is an event that I anticipate and dread in equal measure.

We're a bit like the family in *All-of-a-Kind Family*, which I read over and over as a kid. Just like in the book, there are five sisters, all roughly two years apart. Allison is the oldest, followed by me. The two of us shared a bedroom growing up—well, from the time Hannah was born—and I feel like my bossy older sister has never forgiven me for that.

Meghan, thirty-one now, shared a room with May. But unlike me and Allison, that seemed to bring them closer together. Meghan is soft-spoken and always smiling, and she's probably the sister with whom I get along best, but she gets along with everyone. She married her high school boyfriend. She kept him a secret from our parents for a long time—dating him was her biggest act of rebellion by far—but then he got into med school and all was forgiven. Her son, Timmy, sits in her lap.

May, the tomboy, is also a pharmacist married to a doctor. She does things like play in a softball league for fun, whereas I would never consider that unless I was being held at gunpoint. Her husband is the only white guy at our table. He looks around the restaurant and gives a curt nod to the lone white man at the table next to ours.

Then there's Hannah. She's missing out on today's fun because of her honeymoon. She was the "wild" one growing up — as in, she wore heavy eye makeup and clothes that could best be described as "interesting." She also had more freedom than the rest of us, as well as her own room, but still chafed at the restrictions. She's incredibly smart and has two degrees in electrical engineering, so she's more respectable than me now.

I've often wondered if my parents would have had five kids if Allison or I had been a boy. Were they trying for a boy, then gave up once they had five girls because that was enough? I asked a few years ago, and my mother denied it. She said she just liked babies and had easy pregnancies. I stared at her in shock. She had, after all, spent all my teens and early twenties instilling me with a deep fear of pregnancy, telling me that it would ruin my life.

For now Timmy is the only grandson. My parents do dote on him, but they're not much different with him than they are with Allison's girls. Mom and Dad are indulgent with all three grandchildren, much more than they were with their kids — even Hannah.

"Have you started earning royalties?" Meghan asks me as she reaches for the lo mai gai.

"I have to earn out my advance before I get any royalty money," I explain, "and I still haven't seen my official royalty statement from the third and fourth quarters of last year."

"But it's almost the end of March."

"Yeah." I help myself to the char siu bao. "Scarlett, no. Don't put the har gow all in your mouth at once."

"But Daddy did it," she protests.

"Daddy's mouth is much bigger than yours."

"Like a giant's!" She giggles.

Yes, I'm spending dim sum simultaneously explaining how money in publishing works to Meghan while preventing Scarlett from making a huge mess or burning herself.

People have a lot of misconceptions about publishing. They might believe, for example, that once you sell one book, you can quit your job and go on a fancy book tour that will take you to Paris and London, and it will be so glamorous! On the other end, some people believe it's completely impossible to make a living from writing.

The truth, of course, is somewhere in between.

When I was young and hopeful and had just started querying my first novel, I believed I could make a full-time income from writing within in three years. Ha. That didn't happen.

"Will you get to go on a book tour for your second book?" Meghan asks.

"Uh, no."

"How's that going? Have you finished writing it yet?"

"My editor is reviewing the second round of developmental edits. The book will be done many months in advance of its release date at the end of the year."

People also tend to have a romantic view of the writing process. Typing on a typewriter in a cozy house on the Mediterranean coast, the sea air wafting through the window, rather than avoiding your manuscript by wasting time on social media, then having a burst of caffeine-fueled productivity at one in the morning while wearing fuzzy unicorn pajama pants and a T-shirt with a giant coffee stain.

Just pulling an image out of thin air there. Nothing that's ever happened to me.

I'm glad I write in the age of computers, though. Sure, writing by hand or using a typewriter might sound romantic, but you could lose your entire manuscript when your little sister gets pissed at you and burns it in the fire.

I will *never* forgive Amy March for that. Never.

Honestly, every time I meet someone named "Amy," I cringe inside, and Amy is totally the name of the villain in my next novel. But don't tell anyone—her nefarious ways aren't revealed until the end of the book.

Of course, there are technology malfunctions that could eat your work, but after losing an entire three days of writing once, I'm careful to back everything up.

I explain page proofs to Meghan as Scarlett stabs her char siu bao into pieces with her chopsticks. Fortunately, my mom doesn't ask me questions about publishing anymore. She was always annoyed by my answers, so it's easier this way, even if part of me wishes my parents showed more interest. I'm the oddball artsy-fartsy one in a family of people with scientific professions.

My nephew starts bawling, and Meghan excuses herself from the table.

"Why is he crying?" Scarlett demands.

"Maybe he's hungry," I say, "or he needs his diaper changed. Or he's tired."

I can definitely relate to that last one.

"Then why doesn't he just say that?" Scarlett asks, exasperated.

"Because he can't speak. Crying is how he communicates."

She shakes her head.

"Emily!" Mom's voice booms across the table. I know she's speaking loudly to be heard in this crowded restaurant—and across the large table that's needed to accommodate everyone in my family—but she doesn't need to speak *this* loudly.

"Po Po needs to learn about *indoor* voices," Scarlett whispers to me.

"Yes, Mom?" I say, hiding my laugh.

"Are you going to see Mark again?"

Well. Here we go. Time to put my plan into action.

I straighten up in my seat. "Yes. We're going to have dinner on Tuesday, in fact."

"You see?" Mom says. "I knew you would get along. You kept rolling your eyes whenever I brought him up, but I *knew*."

Ugh, whose fun idea was this?

Oh, right. Mine.

I tell myself that once this meal is over and she gets the bragging out of her system — okay, fine, that will probably take more than a day — things will improve. If she believes I'm dating Mark, I'll no longer be blindsided by surprise dates at brunch. A few lies here and there, and all will be well.

"It's still early," I say, "but I figured a second date — one we arrange ourselves — wouldn't hurt. I'm looking forward to it."

In reality, my plan for Tuesday evening is to hang out with Paige and ignore all the emails that have piled up in my inbox, but what Mom doesn't know won't hurt her.

"I hope it goes well," May says encouragingly.

Allison, however, narrows her eyes at me. "You and Mark? Really?"

Everyone else seems to be buying it, but not my oldest sister. She probably believes he's too good for me, Mark who owns property and a car and has a "real" job.

Allison has no respect for my time. She thinks that everything in her life is more important than everything in my life. If she needs me to babysit my nieces, I should be happy to drop everything because I don't have kids of my own, and writing isn't really "work." Neither is slinging coffee.

Sure, sometimes when I ought to be writing, I'm actually admiring pretty notebooks or refreshing social media, but I do have my own life, and it's important to *me*.

If she was skeptical due to the complete lack of interest I've previously shown in Mark, I'd respect that, but I know that isn't the only thing going through her mind.

"Yes!" I say cheerfully. "He's a significant improvement over any of the men I could meet on an app."

Not necessarily true, though you have to wade through a fair bit of crap, which is why I haven't bothered in a while. There isn't enough brain bleach to deal with the things I saw the last time I tried using a dating app. One day, maybe I'll try a different app, but the dating pool is a sad state of affairs when you're a straight woman over thirty who refuses to lower her standards to the basement. Sure, there are decent men in the world, but not enough of them, and it seems like the good ones are already married. My sisters all met their husbands-to-be by the age of twenty-three, so they don't really know what it's like.

Meghan returns with the sleeping baby in her arms and starts shoveling turnip cake into her mouth. A small piece falls on Timmy. She looks down and seems to consider whether to remove the food, then decides it's not worth the risk of waking him.

"What did I miss?" she asks.

"Emily has another date with Mark," May says.

"That's exciting! Where are you going?"

Before I can make up an answer, Scarlett pokes me. "You look very old today."

"I didn't sleep well last night," I mumble.

"Scarlett, be nice to your aunt." Allison makes it sound like I'm a poor creature to be pitied for her terrible choices in life.

It will be interesting to see how my sisters parent their kids as they get older. Will they be the opposite of our immigrant parents . . . or exactly the same?

I think Allison will be the latter, more or less, and I will serve as a cautionary tale. But hopefully my nieces and nephews will see me as the "cool" auntie, once they stop talking about how old I am.

I reach for the siu mai and glance at my mom, who nods at me approvingly—a rare sight, and I presume it's thanks to the man I'm supposedly dating.

I can't help enjoying her approval, even if it's over a lie.

"So you're actually doing this?" Paige asks on Tuesday. She tosses some chips into her mouth.

"Yep," I say. "I told them at dim sum that I have a date with Mark tonight. So right now I'm supposed to be getting ready rather than sitting here in fuzzy unicorn pants with you."

I'm stretched out on our old couch (a hand-me-down from my parents), and she's leaning back in our recliner (a hand-me-down from her parents).

"For the record," Paige says, "I think this is a terrible idea."

"Why? Fake dating is a more efficient use of my time than going on real dates."

"But now she's going to bug you about when you're getting married. You're just shifting your arguments to a slightly different topic."

I wave this off. "We only recently started seeing each other. I think I have a solid six months until she starts bugging me about marriage."

"Are you sure? She might have waited six months when you were a young twenty-eight-year-old, but I'm not convinced she'll be so patient now."

"Whatever. Our relationship will last three or four months. Then I'll say we aren't suited to each other and broke it off, and she won't be able to bug me about Mark again because I've already given him a shot."

"Unless she wants you to reconcile."

"Well, then I'll have to say he did something not so great."

"And she'll confront his parents about it."

I'm getting a headache. "Look, I can handle this. I was just so tired of her throwing him in my direction. I had to do something. You know 'I'm not interested' isn't enough to dissuade my mother. A little pretend dating? It's easier this way."

"I think you need help," she mutters.

"You're in a cranky mood today."

"I don't want to go back to work tomorrow. Why do I have to go into the office? Other people's jobs switched to remote permanently during the pandemic, but not us. My boss seems to believe that nobody does any work when they're home, even though our tasks get completed. If he doesn't physically see us working, he doesn't believe it's happening."

I'd tell her to look for a new job, but I know she's tried. Last time she got an interview, they refused to tell her the salary until they made an offer, three interviews later . . . and it was lower than what she's presently making. When she tried to be assertive and ask for more, they thought she was being greedy.

She passes me the bowl of chips and goes to the kitchen to make her lunch for work tomorrow. I'm about to watch something on Netflix when my phone buzzes.

MARK: How's our date going?

I smile faintly as I type.

ME: Very well, thank you for asking. Did you tell your parents?
MARK: Yes. My mom was happy to hear we're going out. What's our next date?

I think about this for a second.

ME: Bubble tea on Friday, after I get off work.
MARK: Sounds good.

Yep, everything is going according to plan.
Paige is wrong. This will be just fine.

7

—♡—

"If you want to be a full-time writer, here's my advice: Be rich.
Or marry rich. Have a spouse who can support you,
so that when you have some lean years, you're not worried
about how you're going to pay your electric bill."

—H. A. Kim, cozy mystery author

Friday afternoon at Coffee on College, I'm sweeping up the assorted candy that a kid managed to dump on the floor. When I stand up, dustpan in my right hand, I knock into something hard, and most of the candy goes flying, landing all over the floor once again. A piece of red candy ricochets off the far wall.

"Dammit," I mutter.

"I'm so sorry. I got in the way."

I turn to look at the man who spoke . . . and nearly swear again.

It's the young East Asian guy who comes in here occasionally. He's ridiculously jacked and quite nice to look at. I've never been so close to him before.

"Large black coffee," I murmur.

"What did you say?"

"That's your order. You always get a large black coffee."

He smiles a smile that I certainly wouldn't call *bland*, ahem Mark, and we get lost in each other's eyes for a moment. Then my gaze travels downward to the very hard body that I hit.

"Emily, right?" he says.

I point to the name tag on my shirt. "Yep, that's me."

"I'm Andrew."

I should say something, but I'm struggling to come up with words. I think this is a proper meet-cute! Sure, we've interacted before, but we hadn't exchanged names, so this counts as our first real meeting. Although dating might not be a priority in my life, I still have romantic fantasies.

Or maybe this connection is all in my imagination.

"Emily," he says, "can I take you out some time? Buy you a cup of coffee you didn't make yourself?" He chuckles. "I know I shouldn't ask a woman out when she's at work, but I promise I won't take it badly if you decline."

So it wasn't just me!

I haven't been asked out in ages, and it finally happened after I arranged a pretend relationship. But there's no reason I can't both fake-date Mark and real-date someone else. If it goes well, I can do a switcheroo at some point.

I'm about to breathlessly agree to a date, but then I remember that the first time he came in, I wondered if he was in high school. I quickly realized my perspective was skewed because I'd been watching a TV show—research, obviously—about high school, and most of the students were played by actors in their midtwenties, but still. I think this guy is even younger than those actors. Gen Z, not a Millennial like me. I doubt he was alive for Y2K.

"I don't know," I say. "I'm afraid you're too young for me."

He smiles again, flashing me a dimple. "You can't be older than twenty-eight."

I'm not sure if he's trying to be nice or genuinely believes that, but I'm guessing the former. After all, I have it on good authority from a five-year-old that I "look old."

"I'm thirty-three," I say.

His smile doesn't falter. "I'm twenty-four. See? Not even a decade apart."

Or, in other words, he hadn't started high school when I graduated from university.

By the very scientific half-your-age-plus-seven rule, the youngest person I can date is . . . twenty-three and a half. So, he's old enough by that measure.

But, no. Twenty-four is just too young. He's a baby to me, younger than *Hannah*.

"Sorry," I say. "I don't think it's a good idea."

He shrugs. "It was worth a try."

I appreciate that he's not pushy, though he's a little more insistent when I decline his offer to help me clean up. But it's my job, and this is way better than some of the other things I've had to clean at Coffee on College over the years.

As I sweep up the candy again, I wonder if I made a mistake. We had such a cute meeting, after all. It would make a great story in years to come.

Oh well. At least I have a fake date tonight.

On the way home from work, I'm scrolling through social media when I see an article whining about how Millennials are entitled because they buy coffee away from home once a day, then complain about how they can't afford property.

You know, the sort of article that I've seen over and over in the past several years.

But if you spend $3 a day on coffee, that's $21 a week or about $1,100 a year. That won't do you much when the median price for a detached house is over a million dollars in your city, like it is in Toronto.

Then there's an article about how Millennials aren't having kids.

Gee, I wonder why.

And an article about how nobody wants to work anymore. Hmph.

I guess I'm also in a bad mood because, in addition to wondering if I made a mistake when I said no to Andrew, a "helpful" older customer said it was embarrassing to be doing this job at my age. She told me to go back to school and make something of myself.

I just responded by smiling and nodding. Why do strangers feel entitled to comment on other people's lives like that?

At least my mother is, well, my mother, not a complete stranger.

When I get home, I make myself a snack and a cup of tea, then head to my room, where I work on revising my third book. Some writers enjoy the first draft the most, but I find drafting vaguely terrifying. I prefer to have existing words that I can work with. Mold.

I'm so engrossed in my writing that when my phone rings an hour later, I jolt in surprise.

"Emily!" Mom says. "Are you back from your date?"

"Just got home."

"You're lying."

Okay, self. Stay calm.

"What do you mean?" I ask innocently.

"You weren't at the bubble tea shop at Yonge and Wellesley. That's where you told me you were going, yes? Near Wellesley Station?"

Oh God.

"Are you there right now?" I screech. "Are you *spying* on us?"

"Ah, silly girl. I wouldn't do that." Her tone isn't convincing, though. "Janie's daughter was just there, and she said she didn't see you."

"Why are you telling Janie's daughter"—her name currently escapes me—"about my plans with Mark?" I rub my temple, then I pull up Google Maps on my laptop. There are multiple bubble tea shops near the intersection, as I suspected.

"She works in the area," Mom says, "so I thought—"

"She could see how my date was going? And she agreed to this?"

"Well, she thinks I'm very . . . scary."

I recall what Mark told me and hold back a laugh. "She said that to your face?"

"No, but I could see her thinking that." Mom sounds pleased with herself.

"Which bubble tea shop did she go to?"

"I forget. One with 'tea' in the name."

"Mom, there's more than one tea shop near Wellesley Station. I suspect she went to the wrong one. And from now on, I'm not telling you where we're going. No intersections or even neighborhoods."

"Ah, fine, but I expect to see pictures on your social media."

I press a hand to my forehead. My head hurts. "You look at my social media?"

"Sometimes."

"I don't post pictures of my friends and family. Certainly not guys who've been on two dates with me. All my accounts are part of my brand as an author."

"Your brand?"

I sigh. "Look, I'm going out with him. Aren't you happy? You don't need to interfere any further."

"I don't understand."

My mother raised five daughters. She's used to being very, very busy. I can't imagine having five kids under the age of ten, but my mom did it and lived to tell the tale. She probably doesn't know what to do with all her time now. Since there are no upcoming weddings and I'm the only unmarried daughter, her attention is all focused on *me*.

I'm not sure how I'm going to survive this.

"Please, Mom," I beg. "I'm thirty-three years old."

She clucks her tongue. "I know."

Perhaps mentioning my age wasn't the way to go. It'll just remind her that I haven't accomplished what I'm supposed to accomplish by this age. House, car, husband, kid (or two). A "real" profession. Sure, a lot of people in their thirties don't have those things, but that doesn't mean I shouldn't be different. I'm supposed to give proof to my parents that it was the right decision to come to this country, and though I don't care about some markers of success, it would be nice to own a little house.

"I can handle this myself," I say, though I doubt that will convince her. "I better go. I'm working right now."

She ignores my words, as expected. "I went to the library yesterday and checked if they had your book. They did not. So I asked—"

"Mom."

"I said you were a local writer, and they showed me on the computer—there's a copy, but someone had borrowed it."

Okay, that's nice to hear, and she must not be too ashamed of me if she looked for my book at the library.

Then I remember Mark saying that my mother had read my book, and every inch of my body tenses.

"I really do have to go," I say. "Talk to you later."

I hang up and spend the next few minutes watching soothing videos of hot men baking. Well, maybe more than a few minutes. The next time I look at the time, a half hour has passed, but those videos were necessary to help me recover from that phone call.

Finally, I go back to writing, and after finishing what I wanted to accomplish for the day, I do a little outlining for my "secret" project. But I can't spend too long on it, because I have to wake up in time for my shift tomorrow.

The other day, an author posted a video in which she said

the key to being a full-time writer is to have a rich spouse or a trust fund. I laughed, but it's kind of true. That would definitely help. Since I don't have a trust fund (ha!) I'd need to go the rich spouse route, but I don't see any billionaires trying to sweep me off my feet. Even though that happens to all the poor girls in Tess Donovan's books, it's never happened to me.

And honestly, there's something nice about doing it on my own, but it would also be nice to have dental insurance. Or to not have to worry about the cost of the dentist because I have lots of money in my savings account.

The next afternoon, my feet are aching and I'm counting down the minutes until my shift is over, when a familiar man walks into the coffee shop. This one doesn't knock into me and send a rainbow of candy flying.

"Of all the coffee shops in all of Toronto," I say.

Mark frowns.

"It was a *Casablanca* reference," I tell him. I'd never watched the movie until I read a book about story and structure that exclusively referenced movies and TV shows from before I was born, so I had to watch a few to know what was going on.

"I'm aware, but it's not a coincidence. Your mother told me where you work."

Of course she did.

"Since I was in the area," he says, "I figured I'd see if you were here."

"Well, here I am."

"I know you can't just stand around and talk . . ."

I wouldn't think he'd want to talk to me for long anyway.

"Actually," I say, "we should speak about our plans. I get off in seventeen minutes. If you can wait that long . . ." I gesture to an empty table.

"Sure."

"Can I take your order?"

"Medium coffee, please. Milk and sugar."

I sneak peeks at Mark as I serve the next few customers. He removes his jacket and sets it on the back of his chair. Underneath, he's wearing an argyle sweater and a collared shirt. He takes out his phone and frowns at something,

I can't help comparing him to Andrew, who doesn't seem quite so serious. Plus, he actually asked me out, as opposed to Mark, who went on a "date" with me because my mom forced him. If only Andrew were closer to my age, but a nine-year age gap just seems too wide.

Once I finish my shift, I take a seat across from Mark, who's looking intently at his phone. He startles and drops it.

"Sorry," I say. "Didn't mean to scare you. Anyway, the reason I want to talk is because my mom thought we were lying about our bubble tea date. She sent her friend's daughter to spy on us, and we weren't there."

Mark frowns again. "You told her which tea shop we were supposedly going to?"

"I gave her an intersection. I thought details would make it more believable, but that was a silly mistake." I pause. "Did your parents ask you about our date?"

"I haven't spoken to them yet."

"You can say we're going on another date next Friday, but we should decide on a timeline for this relationship. Lying to my mother about this is a little more work than I expected. Let's say three months?"

Strangely enough, he hesitates before saying, "Sure. Three months."

"If you meet someone you like in that time, feel free to date them, just be discreet so our parents don't notice. We can end this a little early if necessary, but let's try for at least two months, okay?"

"Very well."

"If we give any specifics about our dates, we have to tell each other so our lies match."

He nods.

Wow. He's being so agreeable. No arguing or anything. A conversation with him takes about 13.2 percent as much energy as a conversation with my mother.

"You're sure about this?" I ask. "You can pretend?"

"I'm great at pretending." His voice sounds slightly off, but I try not to read into it.

"All right, well, see you around," I say. "Time to watch videos of Shetland ponies prancing and men baking donuts and cats playing instruments."

Mark's lips part, and he looks vaguely horrified.

There we go. I got a reaction out of him. Before he can judge my time management skills, I head out the door.

I hope, from now on, our fake relationship will be more straightforward.

It should be, right?

8

—♡—

"Like it or not, you do have to suffer for your art."

—Randy Cooperson

The following Sunday, I'm taking transit up to Richmond Hill to visit my parents, when a headline on social media catches my eye.

HOW I BOUGHT A HOUSE IN VANCOUVER BEFORE MY THIRTIETH BIRTHDAY

Ooh! Maybe this will include some good tips. I click on the article.

Approximately 2.9 seconds later, I mentally kick myself for being drawn in by that headline. It was foolish of me. At the beginning, such articles always make it sound like anyone can do it, but once you read a few paragraphs, you realize that the truth is quite the opposite.

For example, my parents did not pay for all my university tuition as well as gift me a hundred thousand dollars upon graduation. Yes, they paid for part of my tuition—I'm very lucky—and I was able to pay off my small student loan in three years, which already put me ahead of many people in my age group.

But a huge monetary gift afterward? Ha!

My parents have five kids. You think they could afford that?

Then this man received an inheritance from his grandmother, and oh, also won fifty thousand dollars from a lottery ticket?

Millennial success stories always read something like this. They're weirdly out of touch. Like, *I paid for my house by laying golden eggs. You can do it too!*

Yeah, no.

By the time I arrive at my childhood home, I'm already annoyed, and I don't think setting up my parents' new printer—the reason for the visit—is going to be a fun time. Or it will take thirty seconds, and I'll be irritated that I traveled all this way for such a simple task.

But at least there will be food.

Sure enough, there are egg tarts and cut-up mango on the kitchen table, and I help myself to the mango before I'm pulled into the "office," aka the bedroom I used to share with Allison.

My parents stand there and watch while I confirm that, yes, the printer is turned on and plugged in and connected to the computer. And yes, there's paper in the tray.

"Could you two maybe, uh, go to another room?" It'll be easier if I have some peace and quiet—my parents' presence gives me performance anxiety. Also, if I swear at the computer or life in general, nobody will be here to scold me.

I check whether the latest driver has been installed before reflecting on the fact that *I'm* the one my parents asked for this favor, even though all four of my sisters live in the Greater Toronto Area, three of them closer to Richmond Hill than I am. (None of us live with our parents now, although they'd let us— I think we all feel that our parents are best appreciated in smaller doses.)

Meghan has a baby, and I suspect they don't want to bother her with trifling matters like printers, and Allison's kids have various activities on the weekend. But Hannah is back from her honeymoon and doesn't have kids . . . and she never works on the weekends and is frankly better at this stuff than I am. Yet I'm the one who's considered "free" because I have neither kids nor a new husband, and while I'm considered too old not to be married, I'm young enough to be considered an IT expert.

Unsure which computer fix to try next, I do a little searching online, in the browser I know my parents don't use—I don't want to be traumatized by their browsing history. Again. (Look, there was an article on spicing things up in the bedroom, okay? I didn't need to see that.)

In the next twenty minutes, I follow some of the suggestions I find, but my attempts to print a test page continue to fail. Hmph.

Visions of being stuck in my childhood bedroom–turned–office at eight o'clock this evening begin running through my head. What if this is the beginning of a horror movie?

The other day, I came across an annoying comment from Randy Cooperson about how writers these days don't suffer enough, but when I saw the size of his first advance thirty years ago (larger than mine, even without accounting for inflation) and how much rent he paid for his apartment in New York City (not very much), it made me almost as annoyed as the article I read on the way to Richmond Hill.

Why the obsession with writers and suffering? If I didn't have to worry about my financial situation, I think I'd write more!

And now I'm trapped in a room with an evil printer.

"Please work. Please," I murmur, tapping the printer reassuringly.

A light turns on and—

Holy shit! The printer is working. It's actually printing something.

To ensure that wasn't a fluke, I go to the word processor, type the opening line of *Pride and Prejudice* from memory, and print it.

Look! I'm a genius.

Of course, I have no idea how I actually accomplished this, but that doesn't matter. Triumphantly, I take the sheet of paper downstairs.

"All fixed," I say, holding up the paper.

Mom grabs it from me. "What is this?"

"Proof that your printer is working."

"Did we do something stupid? How did you fix it?"

"It requires, uh, very technical computer terms to explain."

Luckily, my mother isn't paying close attention to the crap I'm spewing out of my mouth. "What are these words?" she asks. "Is this from your next book?"

I suppress a laugh. "No."

"Good. Because it needs work."

Even Jane Austen's writing isn't enough for my mother.

She pours some water from the kettle into the teapot. "Have some egg tarts."

I don't need to be told twice. I sit down at the table and reach for a tart. They're from my favorite bakery, which I know isn't an accident.

"You got the printer working?" Dad asks, coming into the kitchen.

I nod.

"So, uh, how's the writing going?"

This is, perhaps, one of the worst questions to ask a writer, as the answer is frequently "I cleaned every square inch of the apartment to avoid my manuscript" or "I only banged my head against the desk once today, thanks for asking." And if I say something like that, my parents will ask me, again, why on earth this is what I decided to do with my life. When I fail to explain it, they'll say they thought I was supposed to be good with words.

"Super, thanks," I reply instead.

My mom frowns. I suppose this didn't pass her bullshit detector. "I'm thinking of writing domestic thrillers under another name," I tell her. "I'm plotting one out right now. It's about . . . a writer."

You see? This is what happens when an author tries to describe their books. But I haven't gotten very far with this story, so I don't feel bad about the fact that I don't have a catchy logline. In fact, this is the first time I've mentioned my secret project aloud.

I know, I know, some people say that books about writers are overdone, and they might complain that the characters are annoying self-inserts, but I always enjoyed such stories. *Little Women*, *Emily of New Moon* . . . I loved those books as a kid, even if I'll never forgive Amy March. I signed them out of the library over and over until Auntie Carmen bought me my own copies.

Of course, a domestic thriller is rather different from *Little Women*.

"Will you have to do research for this?" Dad asks.

"Um, yes, there will be research about crime scenes and such." My research methods tend to involve feverishly googling things while hopped up on caffeine, but sometimes I use books too.

"Hmm." Mom starts pouring the tea. "Will you have to commit any murders?"

"Mom!"

"Ah, what do I know about being a writer? I'm just asking a question. If you had a normal job, I wouldn't have to ask."

I bite into the silky filling of my egg tart and hope my parents will move on to another topic of conversation.

"How's it going with Mark?" Mom inquires.

Okay, preferably not that topic.

"It's going well," I say. "He visited me at Coffee on College last weekend." That's not even a lie.

"Have you seen him since then?"

"Yeah, I saw him Friday night." I decide to have some fun. "We went to a cake-decorating class for couples."

The thought of Mark, sleeves rolled up, hands around a piping bag of bright green buttercream, makes me want to laugh. I can't imagine him doing something like that.

"Can you show me pictures?" Mom asks.

"Another time. We took them on Mark's phone. I was busy taking notes as, uh, research. Research for my thriller."

Could this book involve cake decorating?

Sure, why not. I always wanted an excuse to take a cake-decorating class.

My mom loads me down with food as I get ready to leave, and on the trip home, I listen to music rather than read articles about how I'm failing at life because I ate avocado toast that one time, thus preventing me from buying a house.

I'm in my apartment, just about to start my laundry, when my mom calls.

"Did the printer stop working?" I ask as I sort through my laundry hamper.

"Where did you take the cake-decorating class?" she demands.

"Why does it matter?"

"I've been scouring the internet, and I can't find a single mention of a couples' cake-decorating class Friday night in Toronto."

For fuck's sake.

"I found one cake-decorating class," she says, "but it wasn't a couples' one, and Sharon's friend was at it last night and she said you weren't there."

I scrub a hand over my face in frustration. I'm so desperate to stop talking about this that I almost mention the spicing-things-up-in-the-bedroom article. For a split second, that seems preferable, but then I come to my senses.

"The instructor, um, has a home baking business," I say. "She runs a few classes out of her house. They're small . . . more intimate that way. Nothing fancy, though. She doesn't have the classes listed on a website."

"I thought everything was on the internet."

"Why are you looking all this stuff up? Do you think I'm lying?"

My heart beats quickly as I wait for the answer to that question.

"Well," she says, "one time you lied so you could go to a party—"

"I was sixteen!"

I've actually lied many, many more times than she realized. I was still a pretty good teenager, but sometimes life was simpler if my parents didn't know the full truth.

Mom chuckles. "I'm just trying to understand what dating is like for kids your age."

"I'm in my thirties," I mutter. "I'm not a kid anymore."

"You can make me a cake sometime to show off your skills."

"We'll see, but I'm very busy, okay? Between my three jobs—"

"What's your third job?"

I massage my temples rather than unleashing a string of expletives.

"Writing is a job." I clench my jaw.

"I didn't forget about writing," she says. "Ah, yes! Tutoring, right?"

"I've got to go. Talk to you later."

I start a load of laundry—I managed to snag the last free machine—then realize I have to tell Mark about our recent "date." Normally I'd text, but for some reason, calling seems easier right now.

He picks up immediately. "Emily?"

"In case anyone asks, we were at a cake-decorating class on Friday night. I know that's something you wouldn't do—"

"Who says I wouldn't do it?"

I frown. "I don't know. It just sounds too frivolous for you."

"'Frivolous,'" he repeats, a hint of amusement in his voice.

"Yeah. Anyway, we went to this class, but it was at someone's home and not listed on the World Wide Web. Just in case your parents have questions. Providing too many details can be a sign of lying—I learned that while doing research for a new writing project—but trust me, those ones were necessary for my mother."

There's quiet laughter on the other end of the phone. I don't know why, but I enjoy the sound of his laugh, and it feels like he's laughing not at *me* but at the general situation.

"Okay," he says. "I believe you."

Once again, I imagine him with his sleeves rolled up—actually, I rather like that image—and a piping bag in his hands. I picture him piping a smiling turtle with terrifying precision.

Yes, I suppose I can see him doing it.

"So, you might actually take a cake-decorating class?" I ask.

"Sure. If the opportunity presented itself."

I wonder what else I don't know about him.

"All right," I say. "That's all I had to tell you. I'll do my best to keep you informed of our relationship. Like, if we have to commit a murder together, I'll be sure to let you know."

"If you're going to commit a murder, Emily, please don't drag me into it. I would prefer to be ignorant of those details."

"You know, I suspect you'd be good at it."

"Excuse me?"

"Very methodical and careful about covering up your tracks."

"I see."

This is a first. Never before have I told a guy I'm fake-dating that I think he'd be good at hiding a body.

"I better get going," I say in a cheery tone. "Hope you're having a great Sunday. Bye!"

Because this is Mark, not my mother, he doesn't take that as a cue to keep talking for another ten minutes. Though as I set my phone down, I'm oddly disappointed he didn't say anything more.

Huh. Why do I feel that way? I don't understand.

Well, whatever the reason, I'm sure another egg tart will help me feel better.

9

—♡—

"The orange stegasaurus screamed! She was hit by an arow!"

—Future author Emily Hung (age eight)

I knew I wanted to write books from the time I was eight. It was February in Mrs. Cullen's grade-three class. I don't remember the precise date, but it was shortly before Valentine's Day, and we had to write a story in language arts. Not the first time I'd written a story at school, but it was the first time I'd experienced the magic of the words just flowing, as I penned a story about Cupid . . . and dinosaurs.

I didn't know much about Cupid; to me, he was a chubby, naked baby with wings and a bow and arrow who made people fall in love. In my story, Cupid shot an arrow at a stegosaurus, who fell in love with an allosaurus. This, naturally, presented a problem because the allosaurus wanted to eat the stegosaurus. I remember giggling in delight as I wrote the words; Amanda Tran, who sat across from me, glared, but I didn't care. Mrs. Cullen said my tragic love story was very creative.

Writing, I decided, was just like playing. Like having my Barbies go to Jurassic Park. You got to make stuff up. It sounded like a better job than being a firefighter, doctor, or teacher.

When I got home that day, Mom was busy breaking up a fight between Hannah and May, but eventually, she had a free minute, and I told her my exciting news. I was going to write books when I grew up!

It took her a few seconds to answer, and in that time, I realized I'd done something wrong. Probably not as bad as the time I tried to flush Allison's favorite doll down the toilet, but it wasn't good.

She was disappointed in me.

I hated how that felt.

"This isn't a good job for you," she said finally, then added something about accountants and engineers and med school.

I agreed to be an accountant, but I felt like I was telling a lie. It's not that I wished to disappoint the people who loved me; I just really, really wanted to be a writer.

Over the years, there were times when I tried not to want it so badly. Being a novelist wasn't something my immigrant parents would consider "acceptable," wasn't the stable career they'd dreamed of for their children.

And today? Well, today feels like it's proving them right.

The publication of my third book, the final book on my contract, has been moved by five months, for reasons that are unclear to me. It has nothing to do with my progress on my book because I'm going to hit my deadline and deliver it to my editor in a few months.

This means I won't have a book release next year. It'll be the following year, which seems impossibly far away, but these timelines are just the way that publishing works.

The children's books I enjoyed about being a writer? None of them mentioned this.

When I was a kid, I preferred *Emily of New Moon* to *Anne of Green Gables*. Emily's books were more focused on how she wanted to be a writer, like I did, plus we shared a name. But even if I'm more of an Emily girl, Anne Shirley's "my life is a perfect graveyard of buried hopes" seems appropriate right now, albeit melodramatic.

On the practical side, I have to worry about money. This will delay part of my advance, the portion paid on publication, and it's not like I'm raking in the cash right now. It'll probably also delay edits, which means a delay on the portion paid when edits are completed and the book is accepted.

When I get home after tutoring on Monday, I flop onto the couch. Mondays are my busiest days because I also have a shift at Coffee on College, and I rarely get any writing done. I'll lie here for a few minutes, then make myself a nice cup of tea and attempt to lose myself in a book.

Unfortunately, my phone has other plans. It buzzes with a text from Allison.

I need you to babysit on Saturday afternoon.

Not "Can you babysit?" but "I need you to babysit."
Yep, that's my older sister.

ME: Sorry, I'm working on Saturday.
ALLISON: Find someone to cover your shift.

I'm not asking a favor of a coworker because my sister needs a babysitter. In an emergency situation, sure, I'd watch the girls, but I'm not changing my work schedule for next weekend.

For a split second, I wonder if I'm doing this to avoid Scarlett's truth bombs, but no, this really would be inconvenient, and I need the money from that shift.

I'm annoyed that I'm likely the first person Allison asked, despite her knowing I work most Saturdays. She never asks May, for example, and it's not because I'm way better with the girls than May is.

ME: What about Mom and Dad?
ALLISON: They have mahjong, remember?

And *clearly* mahjong—possibly with Mark's parents—is more

important than my ability to make money to feed and shelter myself. Ugh.

One aspect of adulthood that I wasn't prepared for: the way your sisters and friends having kids can change your relationships.

I have a friend from university who has two boys, and it's like her entire personality has become Motherhood. I've seen her once without her kids in the past five years. Even then they were all she talked about—I swear she went on about potty training for forty minutes, no matter how desperately I tried to change the topic—and I felt like we had nothing in common anymore.

Another friend, the only good thing that came out of the ill-fated job I got after graduation, has three kids. We still get along fine, but she's so busy that I almost never see her.

Allison and I were never close. Growing up, she was often annoyed with me, and she regularly assumed things were my fault, even when they weren't. For example, she accused me of stealing her lip gloss, and when I insisted I was innocent, she didn't believe me . . . until nine-year-old Hannah sheepishly revealed that it had been her. But at least Allison didn't used to act like her time was precious and mine wasn't.

Anyway, it's fine. My life is totally fine. I'm not feeling old and unsuccessful and broke and frightened about the state of the world after that climate change article I read earlier. I also saw a picture of some newly discovered deep-sea creature that I swear is going to give me nightmares, but yep, I'm just fine and dandy.

Tuesday afternoon, Andrew comes into the coffee shop and orders his black coffee, a winning smile on his face.

Is it just me, or have his shirts gotten smaller? Or perhaps his arms have gotten bigger?

As I'm discreetly checking out his muscles and wondering

whether he could save me from any of the many natural disasters that climate change could cause, I start regretting the fact that I said no to him . . . because he's too young? It's not like he's nineteen. If the world's going to end, I might as well have some company while I'm here. Maybe I'm also in a lovey-dovey mood because I just finished reading a romance novel about a baker in a witness protection program who meets a handsome cowboy.

"Andrew," I whisper so the other barista doesn't hear, "does your offer still stand?"

"My offer?"

"You know, when you asked me out the other day . . ."

"Yes!" He beams. "Did you reconsider?"

"Uh, yeah. If you're interested."

"Are you free tomorrow night?"

"Sure," I say. "I'll give you my number, and we can figure out the details later?"

When he leaves with his coffee in hand, I feel rather giddy. Sure, I may not have any of the things I'm "supposed" to have in my thirties, but I've got a date with a hot younger man tomorrow night. Age is just a number, and we're much better suited than, say, a stegosaurus and an allosaurus.

Yep, this is going be great.

Andrew's idea of a midweek date is to go out "early."

As in, 9 p.m.

When he tells me he wants to go to suave, I point out that happy hour ends at nine, so maybe we could go at eight?

Thankfully, he agrees.

After I put on my favorite jeans and my lucky red top, I stand on my toes to reach the black clutch on the top shelf of my closet, and—

"Ahhh!"

Paige rushes into my room as I'm gripping my shoulder. "What happened?"

"I think I pulled a muscle trying to get my purse."

Ten years ago, I would have done three seconds of stretching and been ready to go, but something feels wrong with my shoulder now. I move my ibuprofen from my everyday purse to my clutch, just in case I need it.

When I get to suave at exactly eight o'clock, Andrew is nowhere to be found. I grab a table and pull up the drinks menu. I order the same thing I did last time — why mess with success? — then scroll through my phone as I wait for my date. I consider texting him, but he's only ten minutes late, so that might seem desperate.

Besides, I worked myself into a frenzy earlier after reading an article about Gen Z and emojis. They regard certain emojis as a sign you're an old fart, so I'm kind of scared of texting Andrew now. I text Mark instead.

ME: Guess where I am? On a real date.

ME: Don't worry, our parents and their friends will never see me here.

MARK: Are you taking a cake-decorating class?

ME: Ha!

ME: Well, I guess I'm not actually on a date yet, seeing as he hasn't arrived, but he should be here soon.

MARK: It seems a bit late for a date on a weekday.

I don't want to admit to Mark that I had similar thoughts, and Andrew initially suggested nine. I'm about to type something about how I don't work on Thursdays — other than writing, which is flexible — when Andrew slides into the chair across from me.

"Hey," he says. He's wearing a dark T-shirt that molds to his muscles. He looks delicious, and I'm definitely glad I agreed to this date. Why did I avoid dating for so long when men like this arc interested in me? I know I had sensible reasons, but they escape me right now.

The server returns with my drink, and Andrew says he'll have the same thing.

When we're alone, there are a few seconds of awkward silence.

"Sorry," I say. "I haven't been on a first date in a while."

"That's hard to believe, since you're . . ." He gestures to me. "Very pretty."

I might be blushing, but it's too dark in here for Andrew to notice.

Unsure what to say, I stammer, "What do you do? Are you in school?"

"No, I graduated a couple years ago. I work for a start-up."

He proceeds to explain what this company does. It doesn't fully make sense to me, but I nod along, not wanting him to think I'm stupid, and suppress a yawn. I'm not bored, just unused to being out so late on a Wednesday.

"What about you?" he asks. "I mean, I know where you work, but—"

"I'm also an author. My first book came out last year."

"That's so cool." He says something else, but it's hard to hear over the noise in the bar.

I lean closer. "Could you repeat that?"

"It's inspiring. I guess dreams really can come true after thirty."

I can't prevent the expression of horror that overtakes my face.

"Sorry, sorry," he says. "It's just . . . I feel like I have to 'make it' by thirty, you know?"

Yeah, I remember being very determined to get a literary agent and publishing deal before I turned thirty, which didn't happen. But would I have said that if my date was almost a decade older than me?

Well, when I was twenty-four, I wouldn't have gone on a date with someone in their thirties, so I can't really answer that question. Some women get swept off their feet by older men, but I was never swayed in that direction. I was once asked out by a much older white man, but he clearly had a creepy fetish for Asian women, so I wasn't the slightest bit tempted.

"Did you go to university?" Andrew asks.

"Of course. My parents wouldn't have let me do otherwise."

"Did you study creative writing?"

"Ha! No. I majored in math."

"Yeah? That's quite a change from what you do now."

He stretches his arms over his head. I think he's just doing it to show off his muscles, and that's fine by me. I can appreciate an attractive guy.

And you know what? Stretching sounds like a good idea. My shoulder feels a bit weird after my earlier mishap.

I copy his move. That feels better and—

Oh no. I think I pulled something else.

I distract myself with a sip of alcohol, then dive back into the conversation.

It doesn't go too badly. We talk a bit about our jobs—I still don't entirely understand this start-up company, but whatever— and our families. Then we get onto the subject of high school.

"Did your parents let you have a phone?" he asks. "Mine didn't until grade twelve, and it felt extremely unfair."

"I didn't have a smartphone until my last year of university," I say, and his eyes widen. "I had a flip phone before that, and when I was in high school, my parents decided my sisters and I could share a single cell phone. Whoever was going out for the evening got to take it so they wouldn't have to use a pay phone."

I appear to be speaking gibberish to him. I feel old, and it's not because of that twinge in my shoulder.

"Smartphones didn't exist when you were in high school?" he asks.

"They existed, but it was more like business people having a BlackBerry."

"Right. I forgot about those. My dad had one, back in the day, and I think a couple of kids in my middle school did too. It's cool that you've lived through so much history."

Excuse me?

He leans forward again, and even though he's definitely making me feel old, I hope he'll put that big hand on my knee and slide it up my inner thigh. It's been a while for me, and he's nice to look at and he's not a complete asshole.

Then I start wondering if this is some kind of social media prank, where you take an old person on a date and see what ridiculous things you can get them to do.

And then he says, "Wow. You're probably old enough to remember Blockbuster."

Yes, Andrew, I remember Blockbuster. When I was a kid, it was a treat to go there and fight with my sisters over which movie to rent.

Actually, it's a little surprising that Andrew doesn't remember Blockbuster. He's not that young, is he? I think Blockbuster was still somewhat popular when he was like . . . six or seven.

But after that comment, I decided I just couldn't take it any more. Thirty-three isn't that old. Sure, I might not stay out as late as I once did, and sure, my body aches more than it used to, but I'm still young.

However, around Andrew, I felt like a senior citizen.

I couldn't go to bed with this guy. He'd probably whip out some newfangled sex moves that I've never heard of and I'd totally embarrass myself.

No, better to go back to avoiding dates. Instead, I'll just enjoy romance in the pages of a novel. Fictional men are much less hassle than real ones, and they don't make you leave the apartment.

"How was it?" Paige asks when I get home.

"He's too young," I say. "I felt like one of those elderly people who tell stories about how they had to walk uphill both ways through a snowstorm to go to their one-room schoolhouse."

Not that my own grandparents told such stories. As a general rule, they didn't talk about their past at all. In fact, I was sixteen before I discovered that my maternal grandparents didn't grow up in Hong Kong, where my mom was raised. It shouldn't have been a surprise to me; my mother spoke a different language with her mom than she spoke with my dad and us kids. Her parents were born somewhere in southern China, and they left under what I presume were bad circumstances circa 1950. When I asked my mom for details, she said she didn't wish to trouble me with them.

"I'm sure it wasn't that bad," Paige says.

"I think I blew his mind—"

My roommate snickers.

I glare at her before finishing, "When I said I didn't have a smartphone for most of university."

She looks disappointed. "Want to watch something?"

"Nah, I'm tired. I'm going to get ready for bed."

But once I turn on my white-noise machine and crawl under the covers, sleep eludes me, and it's not because my shoulder hurts.

No, I'm suddenly anxious.

What if news of my date with Andrew somehow gets back to my mother? It seems ridiculous to worry about it, yet after everything that's happened lately, I can't help it.

10

♡

"Truth is stranger than fiction."

—A writer who's just been told
their story is unrealistic

After I spend a long day updating my website and revising the book whose publication date has been delayed, my phone rings. It's my mother, and I'm convinced that this is it. The jig is up. One of her acquaintances saw me last night, when I was at suave with Andrew, and I'm going to get in trouble.

I sigh and answer the call. "Hi, Mom."

"Ah, Emily, what is with that *tone*?"

"I have no idea what you mean."

"And where were you on Tuesday morning?"

Okay, this isn't what I expected.

"At work?" I'm not sure why it comes out as a question; I know I was at work on Tuesday morning. But my mom has a way of making me doubt things that I know are facts.

She goes on to describe how her friend's niece's cousin's brother-in-law's barber—or something like that—saw me at Coffee on College on Tuesday.

"What's the problem?" I ask my mother. "That's exactly where I told you I was."

"I hear you were talking to a *man*."

"Am I not allowed to talk with men now? Serving customers is part of my job."

"I hear it was a very attractive young man, and you were *flirting*."

Oh. Now I know what happened. This acquaintance of an acquaintance, whoever they are, saw me talking to Andrew.

"I thought you were seeing Mark," Mom says.

"Yes, I am, don't worry. I wasn't flirting with Andrew—"

"Andrew! So that's his name."

"He's a regular, we're friends, that's all. Whoever said I was flirting clearly misunderstood the situation."

There's a long pause, and I wait with bated breath to see if she'll buy this explanation.

"Well, Winnie *is* known for exaggerating," Mom says at last.

I exhale in relief.

"But is this guy interested in being more than friends?" she asks. "I very much hope it works out with Mark, but if not, it wouldn't be a bad idea to have someone waiting in the wings."

"Look, Mom," I say, jaw clenched. "I don't need to have anyone *waiting in the wings*." This conversation is testing my patience.

"Oh? Is it going that well?"

"Yeah. Sure. But I don't want to talk with you about it, okay? It's early days, and my dating life is private."

She actually laughs. "Are you going out this weekend?"

"He's busy. I'm not sure he'll have time." After that painful real date, even pretending to have a date is too much for me, apparently. I make a mental note to text Mark and tell him to pretend to have a busy weekend. Dungeons and Dragons. A big project at work. Bottle-feeding a litter of kittens. I don't care.

"Hmph. Maybe he's blowing you off." Mom mentions something about telling his parents, and my skin feels like ice. I don't need more complications; I can barely manage my life as it is.

"He's not *blowing me off*. Could you please not interfere? It's going well, like I said."

"If you say so." But there's a note of skepticism in her voice.

I finally manage to get her off the phone, then go to the kitchen to make myself some tea, just as Paige arrives home.

"We're going out on Saturday," I say, "and getting drunk. I'll text Ashley."

"Did you just get off the phone with your mother?" she asks.

"How did you know?"

"Lucky guess." She quirks her lips. "Where should we go?"

I don't know why this is always such a hard question, but it is. Yes, there are lots of restaurants and bars in Toronto. Yes, I've been to many of them and enjoyed myself. But for some reason, this is almost as bad as when people ask me what my book's about.

I can see why people adopt a usual hangout, like Central Perk or MacLaren's. It cuts down on all the pesky decision-making. In theory, I like going to different places, but in practice, it involves too much thinking.

Since I'm feeling poor these days—thanks to my book being delayed, inflation, and the fact that I paid for my drink at suave as well as a cake-decorating class in the past week (okay, nobody paid for the class, but I'm really getting into this fake-dating act)—I try to think of cheap places, and eventually come up with Zed's. We used to drink there when we were younger, but it's been a few years.

It also has another advantage: I've never seen anyone who knows my mom there.

When we get to the bar on Saturday, the decor is exactly the same as before, and there's something comforting in that. The average age of the customers also hasn't changed, which means we're now older than most people here. Yep, for the second time in a few days, I feel old when going out for drinks.

But inflation hasn't touched the drink prices, which is nice. Paige and I each get a rum and Coke and grab a table in the corner.

"You're lucky you have four sisters," Paige says after we each take healthy swallows of our drinks. "It spreads the expectations around."

"Yeah, it does cut down on the guilt."

Not that I don't feel guilt, but it would be worse not to meet parental expectations if I didn't have sisters with kids and husbands and respectable careers. Signs of success to make my parents feel like coming to this country was worth it.

But Paige has only one sibling: a coddled younger brother. It made it easier for her family to travel—they went to Hong Kong every two years, whereas my parents managed that trip with us only twice—and she didn't need to share a bedroom, but yeah, there are advantages to my situation now.

"We're both over thirty," Paige says, "and neither of us is married or has kids. Or makes a lot of money. My parents keep asking themselves where they went wrong. I had to endure yet another conversation about that today."

"Did you mention your tattoo?"

Paige gives me a scary *are you kidding me?* look, and I laugh.

"The problem is that I get compared to my sisters," I say. Although come to think of it, Mom and Dad haven't done much of that lately. "Is your mom throwing men at you, like mine?"

"She keeps dropping 'subtle' hints about one man or another. Well, she thinks she's being subtle, but it's more like she's shouting things from the rooftops. Anyway. Ashley's here."

I stand up and wave Ashley over.

She sets down her stuff at the table. "Was the floor always this sticky?"

"Yes," Paige says. "It just didn't bother us when we were twenty-five."

"Gross."

However, after Ashley goes to the bar and comes back with a set of tequila shots, she's singing a different tune.

"Wow, it's so cheap! We should come here more often."

"You want me to do a shot?" I ask.

"Yeah, why not?"

"I'm too old for shots."

"You're never too old for shots," she says.

"Fine, but just the one."

We do the shots—salt, tequila, lime—and I decide that I wasn't wrong; I'm too old for this, but the rum and Coke is good.

"How's Frank?" Paige asks Ashley.

"He's just always . . . there. I wish we each had our own room, separate from the bedroom. Like a man cave and a woman cave."

"You could move," I say. "Get a three-bedroom place."

"Haha, very funny. In this rental market?"

I consider the housing situation in Toronto and take a healthy swallow of my drink. Okay, maybe two healthy swallows. Being able to pay for an extra room? That seems like an impossible luxury, plus competition for rental units can be fierce. I'm thankful that Paige and I have lived in our apartment for five years, even if the place has some issues. It's been a while since I had to deal with moving, and I appreciate that I wasn't living alone when the pandemic started. We'll probably live together in that apartment forever, since I don't know how we'll ever afford to move.

Ashley goes up to the bar to get another drink, one that isn't a shot.

"So, how was your date on Wednesday?" she asks when she returns.

Right. I haven't told her about that yet. I describe what happened, how he was amazed that I lived through so much history and remembered Blockbuster, and she can't help laughing.

Then I tell my friends that one of my mom's friends (or friend of an acquaintance of an acquaintance?) saw Andrew and me "flirting" at Coffee on College on Tuesday morning.

"I don't know how I'll pull off this fake relationship," I say.

Someone at the next table lets out an extra-long burp— Scarlett would be impressed—and I start feeling positively ancient.

I wait for him to finish before I continue. "I thought it wouldn't be so hard. We'd tell lies for a few months, nothing more, but my mother seems to know everyone in Toronto."

"You need to step up your game," Paige says. "Go on actual dates with him. Take pictures together and share them with your mother. Commit to this role."

"How much free time do you think I have?"

"Or you could just say it didn't work out," Ashley suggests. "'Mom, I gave it my best shot, but Mark Chan and I simply aren't suited for each other.'"

My entire body cringes. I can't admit defeat, not yet. That would make me feel like too much of a failure. If I can't have a successful real relationship, the least I can do is have a successful fake one. I imagine my mother's disappointment if I told her that it didn't work out with Mark. I'm not in the mood to make her even more disappointed in me. Sure, my more accomplished siblings take some of the pressure off me, but it's no picnic feeling like you're the most inadequate one in your large family.

I know, I know, I shouldn't care so much about what she thinks, and it hasn't stopped me from pursuing my dream, but still. I'm the child of immigrants, and there are certain expectations, even if they're not regularly spoken aloud.

"Paige is right. Mark and I need to go on real dates." I cringe again as I say it, but not as much as I thought I might. Brunch with Mark wasn't completely terrible, and at least he's about my age and doesn't think I'm a living relic.

"This seems a little excessive," Ashley says.

"Maybe." I sigh. "But it's my best option at this point."

"Ooh. Are you okay with it because you actually like Mark and want to spend time with him?"

"No," I scoff. "He's more tolerable than I initially thought but no. I'm not interested in Mark. I'm just interested in making my mother *think* I'm interested in him."

That makes sense, right? Everything is starting to seem a little fuzzy around the edges.

Mmm. Rum.

I'm too old for this.

When I wake up the next morning, my room is too bright. Which is weird, because it doesn't get any direct sunlight.

I didn't drink that much yesterday, did I? I swear I've had that much to drink many times before and felt perfectly fine—or close to fine—the next morning. I guess my body can't handle booze like it used to. I shouldn't have had that last amaretto sour.

I stumble into the kitchen, where Paige is making coffee. She looks similarly unhappy with the decisions she made last night.

"Good morning."

We both wince at her loud voice.

"Sorry," she says more quietly.

I stretch my arms over my head. I think I slept funny. Ugh. I down a painkiller, then pour myself some coffee, adding more milk and sugar than usual.

"Did I dance last night?" she whispers.

I think back. "I have a vague recollection of you dancing to a Taylor Swift song. In fact, I believe you were doing the Macarena, but don't quote me on that."

I pick up my phone to check if I have any photographic evidence of last night.

I do not.

After a night of drinking, I used to be able to bounce back easily, but now all I want to do is snuggle under a blanket, drink coffee, and watch baking shows. Maybe I'll also soothe my aching muscles with a hot-water bottle.

But before I allow myself to do that, I should text Mark. I settle on the couch, open up our messages, and . . .

I gasp as I read our last texts.

ME: HEY BABY
MARK: Are you drunk?
MARK: Do you need me to pick you up?

Huh. I don't remember this.

"Why are you making weird noises?" Paige asks. "Is your hangover that bad?"

"I drunk texted Mark." I cover my face with my hands as she comes over to the couch and reads the texts.

She snickers, then tries to paste on a serious expression. "It's not that bad. You sent him a grand total of two words."

"I called him 'baby.'"

I'll never be able to appear in public again. I cannot get over this.

I consider my options. I could retreat to a remote cabin in northern Ontario, hunting and foraging for my food as needed so I could avoid humanity. Unfortunately, the fact that I'm an extrovert puts a bit of a damper on this plan. I'm not sure how I'd manage the isolation. Plus, I know nothing about surviving in the wilderness.

For example: bears. I know nothing about bears.

Banishing myself from society is a bit much, but I'm not sure

I'll be able to face Mark again. How I can ask him to go on real fake dates with me?

Maybe I should pretend that a friend stole my phone.

Sorry about last night. I was out drinking with my friends,
and my roommate thought it would be funny to text you.
(She knows the truth.)

I add a winky face for good measure before sending the text.

"Why are you smiling?" Paige grabs my phone. "I can't believe you threw me under the bus."

"It's not like you and Mark know each other. You'll never have to meet him."

"You owe me," she mutters.

"Fine. I'll make you dinner tonight."

"All right."

Well, that was easy. I'm not surprised, though. One of the things that I did not anticipate about being an adult? It's a huge pain in the ass to have to plan for multiple meals every day, even when you love food as much as I do, and sometimes you get so overwhelmed by the thought that you eat cheese and crackers and Froot Loops for dinner.

Except Mark Chan. I bet he doesn't do things like that.

Paige heads to her room, and I head to social media as I wait for Mark to reply. I'm halfway through my second video of baby pandas terrorizing a zookeeper when he responds.

I was genuinely worried about you.

I feel warm inside.

Am I about to puke?

I dig my fingers into a throw pillow and steady myself. My head isn't in great shape, but I'm definitely not going to vomit.

ME: I'm sorry. It won't happen again.
ME: I have to ask you something and I think it would be faster
    if I called. Is that okay?
MARK: Yes.

That period seems vaguely threatening, but I decide to ignore it. I make the call. He picks up on the second ring.

"Hello." He doesn't sound like he's nursing a hangover. Lucky him.

"Hi," I say.

"Could you speak a little louder? You're very quiet."

"Sorry." I increase my volume slightly. "My head hurts, and I'm trying not to make it worse." I pause. "I think we need to start going on dates, rather than just saying we're going on dates. We need pictures. We also need to fool my mother's many friends and acquaintances, who might see us when we're out and about."

"I agree."

I have further arguments lined up in my semifunctional brain, but it turns out that I don't need to use them. I'm almost disappointed.

"Really?" I say. "You agree?"

"Yes. It'll be simpler this way."

"How about we go out for dinner this Tuesday?"

"Fine," he says.

"Do you have any restaurants in mind?"

"There are a few I've been meaning to try. I'll make a reservation."

"Okay, *baby*."

I'm not sure why I added that last part. I was embarrassed beyond belief when I saw what I'd drunk texted him, but using that word for the second time doesn't have the same embarrassment factor, and for some reason, I want to get a response out of him.

"I hope you don't expect me to call you that when we're out," he says, rather sternly.

"Of course not."

"Is there anything else you wished to discuss?"

"No."

"Very well. I'll see you on Tuesday." He pauses, then adds, "Baby."

I'm too stunned to say anything else before he hangs up.

Is Mark trying to have fun? Get back at me?

How peculiar.

11

———♡———

"Never, ever edit as you write, no matter how strong the temptation might be. You have to finish the whole manuscript and let it sit for a week or more. Then read it over, all in one sitting—you'll be seeing it as a reader, and you'll know what needs to be changed. Editing as you write is a complete waste of time."

—Tess Donovan

I ought to be writing tonight, but since I'm seeing Mark, there's no time for that.

After my shower, I debate what to wear. Considering that I've been picking out my own outfits for over thirty years—my mom (mostly) let my pick my clothes starting when I was a toddler—I should be better at this. Alas.

I've never been on a real fake date before, which is part of the problem. An additional complication: I'm not exactly swimming in cash, so my wardrobe is the opposite of impressive.

Paige is at the gym, working out her frustration at being told she wasn't a "team player," so I can't ask for her opinion. I'm flying solo. Eventually I settle on gray pants and a slightly low-cut purple sweater—not for Mark's benefit; I just like the way it looks—with a simple necklace.

When I get to the Peruvian restaurant on Harbord, my heart is beating quickly. Why am I nervous? It's not like this is a real date and I care what he thinks of me. This is all part of our act.

Mark is already seated at a table for two. He's wearing a sweater-vest, like he did for our brunch at Lily's Kitchen, and he's studying the menu. When I pull out the chair across from him, he glances up and seems momentarily surprised by my presence.

"Hello, Mark," I say.

"Emily." He nods.

The restaurant is small and dimly lit. Mood lighting, I suppose. It's not very busy, perhaps because it's a Tuesday.

I open the menu. The prices are, unfortunately, as high as they were online. Not that bad, really, but it'll cut into my budget for the week, and I grimace.

I definitely won't be having any alcohol tonight. I'll stick with a main course and nothing more. Well, maybe I'll try some chicha morada.

"Don't worry, I'll pay," Mark says. "I chose the restaurant."

"And I was the one who said we had to start going on real dates. So in a way, I'm the one who invited you out."

He gives me a look. "You can pay next time."

I'm a bit relieved, honestly, though I try not to show it.

The server comes around and fills up my water glass. He recites the specials for the day—also written on a chalkboard by the entrance—and asks if we want anything to drink. I order the chicha morada, as does Mark.

Once we're alone again, he asks, "Shall we get an order of ceviche to start?"

I start to say no, then remind myself that he's paying, and this is his idea. "Sure. Which one?"

I consider getting lomo saltado for my main, but ultimately decide on arroz con pato. The server returns with our deep purple drinks and takes the rest of our orders.

Mark reaches for his glass. "So, what made you decide to be a writer?"

I sip my drink as I prepare to answer. The intense color is

from purple corn, and it has a pleasant, light sweetness with a little spice.

"I really enjoyed reading as a child," I say. "I could get lost in a book so easily, and I fell in love with writing stories in grade three. But creative writing wasn't a practical thing to study in university, so I didn't ever consider it. These days, I sometimes wish I had a better humanities background—a major in English or history, maybe—but that would only have been acceptable to my parents if I was planning on law school, and I never wanted to be a lawyer." I pause. "I started writing my first novel when I was twenty-four. I mean, other than the 'novel' I wrote when I was eleven."

"What was that one about?"

"Let me give you a tip for the next time you meet an author: don't ask what their book is about. But that one was a rainforest adventure. With aliens."

In the flickering candlelight, his lips curve into a smile. There's an odd flutter in my chest, and I instinctively smile back.

Mark Chan is more than a little handsome.

Disconcerted by that thought, I swallow some chicha morada and glance around the restaurant, trying to see if there's anyone here who might know my mother.

Nobody looks familiar.

"When did you decide you wanted to be a computer engineer?" I ask.

"When I was twelve. After I gave up on my dreams of being a video-game tester for Nintendo and also decided that I was too distressed by the sight of blood and needles to consider being a doctor."

I find that confession rather endearing. Mark seems like the kind of person who'd be stoic in the face of gushing blood, and the fact that he isn't makes him seem less like the perfect bland man chosen by my mother.

Yes, I'm aware that sounds silly, but it's true.

"Is being a writer everything you thought it would be?" he asks.

"Ha! I wasn't prepared for the publishing industry."

"In what way?"

"Would you like a three-hour speech?"

"Some other time, perhaps."

"I'll hold you to it," I say. "And although I do like writing, I wasn't prepared for how much time I'd spend avoiding it by mopping the kitchen floor and watching cute puppy videos. The other day, I even spent an hour researching poison in the Victorian era, although there's no poison in my book and it's contemporary."

There's unexpected mischief in his eyes as he leans forward. "Do you still think I'd be good at covering up a murder, *baby*?"

"Stop teasing me!"

"I'm not teasing you." He lowers his voice. "I'm just playing the part, in case someone sees us together. You told me it wasn't necessary to call you 'baby' in public, but it makes sense for me to use a term of endearment."

"That one seems woefully out of character for you."

He arches an eyebrow. "So if I were a character in one of your books, which term of endearment would I use?"

I can't help squirming in my seat. I'm unsettled by this conversation, and I don't like it. His serious-yet-teasing tone is *seriously* annoying.

"'Sweetie,' perhaps," I say, rather irritably. "Or 'darling.'"

The corners of his mouth quirk up, as if he's amused that he's made me irritable. Perhaps Mark isn't as bland as I thought, but he's more aggravating than expected.

Our ceviche arrives, and I eagerly dig in.

"By the way," I say, "I'm sorry about drunk texting you and later blaming it on my roommate."

"Next time, please have the courtesy to reply so I know you're okay."

"I promise I won't do it again. I rarely drink like that." I don't want Mark to think I drink as much as, say, Bridget Jones. Not that I really care what he thinks, but I'd prefer if my fake boyfriend didn't wonder if I'm an alcoholic.

When my duck arrives, I take a picture of it, my half-finished chicha morada in the background. I know Mark doesn't approve of the pictures, but first of all, I don't care what he thinks, and second of all, I need evidence of our date.

I hold my phone up in his direction.

He frowns. "I don't like having my photo taken."

"It's proof that we went on a date."

"I do not give you permission to put any pictures of me online."

"I won't, but if my mom asks, I need to have something to show her."

He sighs. "Very well."

"You can smile, you know."

"No, I can't. I'm highly allergic to smiling."

"I've seen you smile before. Not often, but it happens."

"You must be mistaken," he says.

"When I said you could call me 'sweetie.' You smiled then."

"Did not."

I'm having trouble getting a read on him. I blame the dim light. Does he genuinely think his lips didn't turn upward then, or does he just enjoy bothering me? Given that I have four siblings, I'm used to people doing the latter, but he's unlike any of my sisters.

And then it happens. I see the tiniest quirk of his mouth again.

This is definitely Mark being playful.

I'm not sure what to do with that. It's disorienting.

Luckily, I regain my wits in time to take a photo while he's still quasi-smiling, and then he pulls out his phone. "I suppose I should have a picture of you too."

I smile and gesture for him to take it.

When he tucks his phone into his pocket afterward, I swear his gaze slides from my eyes to my cleavage for a split second.

Nah, I was probably imagining that.

Finally, I dig into the duck, which falls off the bone with ease. It's just as delicious as it looks. The rice—which has cilantro, bell pepper, and peas, among other things—is also amazing. The raw red onion on top is thinly sliced and works perfectly.

"How is it?" Mark asks.

"It's very good," I say. "How's the lamb shank?"

"Delicious."

I'd like to come back here sometime—on a *real* date—and try the lamb. I don't think I can ask my fake date for a taste of his meal.

He picks up an unused spoon, breaks off a piece of tender lamb, and puts it on my plate.

Okay, I didn't think I was that obvious, but I'm not going to say no.

It is, indeed, quite tasty, and I feel obligated to give him a bite of my food too. In fact, it's not entirely obligation—I do genuinely want him to try it.

We eat in contented silence for a few minutes.

"So," I say, "how's your first 'fake date' going?"

He winces at my use of air quotes, then says, in a mild tone, "What makes you assume this is my first?"

"Lucky guess."

He looks at his plate. "The food is excellent."

"And the company?"

"Acceptable." He accompanies his response with one of those smiles he claims to be allergic to, and I feel an odd warmth in my chest. Being on a date with Mark isn't so bad. It won't be a problem to do this a few more times.

Although the restaurant is slightly expensive by my standards, it's not one of those expensive places that skimps on portions. By the time I finish my food, I'm quite full.

A few seconds after I set down my fork, my phone buzzes twice.

"Sorry, let me check this." I take a peek at my phone. It's Paige, making sure that my date is going okay and sending me a puppy video in case it isn't.

I put the phone back in my purse.

"You can respond if you like," Mark says. "I know my mother gets antsy if I don't answer a text promptly."

"No, no, it's fine. Just my roommate. I'll watch the puppy video she sent me later." I feel a twinge of annoyance that he feels the need to give me permission to text, when he spent so much time texting at Hannah's wedding.

"Tell me more about these puppy videos that prevent you from writing."

"You must have wasted time watching animal videos when you had better things to do. Actually, no—you've probably never done anything foolish like that."

"You seem to have a rather particular view of me. Maybe I have hundreds of puppy or kitten videos bookmarked."

"Are you more of a cat person or dog person?"

"Cat person, I suppose. And I've wasted time watching videos of kittens playing with string, I'll have you know." His low voice isn't quite as calm as it was before, and he no longer has that spark of playfulness. I think this conversation has taken a turn. "You seem to think I can't do anything frivolous or fun, like when you made that comment about the cake-decorating class."

I appear to have struck a nerve. "Given the way my mother talks about all the great things you've done, I don't know how you have time for anything else."

"I'm sure she's exaggerating, or you're exaggerating what she says. Perhaps both."

"Are you calling me a liar?"

"We're both liars." His tone is back to being annoyingly mild. "We're not in a real relationship, but we're pretending to be."

I look around. I hope nobody is listening to our conversation. "You didn't have to agree to my plan, but you did."

He sighs. "I did."

"It must be *such* a hardship," I say, "for you to pretend to date someone who isn't making use of her degree and doing calculus at her job. Someone who lives with a roommate."

"What are you talking about?"

"Come on. You were judging me the first time we met."

"Your imagination is running away with itself. A hazard of your occupation, I presume."

I glare at him. I can't believe that, ten minutes ago, I thought this fake date wasn't so bad after all. He really is irritating . . . in an entirely different way from how he irritated me earlier.

"Once again," I say, trying to keep my voice steady, "you're calling me a liar."

He shrugs.

"You're not going to refute that?" I ask.

"Whatever you say, however I respond, you seem to take it the wrong way."

"Then maybe you should be clearer."

He scowls.

I'm not sure how this got so off the rails, but I don't see the point in continuing our conversation. I just need to pretend we're having a half-decent time for the sake of our act.

The server clears our plates. "Would you like to see the dessert menu?"

"No, thank you. Just the bill, please," I say with a forced smile.

When he walks away, Mark leans forward. "Is dessert too frivolous for me?"

"I thought this sort of snippiness was below you."

"Clearly you were wrong, as you've been wrong about many other things."

There's something refreshing about him arguing with me like this—and the sense of humor that he displayed earlier. He's not unflappable.

But the fact that he can get under my skin doesn't mean I *like* him.

He pays the bill, and neither of us attempts to linger afterward. We put on our jackets and head out into the cold night. He starts walking toward Bloor.

"Are you coming?" he asks, looking back. "To the subway?"

"No, I'll wait for the bus. It stops closer to my apartment."

He walks back. "I'll wait with you."

"That's not necessary."

"It's dark and my mother would kill me if I didn't make sure you got safely on the bus."

I wonder if his mother is as overly concerned about kidnapping as mine.

"Fine," I say. "If you insist."

We stand in frosty silence for a very long three minutes before the bus approaches. I take my PRESTO card out of my purse, then decide, for the sake of our "act," to give him a hug. He appears startled, but his arms come around my back. To my annoyance, it's not unpleasant.

Then he whispers, "I'm going to kiss your cheek, okay?" His voice is serious, suggesting that he doesn't take any pleasure in this but believes it's necessary.

Yet when his lips brush my cheek, he lingers long enough for me to wonder if my assumptions are wrong.

I get on the bus in a daze.

———————

Wednesday afternoon, I'm about to start writing when my mom calls.

"Did you have dinner with Mark yesterday?" she asks. "I seem to recall you mentioning it. How did it go?"

The one time we actually went on a date instead of pretending we went on a date, we weren't seen putting on a performance.

Hmph. I went to all that effort for nothing.

I touch my cheek, where he kissed me last night, then slap my hand down on my desk. Why am I thinking about the press of his lips against my skin? It's not as if I liked it.

"Yeah, it was lovely," I say through gritted teeth. "The food was great." Not a lie. *And if you need a few pictures for proof, I can send them to you.*

"I'm glad." She doesn't ask for pictures. "We're hosting a gathering for Wayne's sixty-fifth birthday party in a few weeks. I'm sure he'd like it if you both were there."

I doubt he'll be too fussed about my presence, but I'll come if I don't have a shift.

"It's a Sunday," she says, "so you shouldn't have to work, right? Mark's parents will be there. The two of you can come *together*." She sounds almost giddy.

Good thing it's not a video call so she can't see my expression of horror.

"Which day is it?" I ask.

She tells me the date.

"Shoot, I'm pretty sure Mark is busy," I say. "He mentioned something about—"

"No, he's free. You must have your days mixed up. I already spoke to his mom, and she said he could come. He shares his calendar with her."

I pinch the bridge of my nose. *Thanks for making my life dif-*

ficult, Mark. Going on a date so we might be seen in public is different from attending a family friend's birthday party as a couple. I'm not looking forward to this.

"I'll do my best," I say, "but one of the other baristas quit, so we're a bit short-staffed. I might have to pick up another shift." Not true, but it sounds believable, doesn't it?

"I'm sure they'll hire someone else in the next three weeks."

If I put up too much of a fight, she'll become suspicious, so I simply say, "Hopefully."

"I'm really glad my little plan worked." She laughs. "I was half-worried you'd get angry and leave Lily's Kitchen without talking to Mark, and now look at you. Your father said it was too much, but I was right after all. One day, you'll be thanking me in your wedding speech."

She's already talking about our wedding! Paige was correct. It didn't take long.

"Yes, you were right," I say reluctantly. This fake relationship has forced so many indignities on me. Like saying that my mother was right to trick me into going on a date with Mark Chan.

"I should be a professional matchmaker! Do you think I could make lots of money?"

"Uh . . ."

"Ah, Emily, why aren't you encouraging my dreams?"

Well, you never encouraged my dreams. You wanted me to be practical.

After ending the call, I watch a kitten video—for the very necessary purpose of lowering my blood pressure after that conversation—before I do some research on poison. For my book, of course.

But my mind wanders back to yesterday's "date," and I find myself wishing I hadn't been so combative.

That's the problem with real life. When I write, I can revise the words on the screen before anyone sees them. Polish them until they shine. After finishing the first draft, I always let my manuscript sit for a while, to help me get some perspective. (That's not the only way to write, though; my critique partner edits as she writes, and it works for her, even if certain authors would say that's a terrible idea.)

And now that more than twenty-four hours have passed since my rendezvous with Mark, it's given me some perspective, and I wish I'd handled it a little differently. I try composing a text to tell him that, but I can't find the right words and soon give up.

Time for more kitten videos.

12

—♡—

*"We are gathered here today to bid farewell to Trunkit,
who was partially eaten by a T. rex on Tuesday."*
—Future author Emily Hung (age eleven)

I loved looking after Hannah when she was little. She was always amused by the stories I told with our dolls and stuffed animals; her delighted giggles made me feel like I was a great storyteller. One of the rare times I was annoyed with her—she ate some of my Halloween candy—I made her favorite doll die in an unlikely accident with a garbage truck and a dragon. But that didn't work as intended because she enjoyed the funeral I staged afterward, and for weeks after that, I kept having to arrange funerals for her toys to entertain her. I can't say that was my favorite, but I gave Trunkit (her stuffed elephant) three violent deaths and funerals nonetheless. And when she accidentally decapitated her stuffed sheep, I sewed him up with care. After the funeral, of course.

Later, however, I was resentful of Hannah. When she was allowed to sleep over at Brooke Martin's house at age ten, it became painfully clear that different rules would apply to her. At that age, I'd begged to go to my best friend's birthday sleepover, but Dad had insisted on picking me up at 9 p.m.

Maybe little things like that shouldn't have bothered me so much, but they did. I would dig my nails into my palms, the sharp pain preventing me from an outburst of anger that would upset my baby sister.

Because I, too, treated Hannah a little differently from my other sisters. I would never hold back from upsetting Allison, for example.

The one time I truly felt badly for Allison was when I was twelve and she was fourteen. Everyone in our family came down with the flu, except me and Hannah. At first, I didn't mind the disruption to our family's routine. Hannah and I ate whatever we wanted, and nobody nagged me about anything.

But at one point, I woke up to my parents having a frantic conversation, and then Auntie Carmen was called to take Allison to the hospital. My big sister was the sickest of everyone, so sick she'd forgotten to be annoyed with me for days.

I started panicking. It was two in the morning, and my parents looked like they needed to be in bed, but they were down in the kitchen making calls. Allison was on the couch with the barf bucket.

"Will she be okay?" I asked.

My parents had taken us to the ER before, but for broken bones, never for the flu.

"Ah, she'll be fine." My mom's weak voice wasn't convincing, though. "I think she needs an IV. She lost too many fluids."

"Why can't you take her?"

"I will go too, but I need help . . . from someone who is well."

"I'm well," I said.

"No, you stay here," Dad said. "Take Hannah to school in the morning."

When we got back from school the next day, Allison was still gone.

"When is she coming back?" Hannah asked.

"Soon," I said. It felt like my duty to make sure she didn't worry, even if I did.

But she must have still been worrying—she didn't want me to tell the kind of morbid stories she usually enjoyed—and she was practically glued to my hip all evening.

When Allison returned home, looking weak but more like herself, Hannah ran to her and hugged her. I said, with total honesty, "Glad you're doing better."

I was relieved. I didn't have words for all I was feeling—and twelve-year-old me usually did have words—but that much I knew.

The Saturday after my unfortunate date with Mark, Hannah visits my apartment.

My baby sister hasn't visited me here in years, and never by herself; in fact, we rarely hang out just the two of us.

I still have some lingering resentment toward her. I'm not proud to admit it, but I do, although I'd never tell her that. She had freedoms that I could never have hoped to have, and I bet if she'd told Mom, at the age of eight, that she wished to be a writer, Mom wouldn't have been quite as disappointed.

But instead, she's the engineer.

I make us tea, and we sit at the tiny dining room table. She shows me pictures from her honeymoon in Mexico, followed by photos of the wedding, where me, Allison, Meghan, and May were all bridesmaids. Brooke Martin was the maid of honor.

As I flip through the pictures on her tablet, I don't think about my niece's horror at my age or my mother's insistence on matchmaking. Instead, I recall Hannah giggling when I made her stuffed sheep eat some magic beans and fly to Neverland.

Shit. I think my eyes are wet.

I didn't feel like crying during the wedding ceremony, but now that I've had some distance from the actual wedding day, I do. Obviously, getting married isn't a necessary part of growing

up, but seeing pictures of her in that wedding dress, the young
woman in front of me now . . . my throat clogs with emotion. I
hope she doesn't notice.

I don't want her to worry about me, like I didn't want her to
worry when Allison was in the hospital.

"You know, I don't remember ever wanting to play weddings
with my toys," she says. "I seem to recall preferring funerals."

"The first doll funeral happened because I was mad at you."

"Oh?" Her eyes widen. "I don't remember that."

"You stole all my Smarties from Halloween."

"But those were your favorite!"

"Exactly. I was pissed. That's why your doll had to die, but
it didn't upset you like I expected. Instead, I had to conduct
funerals on a regular basis to amuse you."

We laugh together, and for some reason, it feels different.

More like it did when we were kids.

I open my mouth, about to tell Hannah that my relationship
with Mark is fiction too, but then I think better of it. The fewer
people who know the truth, the better.

And then my fake relationship whizzes out of my head at my
sister's next comment.

"I should warn you," she says.

"About what?"

"Mom and Dad are concerned."

"I know, I know, I don't have a proper job, I'm not married—"

"I'm not talking about that. They're worried you think Dad's
not . . . your bio dad."

"What?" I shriek. "Why would they . . . *oh*."

My parents have definitely read my book. I thought my mother
might ask which characters were based on her, but I didn't anticipate *this*.

"It's fiction," I say. "Just like an elephant getting eaten by a

T. rex is fiction. Don't they understand that I make things up? It's not like I wrote a memoir."

"I told them that, and besides, your chin looks exactly like Dad's—"

"Yes, multiple people have commented on that, weirdly enough."

"—but Mom countered by saying writers often draw inspiration from their real lives. It sounds like they've been worrying about this for months. May told me they've mentioned it to her too."

I'm getting a headache.

"I thought you should know," she says, "in case they make any weird comments."

"Uh, thanks."

We both sip our tea, and there's an awkward silence in the apartment. Paige is out with a friend, so it's just me and my sister.

Then we look at each other, and when her lip twitches, I can't help bursting into laughter at the ridiculousness that is my life.

And as she joins me in laughter again, I feel the last of my resentment leave my body.

But that doesn't mean I'm going to tell her the truth about Mark.

In the next few weeks, I cook for Mark one sunny Sunday afternoon—at least, that's what I tell my mother, who fortunately doesn't ask if I have any questions about my paternity. We also go out for fried chicken (supposedly). I'm not in the mood for more real fake dates. Aside from some brief texts to communicate the details of our so-called relationship, we don't speak. I tell him that our "relationship" will end right before the Canada Day weekend, and he agrees.

I don't feel disappointed that he doesn't argue.

As Uncle Wayne's birthday approaches, I become more worried about our ability to pull this off. Rather than googling things that I fear will get the authorities interested in me, such as how to hide a body—research for my writing, obviously—I search for silly things, such how to tell if a woman likes you. I need to know how to act around Mark so everyone believes I'm falling for him. Of course, I have my own personal experience, but it's been an exceedingly long time since I've had a serious crush. I need a refresher, and some unbiased sources might be helpful.

The results are, however, confusing. One listicle suggests that a woman acting nervous and avoiding eye contact is a sign she's interested in a man; another listicle says that making clear eye contact is a sign she's interested.

Being touchy-feely is a good sign, according to multiple sources, but I'd never be too touchy-feely with a guy around my family. That would be suspicious.

Another article—a very scientific one, of course—says that to show a guy I like him, I should laugh at his jokes.

Except the only time I've ever really laughed with him was when he called me "baby," which I probably shouldn't do when we're around other people. If we were actually in a relationship, a term of endearment wouldn't elicit a laugh, right? But having inside jokes is very relationship-y . . . isn't it?

This is all very complicated.

Eventually, I work myself into such a state that I need to read about household poisons to calm myself down.

A few days before the party, my mother asks if I'll come early to help her prepare. I hesitate, a bit afraid she's going to ask questions about my book and who I think my dad is, but ultimately, I agree to come early. This will give me an excuse not to arrive with Mark, which would probably involve him picking me up at the subway and sitting in uncomfortable silence for twenty-five minutes. Or forty minutes, depending on how awful the traffic is.

On Sunday morning, I deal with a nauseatingly bumpy bus ride and arrive at my childhood home before ten. It's an unusually warm day for early May, warm enough to enjoy the backyard, so I help my parents clean off the patio furniture. Then my father and I drive to a bakery to pick up a cake, followed by two different restaurants to pick up food. I'm concerned that we won't be able to fit everything in the car, but somehow, we manage.

"How's it going with Mark?" my father asks on the drive back.

"Mom asked me that question an hour ago, while we were taking tables outside. If I remember correctly, you were there for that."

"I was."

"Are you hoping I'll give you details that I wouldn't share around her?"

"I want to make sure he's treating you right. Your mother seems to assume he is, but I want to check."

Okay, I'm rather touched.

"Yes, Dad, you have nothing to worry about. No need to bring out your shotgun."

"Shotgun?" He glances over at me, then turns back to the road.

"The stereotype about fathers . . . never mind."

Asian parents can be scary enough without weapons.

"You know," he says, eyes fixed ahead of him, "I *am* your father."

Oh dear. Here we go.

If I were less appalled by the situation, I might make a *Star Wars* joke, but I don't.

To be honest, I'm surprised Dad is the one bringing this up. Usually, Mom is responsible for the difficult conversations—and

I think this falls into that category, even if it's absurd that it's occurring at all.

"I never questioned it," I say. "Don't worry."

"If you want, we could do a test."

Oh, for fuck's sake.

"That's not necessary," I tell him. "I have no doubts, I promise. My book isn't based on my life."

"It was just hard to believe at times, because you write so well about things that haven't happened to you."

"Well, uh . . . thanks?"

I appreciate the compliment, but it's difficult to sound appreciative after suffering through that conversation. I'm glad Hannah warned me it might be coming.

"Could you do me a favor?" I ask.

"Of course."

"Can we never, ever talk about this again?"

He chuckles. "Sure."

Now I just have to look forward to surviving a party with my fake boyfriend.

13

♡

"The course of fake dating never did run smooth."
—Me, with a little help from Shakespeare

When we return to the house, the party is already in full swing. Auntie Sharon and Uncle Wayne are in the backyard, and my uncle is drinking what I suspect is his second beer.

"Happy birthday," I say to him, and a moment later, I sense someone else beside me. I turn to see Mark. He lays a hand on my shoulder before also murmuring his good wishes.

"It looks like you're going to be next after all, Emily," Wayne says.

Someone pulls on my leg. "Is Mark your boyfriend?" Scarlett asks once she has my attention. "When are you getting married? Next month? You promised I could be your flower girl."

I didn't actually promise her that, but I'm not going to argue with a five-year-old.

"Me too!" Scarlett's three-year-old sister, Khloe, jumps up and down with her hand in the air.

Scarlett glares at her. "You'll mess it all up again, like at Auntie Hannah's wedding. You weren't supposed to run to Mommy after you made it down the aisle. You were supposed to stand at the front, like I did."

"Scarlett," Allison says, "be nice to your sister."

Khloe, however, has already moved on to the next thing. She

runs around the yard in her dress, picking up sticks, then zooms back and presents one to me. I'm not sure what I've done to deserve this gift, but I thank her for it.

"It's a fairy wand," she says.

"Can I turn you into a frog?" I wave the stick around, then tap it on her shoulder.

She giggles. "What sound do frogs make?"

"Ribbit," I say. "Ribbit."

"Ribby! Ribby!" She starts hopping on the ground.

"So you and Mark really are together," Allison says, but she sounds skeptical, like she did at dim sum.

"Yes!" I say brightly, wrapping my arm around him. He doesn't flinch, thankfully.

"You make a rather unusual couple."

"What's so unusual about us?"

"You know what I mean," she says. "You're the one who refuses to follow the rules, and he . . .." She gestures at him.

"Ribby! Ribby!" Khloe hops in between us.

Allison touches her younger daughter on the head. "You're a human again."

"No!" Khloe says. "Only Auntie Emily can turn me back. Ribby! Ribby!"

Allison looks at me. I consider leaving my niece as a frog for a little longer—she doesn't seem to mind—but then I tap Khloe with the stick.

"Now I'm a pig!" Khloe shrieks. "Oink! Oink!"

Scarlett rolls her eyes. "You're such a baby." She's as unimpressed with Khloe as Allison is with me.

At that moment, Mark's parents arrive, and seeing as I'm supposed to be his dutiful girlfriend—ha!—I need to say hello.

"Emily," Cilla says warmly. "How nice to see you again. Mark has been telling us so much about you."

Oh, has he? I'm very curious to know what he's said. Presumably he hasn't been telling his mom that I take everything the wrong way.

"I must see these cake-decorating skills put to use one day," she continues. "I was very intrigued when he told us about the class."

"Yes. Right. Of course." Fake cake decorating has come back to haunt me yet again.

While Cilla seems keen to talk, her husband stays quiet, his posture rigid. I've met Terrence Chan only once before—at Hannah's wedding—and now I note the strong resemblance between him and Mark. I suppose this is what Mark will look like in thirty years. It's partly their features, but it's also the way they carry themselves. It's easy to see where my so-called boyfriend got his slightly stiff, formal manner. According to my mom, Terrence comes from a wealthy family in Hong Kong, and he does some kind of business thing that she doesn't understand.

"Oink! Oink!" Khloe says from somewhere on the ground, interrupting my thoughts.

"I'm going to get a drink," I say. "I'll be back."

I hurry to the other side of the backyard, where there's a selection of crappy Canadian beer that Wayne is, for reasons unknown to me, a dedicated fan of. I could drink it if I have to, but then I see a bottle of wine. Excellent. I pour a generous amount into a plastic cup.

"Hi, Emily." Auntie Janie speaks to me before I can return to Cilla and Terrence. "I hear you and Mark are dating?"

"We are."

"Are you engaged? When are you getting married?"

We've been "dating" for less than two months. If I ever get engaged to someone, it would be after a minimum of one year of dating. And I'd want to live together before we actually tie the knot, just in case that turns out to be a disaster and I have to call the whole thing off.

I gulp some wine, then paste on a smile. "I haven't been in a relationship for a while. I'm taking things slow."

Janie looks rather horrified. "Don't take things too slow. You're thirty-two, aren't you?"

"Thirty-three."

"If you want to have babies, you'll have to start soon."

I recall what it was like when I was nineteen and brought a boyfriend—whom I'd been dating for seven months—to a family gathering. Let me tell you, nobody was talking about marriage and kids then. Some people were appalled that my parents "allowed" me to date while I was still in undergrad.

"Oink! Oink!" Khloe says.

I tap her head. "Now you're a little girl."

"Moo! Moo!"

"Is that the noise little girls make?"

"Moo!" she says as she runs away. "Moo! Moo!"

I assume that means "yes" in cow.

"You're very lucky," Auntie Janie says, ignoring the barnyard noises. "I know a girl who stayed single until thirty-three, and when she wanted to settle down, the only man she could find was a dental assistant." She says that as though it's embarrassing, but there's nothing wrong with being a dental assistant. "Mark is a good catch. Hard to believe he isn't already married."

"Probably because he's too annoyingly perfect," I mutter.

"What did you say?"

I take another glug of wine "Yes, it is. I'm *very* lucky."

Remembering that I'm supposed to act like I'm besotted with Mark, I glance around the backyard until my gaze lands on him. He's having a conversation with my father. He immediately looks at me and gives me a curt nod. I'm not sure how long I should maintain eye contact to convince people that I'm *besotted*. The advice is getting a bit jumbled in my head, so I decide to go for 2.4 seconds and flutter my eyelashes for good measure.

"Do you have something in your eye?" Auntie Janie asks.

"Just a bit of dust, I think." So much for a sexy flutter of my eyelashes.

Speaking of eyelashes, you know what's always confused me? When cartoon animals or objects are used to represent a man and a woman—say, on a greeting card—you'll know which one is the "woman" by her long eyelashes. Who decided that a female cactus or pig should have long eyelashes and a pink bow in her "hair"?

I have no idea why I'm thinking about that now. I blink, attempting to get the "dust" out of my eyes, and ask my auntie about her kids, both of whom are too busy to be here. Letting her brag about her kids? Always a safe topic. Her oldest is doing his residency, and she'll never let my parents forget it. She has a son who's going to be a neurosurgeon, and my parents do not.

Khloe runs by and knocks into me, nearly sloshing my wine.

"Say sorry when you bump into someone," Allison calls.

"Moo!" Khloe cries.

The next time she gets close to me, I tap her with my hand. "Now you're a cat."

Apparently, these are the magic words that turn her back into a human. Instead of meowing, she says, "Auntie, your dress is so pretty."

I don't usually wear dresses until the summer, but I figured today was warm enough. I'm also wearing a pink cardigan on top of my flowered dress.

"Thank you, sweetie," I say.

"Is it a wedding dress?"

"No."

Does everyone need to bring up weddings? It makes me want to drink more, especially since it's so warm outside—really, why is it so warm?—and the white wine is quite refreshing.

"I read your book," Auntie Janie says. "I meant to read it earlier, but I'm so busy—I barely have time to read these days."

Oh no. Is she going to ask who I think my father is?

I drain the rest of my wine instead of screaming, *It's fiction!*

"Your mother and I were talking about it."

"Were you?" I murmur.

Why does the ground feel like it's moving?

"And we were wondering if the one character was based on—"

"Sorry," Mark says, coming over and taking me by the arm. "I need to steal my girlfriend away for a moment."

He sounds different than he usually does, artificially upbeat, but maybe this has something to do with the whole acting-like-my-boyfriend-around-our-families business. He leads me through the back door, where we both instinctively take off our shoes.

"That was good timing on your part." I wobble after I slip off my second shoe.

He grabs me before I fall. "I was worried. You're unsteady on your feet. How much did you drink?"

"Don't sound so accusatory. It was just the one cup of wine. Yes, I know that's probably more than a regular glass of wine, but . . ."

"When did you last eat?"

"Um . . . last night I ate a bag of popcorn while watching a movie."

He shuts his eyes, as if this is too much for him to bear.

"What?" I say. "There's nothing wrong with the occasional bag of popcorn."

"But it's one o'clock in the afternoon. The next day. You didn't eat breakfast?"

"Does the sugar in my coffee count as food?"

He gives me a look.

"I don't always eat breakfast on Sunday," I say. "Have a problem with that?"

"No, but I'm not surprised that wine went straight to your head. You should eat something." He pushes me onto a chair by the kitchen table and walks away. The next thing I know, my mother is setting a plate with cheese, crackers, and fruit in front of me.

Ooh. Cheese.

It actually does feel nice to be sitting down and eating, rather than standing as I listened to Auntie Janie talk about my book. Mark was right—this is exactly what I needed.

"Why are you arguing with Mark?" Mom asks.

"I'm just hangry," I mutter.

"Hangry? What is this new word?"

"Never mind."

"Well, you've always been irritable when you're hungry."

Mark returns with a glass of water. He kneels in front of me and places a hand on my shoulder. I suppose he's doing a good job at being an attentive boyfriend.

"I'll leave you here with Mark," Mom says. "I've got to bring some stuff outside."

He pulls up a chair next to me, and I enjoy my cheese and grapes.

"That conversation sounded like it was about to get painful," he says. "The one you were having with Janie."

"Is that why you rescued me, or was it just because I was wobbly?"

"Bit of both. You were also doing something weird with your eye when you looked in my direction."

"I was trying to appear *besotted*."

"It was a valiant attempt, but I think you missed the mark." He studies me for a moment. "How are you doing?"

"I'm fine, but perhaps I shouldn't have any more wine. You can go out now, if you like. No need to stay here with me." If I wait a little longer, maybe Auntie Janie will have forgotten that she was asking about my book.

"I'm your boyfriend. I should stay with you if you feel a little off."

I doubt every man I've dated in the past would have done that, but I don't argue.

"Besides," he says, "Wayne was extolling the virtues of crappy beer, and I wasn't sure how much more I could take. That, and people kept asking when we're getting married."

"Yeah, the marriage talk is a bit much, but I do like it a little better than my mother constantly singing your praises and telling me that I need to go out with you."

"Ah. You don't like people singing my praises?"

"It was getting repetitive, and it had reached rather fanciful proportions. Plus, now she's not quite as disappointed in me, so that's nice."

Dad and Hannah come in the back door, and Mark and I lapse into silence until after they've checked on me and returned to the backyard. Later, I'll have to tell Hannah about the conversation in the car.

"I don't think your parents are as disappointed in you as you think." Mark touches my shoulder, and I'm not sure if this is all part of the act—although I doubt anyone can see us from the backyard right now—or if he's genuinely trying to be comforting.

Despite our argument last time, I think it might be the latter?

Huh.

The good thing about nearly passing out is that my mother loads me down with even more food than usual to bring home.

Unfortunately, when we're alone in the kitchen together, she suggests I was woozy because I'm pregnant.

"Pregnant?" I yelp. "I was drinking."

"You should stop doing that immediately."

"I'm not pregnant. I'm not having—"

"You're thirty-three. You don't have to pretend you're not . . . you know."

This entire conversation is horrifying, to put it mildly. Mom thinks I'm having sex with Mark Chan! If I were nineteen and having sex, I'd be getting a lecture, but now I'm so old that she's not bothered by premarital sex and possibly pregnancy. She might even be *happy* if I were pregnant because it would speed up the wedding that she's hoping for.

"Look, it's my period." A lie, but whatever. Not like I haven't been telling any of those. "I promise I'm not pregnant."

"Are you sure?"

"I'm positive. I mean, I'm positive a pregnancy test wouldn't be positive."

She finally stops this horrid line of questioning and lets me leave. I go out to the backyard to wish Wayne a happy birthday once more, then walk to Mark's car with him.

"How are you doing now?" he asks.

"I'm fine," I say. "You were right. It was the alcohol on an empty stomach, and now I'm very full." I pat my belly.

We're quiet as he starts driving, and I'm about to doze off when I realize, with a start, that he's not heading the right way.

"Where are you going?" I ask.

"I'm driving you home. You'll have to tell me your address, but I know the general area."

"I thought you were driving me to the subway."

"With all that food? Besides, you weren't feeling well earlier."

"Thank you," I mumble, deciding there's no point in protesting. "And thank you for being an attentive fake boyfriend at the party."

"You're welcome," he says gruffly.

I hesitate. "What did I take the wrong way? When we first met?"

He doesn't answer for a long time, and right when I think he won't, he says, "You thought I was judging you for not owning your place and living with a roommate. I was just cringing at the thought of living with a roommate myself—I did, briefly, and it was a nightmare."

Okay. Fair enough.

"I know I'm lucky to have parents who could help me with a down payment." He pauses. "I'm not judging you for your job either."

"No?"

"No." He slows down to a stop on the highway. Toronto traffic is rarely good. "It's admirable that you didn't do what was expected of you. I could never do the exact opposite of what my parents wanted."

"Is there something you want to do other than be a computer engineer?"

"There isn't," he says.

"No desire to be a fitness influencer? Perform on Broadway?" His lips twitch. "No."

"You know, I meant to keep the job I had after university until I could make a living as an author, but . . ." I look out the passenger window. "I hated it. I was too miserable and drained to write most of the time. There weren't many women in the office, and men with the same job title as me made more money—though it took me two years to realize that. I was also expected to make the coffee and take notes during meetings, and there was this one guy . . ." I shake my head. "My boss didn't care. Or didn't believe me. And they wonder why so many women leave STEM."

"I'm sorry," he says quietly.

"I was a barista in university, to help pay for my living expenses, so I went back to doing that. I don't like it, but when my shift is over, I feel like I can leave it behind. My manager doesn't expect me to cater to customers who are complete assholes—he's banned a couple of troublemakers. So it's not too bad. I used to do more math tutoring, but now I only have a couple of students. I'm not a natural when it comes to teaching." Though since I make more money an hour at it than slinging lattes, I haven't completely given it up. "I know I could have tried to find another full-time job that made use of my degree, but I had no interest. I couldn't make myself apply."

I can't believe I told Mark all that. Now he knows more than my mother does.

And now I know that I judged him unfairly at first.

If I hadn't heard about him ad nauseum from my mother, I probably wouldn't have done that, but by the time I met him at Hannah's wedding—I still can't believe my mom invited him—I was so sick of hearing about the great Mark Chan.

I'm not saying I would have been interested in him, but I wouldn't have hated him on principle. I expected him to be rather like my big sister in his opinions on my life, which made me feel defensive, yet he's surprised me. He really was kind today too.

Though there is one thing that still niggles at me.

At the wedding, he spent a lot of time texting, which was another reason I was annoyed with him. I haven't seen him do that since, however. His attention isn't usually glued to his phone when we're together.

"Who were you texting at Hannah's wedding?" I ask. When he doesn't immediately reply, I say, "Never mind. You don't owe me an answer. I just—"

"My sister. She wasn't feeling well, and her husband was out of town for work. She was trying to decide whether to go to the ER. I encouraged her to go."

I still. "Did she?"

"Yes. She needed to get her appendix out. She's fine now."

I release a breath. "I'm glad. Your parents must have been so worried during the wedding too."

"Cassie didn't tell them until later. She doesn't want to worry my mom, and my dad . . ." He shakes his head.

Ah. I get the sense that this might be part of the reason his sister doesn't live in Toronto.

"I'm sorry," I say, "for all the assumptions I made about you." It's a bit uncomfortable to apologize like this, but it needs to be said. I can't just ignore it.

He acknowledges my words with a brisk nod.

"I mean it," I continue. "I shouldn't have—"

"It's okay, Emily. I understand."

I sigh and look out the window. "It's been a long day. My dad felt the need to assure me that he really is my dad, even offered to do a DNA test if I thought it necessary."

"Um . . ."

"Don't ask. And my mother thought I was pregnant."

"Your mother *what?*"

I've never heard him speak so loudly before.

"You know, because I was lightheaded," I say.

"But we're not sleeping together." He pauses. "Though I suppose you could be sleeping with someone else. It's none of my business."

"I assure you, I'm not pregnant, either with your baby—"

"Thank God. That would have been more of a miracle than I can handle."

"—or anyone else's baby. But saying that I wasn't having sex wouldn't have convinced my mom, so I didn't bother, though I told her I'm not with child. Hopefully, she doesn't bring it up with your parents."

I wonder if the thought of having sex with me appalls him. That shouldn't bother me—it's not like I want to sleep with Mark, even if I like him more than I did before and he *is* quite attractive—but I feel the strangest sense of disappointment.

I think that wine is still going to my head.

14

—♡—

"Midlist authors, midlist authors,
wherefore art thou, midlist authors?"

—Me, with apologies to Shakespeare (Nah, he's been dead for
four hundred years; he doesn't need apologies, and I'm sure
he's already turned in his grave thousands of times from
the things people have said over the centuries)

It often feels like publishers are just looking for the next big
thing, the next book that will top the bestseller lists, rather than
caring about authors who might be slow and steady performers.
It isn't difficult to find blog posts, etc., dating back several years,
that lament the sorry plight of the midlist author.

When you're an aspiring author, you might think that once
you get a book deal, you'll be set! I sure did. But one contract
doesn't guarantee that you'll ever get another. A publisher may
drop you to make way for something new. I now live in terror of
never getting another shot once I finish this three-book contract.
My first book has sold okay, but nothing super impressive.

On this gray Saturday afternoon, that's one of the many things
getting me down.

Others include: the underfunded health-care system and the
lack of action on climate change. And another billionaire pissing
away money instead of paying his workers a proper wage.

On the bright side: a gelato shop opened near our apartment.

Though this is, perhaps, a bad thing because I might spend too much of my hard-earned cash there. But I've gone only twice in the past five days, which feels like a remarkable level of restraint.

Also on the bright side: I'm going out tonight. A double date. Paige has started seeing someone whose friend is a writer, and I guess they decided they should set us up. Since Mark isn't actually my boyfriend, I'm free to go. If one of my mother's acquaintances happens to see the four of us in public, I'll claim I'm having dinner with a group of friends. No big deal.

The last time I went on a real date, I felt like an old fogy, but Paige really wants me to go, so I'm trying to be optimistic. It seems to be working because I'm beginning to feel genuinely excited, although that's partly because we're having hot pot.

When we meet up at the restaurant, we're promptly shown to our table, and I can't help wondering if some of the Asian customers are rolling their eyes and assuming that Paige and I are the sort of Asian women who refuse to date Asian men, since we're with two white guys.

Whatever. Clive the Writer works in sales and isn't bothered by the fact that I'm a barista. Now it turns out Mark wasn't put off by that either, but I feel like Clive gets me in ways that Mark does not.

Or maybe I just find him attractive. He has blue eyes and floppy brown hair that is, for some reason, really doing it for me today.

He's also not giving off any weird I-want-a-submissive-Asian-wife vibes, and we bond over the fact that we're glad computers are a thing and it's not possible for the only copy of our manuscript to blow into the lake, as happened to Colin Firth in *Love Actually*. When I talk about my family's first computer—which we got when I was in kindergarten—unlike Andrew, he doesn't look at me like I'm positively ancient.

By the end of dinner, Paige and Jeremy aren't quite necking

on the other side of the booth, but they look like they want to. I'm not surprised when she says they're going back to our apartment.

I'm enjoying my time with Clive, but I'm not ready to go home with him or bring him home with me, so I suggest we have a drink. He agrees. He mentions a cozy place known for its craft beer, and although I'm not a beer kind of gal, I figure that'll work for tonight. Maybe I'm overwhelmed by that hair and easy smile, I don't know.

When we step inside, we're quickly shown to a table. The waitress comes around, and Clive asks her some questions about what's on tap. It all goes over my head—I don't know anything about hops—and I pick something at random based on the name. It seems to impress him, which I shouldn't care about, but I do.

"Is it super hoppy?" he asks, once we have our drinks in hand.

"Uh, yep!" I say. "Extremely. Mmm."

In all honesty, it tastes a bit like piss, but whatever. It's just one drink.

He lists a bunch of hoppy beers that I might like, then says, "So, what are you writing right now?"

"A domestic thriller," I reply. "A little different from anything I've written in the past."

"What's it about?"

"Well . . ."

"You should always have a logline ready," he says. "It's important to know how to promote your book."

"Yes, but I've only just started the first draft. I'm a plotter—"

"Me too."

"But I still need to write a few chapters before I really get a feel for the story, and that's when I try my hand at the blurb and synopsis."

"It's good to have a logline early on—it can also help guide your writing—but you don't need a synopsis until you're ready to query. Why bog yourself down with that now? The most important thing is to finish what you've started. Get in the habit of finishing things. Just some friendly advice."

My hand tenses on my pint.

"There's this great app I found," he says, "to stop you from getting distracted." He prattles on about something I first heard about five years ago, this man who assumes I'm not published and probably haven't finished anything.

There's no shame in not being published, and it's not like I think I'm better than him, but I hate that he's making these assumptions. It reminds me of a post I saw online, about a woman who was subjected to a man trying to explain her own journal article to her, not realizing she was the author.

Actually, I think I've seen multiple such posts.

"What are you working on?" I ask Clive.

"I'm about to start querying my three-hundred-thousand-word epic fantasy. I know, I know, the word count's a bit high, even for epic fantasy, but I promise you, all those words are very necessary."

"I bet they are," I murmur, trying to keep the sarcasm out of my voice.

"You can't give up, Emily."

"I'm not."

"The other day, I discovered a great resource for querying writers. Let me share it with you, for whenever you're ready to query."

"No, that's okay."

"Are you planning to self-publish?"

"Not at present. Maybe one day, but I don't think it really suits my skill set."

"Some people do well with it." He prattles on while I sip my disgusting beer, then says, "I sense you're a bit discouraged."

Well, I'm a little discouraged by this date.

"The industry is a bit of a mess," I say, half expecting him to tell me that I have so many advantages as a non-white woman because everyone wants diversity these days.

Fortunately, I'm saved from that indignity. Thank God for small mercies.

Instead, he says, "Let me give you another piece of advice—"

"No, it's quite all right. I know what I'm doing." Yes, there are always things to learn, but I don't think unsolicited advice from Clive will be helpful.

"When you're ready to query agents, like I am—"

"I already have an agent."

"You do?" His eyes widen, but then he composes himself. "Are you sure you didn't get taken in by a scammer?"

"My agent isn't a scammer. She got me a contract, and my first book came out last year."

"Doesn't mean she isn't a scammer. Did you have to pay for it to be published? Did she sell your book to a vanity press?"

"No. I got an advance. You can find the book at Indigo."

He blanches.

I can't believe I liked him at the beginning of the evening. I bet he's the kind of guy who needs to be in a relationship with someone he regards as less successful than him, which is why he was quite happy with me being a barista who hadn't published anything—so he thought.

But now . . .

"Why did you let me give you advice?" he asks.

"I didn't ask for advice. You assumed I needed it."

"You could have stopped me."

"I eventually did."

Men might accuse women of being overly sensitive and emotional, but have you met men? Some of them have extremely delicate egos. I'd never want to be with a man whose ego constantly needed to be soothed. A man who'd feel like his, well, manhood was under threat if I had any modicum of success.

I have a feeling Clive is that kind of guy.

Bummer. I really do like that hair.

I down the rest of the beer and when the waitress comes around and asks if we want another, I say I'll pay for my drink—and just my drink.

Clive scowls at me.

When I leave the bar, I don't feel like going back to my apartment, where Paige and Jeremy are probably getting it on. Instead, I head to a café that's open late and order some tea. I text Ashley, but she doesn't reply. And then, for some reason, I find myself texting Mark.

I had a bad date tonight.

He replies immediately. Are you okay? Do you need me to pick you up?

I'm not sure what reaction I expected, but it wasn't that, even if it's similar to his response to the infamous *hey baby* text. But what do I know about telling my fake boyfriend that my real date didn't go well?

ME: I'm fine. Having tea in the Annex. Will head home soon.
MARK: I can meet you. I'm in the area.
ME: That's not necessary. Don't feel obligated.
MARK: What's the address?

Well, if he insists. It'll be nice to see someone familiar, since I won't be able to talk to Paige tonight. I tell him where I am, and he says he'll be here in fifteen minutes.

I waste time on my phone until Mark walks in. He sets down his jacket on the seat across from me, then goes to get some tea for himself.

"Are you okay?" he asks when he returns, his eyebrows drawing together slightly.

"You already asked me that."

"I wasn't sure you were telling the truth."

"Why wouldn't I? Sure, we're lying to our families, but I've been truthful with you."

"You texted me after your date," he says, "even though you don't know me very well. I was concerned."

I shrug. I'm not entirely sure why I texted him after Ashley. I mean, I have sisters. Other friends. Yet I chose Mark. "Really, I'm fine."

"A bad date for a woman can be dangerous."

He's not wrong.

"I didn't feel like I was in danger," I say. "It was a double date with Paige. Dinner went fine, so Clive and I headed to a bar together afterward, and that's when it went downhill." I provide some details, and Mark listens without comment. "I feel like a failure in my parents' eyes, but apparently, I was too successful for him. He didn't *say* that, but . . ."

"You should be with someone who can be happy for you."

"Exactly. I guess a part of me had this romantic notion of being in a relationship with another writer. We'd have so much in common. Be able to discuss craft and the publishing industry. Write side by side. I don't know, it sounded fun." I sigh. "Of course, not every male writer is like Clive, but . . ." I shake my head. "Where were you tonight? Were you on a date too?"

"No. Visiting a friend."

"Sorry if I made you worry." It never occurred to me that Mark would be worried, though he was kind when I drank on an empty stomach at my parents' house, and he was concerned when I drunk texted him.

Yeah, I shouldn't have been surprised.

"It's fine," he says gruffly.

"Are you annoyed that I'm going on dates with other men?"

"Why would I be annoyed?"

I feel a tiny sliver of disappointment at his words, which makes no sense.

"I don't know," I say. "Because given my luck, your parents would probably see me?"

"It's a big city."

"Yet sometimes, it's really not. If I were to actually kiss another guy in public, I bet Auntie Janie would be standing right there, ready to ask me questions about my book." I pause. "I've been on two real dates in the past couple of months, and they reminded me why I didn't bother for so long. I'm not going to date anyone else until our 'relationship' is over. It's not worth the trouble."

"Okay, baby."

"You're running that joke into the ground," I mutter. "Next time I'll have to k—"

I slap a hand over my mouth.

Oh shit.

I was going to make a joke about kissing Mark to shut him up.

It would be obvious it was a joke . . . I think? But there's something about his expression that makes me wonder otherwise.

Nah, he normally looks serious. It's just the way he is.

Flustered, I say, "I should be getting home."

He stands up.

"You don't have to go," I tell him. "You can stay here and finish your drink."

"I assure you, I can drink tea and walk at the same time."

"Suit yourself."

We head into the cool night and start walking toward the subway, which is thankfully a quick five minutes from here. I don't know if I could stand to be in his presence any longer, my shoulder nearly brushing against his arm.

After we enter the station and tap our cards, we come to a stop at the same time.

"I'm going east," he says.

"I'm going west."

"Text me when you get home." He turns and heads down the stairs.

I take the other staircase to my platform, feeling out of sorts. To my distress, I think it might have more to do with Mark than my failed date.

When I arrive home, Paige's door is closed, but I can see the light underneath it and hear the quiet murmur of conversation.

Me, however? I'm alone tonight.

I send a *home safe* text to Mark before getting ready for bed.

The next morning, there's a man in the apartment. It's been a very long time since we've had a guy here in the morning. Jeremy drinks his coffee with a little milk and a lot of sugar, and he keeps kissing Paige on the cheek.

Ugh. Why are they being so sickeningly cute?

I shouldn't be bitter. Yeah, it's been a while since I've had sex, but whatever.

"How'd it go with Clive?" Jeremy asks as he pours himself some cereal.

"Thanks for setting us up," I say breezily, "but I don't think it'll work out."

Apparently, Jeremy isn't the sort to ask why, which is lucky. He and Paige venture back to her bedroom after breakfast, and it's also lucky that I don't have Paige's elephant-like hearing. I pour myself some more coffee, then head back to my own room.

I start up my computer, crack my knuckles, and get down to work. Last night's encounter with Clive has lit a fire under my ass, and I'm determined to write the best fucking book ever that will make him weep with inferiority.

Something about our interaction makes me think about the plot of this thriller in a new way and—aha! I've got it.

I open my outline, save it under a new name, delete most of the words, and bang out a new outline. Then I go to the document where I've started the first two chapters, make a few tweaks to the existing text, and continue drafting.

I love days like this. Days when the writing just flows, almost like magic. Yeah, today the flow is happening partly due to spite, but the reason doesn't matter. It's all good.

When my stomach rumbles at a disturbing volume, I check the time. It's two in the afternoon, and I've been typing for four hours straight. I don't really want to take a break, but I know it's for the best. I stretch my arms over my head and go to the kitchen, where I heat up some leftovers. Paige appears to be out—probably at the gym.

I'm about to head back to my room when my phone rings.

"Hi, Mom!" I say.

"You're in a good mood. Are you sure you're not pregnant?"

I never thought being in my thirties would involve my mother repeatedly asking if I'm pregnant. Normally this would make me want to curse, but right now I'm unable to feel anything beyond mild irritation.

"I'm sure," I say. "I'm having a good writing day."

"Ah, you're in love. That's why you're happy."

"I'm not . . ." I don't want to protest too much; I am, after all, "dating" Mark. But our so-called relationship is fairly new, so it's reasonable I wouldn't be using the L-word yet. "Yes, it's going well," I tell my mom.

Fortunately, I'm able to get her off the phone fairly quickly. She doesn't say anything about last night. I guess nobody saw me with Clive at the bar, or with Mark at the café.

Before I can return to my writing, I receive a text from him.

Shall we go on another date next weekend? Rather than just pretending we went out?

Why do I feel momentarily excited by those words? It's not because I want to see him again. I mean, I don't mind spending time with him—he's not so bad after all—but there are probably better things that I could do on a Saturday night than whatever he has planned.

ME: Did you have something in mind?
MARK: I thought you could come over and I'll cook dinner.
        How does that sound?
ME: Works for me.
MARK: Just one thing. Are you allergic to cats?

15

———— ♡ ————

"Happiness in fake relationships is entirely a matter of chance."
—Me, with a little help from Jane Austen

Friday after work, I decide I should bring something nice to Mark's for dinner tomorrow.

A homemade dessert—wouldn't that be lovely?

I haven't baked since 2020, when many people were trying their hand at baking and the stores were running out of flour. Paige and I attempted to make pineapple buns, and I still have nightmares about how badly they turned out and how much of a mess we made.

But that's okay! I'm older and wiser—and I won't make anything with yeast. Or more than ten steps.

Lately, the manager at Coffee on College—who's a little older than me—has been playing his hair metal playlist over and over. I heard "Cherry Pie" four times today, which is perhaps why cherry pie is the first thing that pops into my mind. That, or the dream I had the other night about the cherry pie milkshake at the Shakerie, which, for inexplicable reasons, grew to six feet and started chasing me.

The way to a man's heart is through his stomach, and I'll impress Mark with my—

No! I don't want Mark's heart. But he's been good to me lately, and I want to thank him.

I spend ten minutes looking at recipes, then go to the store to buy ingredients. Since fresh cherries are expensive—and besides, I don't have a cherry pitter—I decide frozen will do.

The pie crust is chilling in the fridge and I'm reducing the cherries on the stove when Paige comes in.

"It smells great in here."

To my annoyance, she sounds rather surprised.

"What are you doing with cherries?" she asks.

"Cherry pie. For my dinner with Mark."

She gives me a look that I don't want to interpret.

"Oh, by the way," I say, "the other front element stopped working."

"But that's my favorite one."

Now it's my turn to give her a look.

"Yeah, yeah, I have a favorite burner," she mutters. "I'll tell the super and he'll get it fixed . . . never."

Ah, the joys of renting.

But I'm not too bothered right now, because I'm making a delicious cherry pie, and tomorrow I'll get to see Mark's place . . . and meet his cat.

I still can't believe he has a cat. He struck me as the kind of guy who'd never own a pet—aside, perhaps, from a fish. I assumed he wouldn't like cat hair or dog hair getting on his floors and clothes, though I concede that many of the things I assumed about him have proven to be untrue.

When I asked what her name is, he told me that would have to wait until we're properly introduced (??). I suspect she has a human name, like Helen or Margaret. Something old-fashioned, as opposed to, say, Madison, which I recently learned only became popular due to *Splash*. It would certainly be something to write a screenplay or book that actually affected baby names.

Paige leaves for the gym, and I spoon the cherry filling into the crust. Now it's time for the lattice. I've never attempted a lattice on a pie before, but I should be able to manage it.

Alas, my first attempt at cutting strips doesn't go well—they're woefully uneven—so I dig a ruler out of my desk drawer and manage a little better on my second attempt. As I try weaving the strips of dough in and out to make the lattice, I decide it's a very good thing that my childhood dream was to be a writer and not, say, a pastry chef.

Finally, I give up and do four strips in one direction and four strips on top in the other direction, then put it in the preheated oven. I set the timer on my phone and go to my bedroom, where I catch up on my email. The less said about the disturbing number of emails in my inbox, the better.

When the timer goes off, I pull the pie out of the oven. It looks . . .

Frankly, it doesn't look much like the pictures that accompanied the recipe. Was the filling too runny? Juice has bubbled over the crust, and there's a faint smell of burnt sugar—honestly, I'm surprised the smoke detector didn't go off.

I open the oven door again and decide I'll need to clean the oven tomorrow.

Well, hopefully it will still be tasty. I want to impress—

No! Why do I keep thinking that? I just want to thank Mark for being a good fake boyfriend. That's all. Nothing more.

I ride the elevator to the ninth floor of Mark's building, not-so-pretty pie in one hand and bottle of wine in the other. I'm feeling slightly anxious, even if there's no good reason for that. It's just a fake date, and nobody is around to see us. We don't have to put on a good act, though I've decided we should take a cute picture together for my lock screen photo. Was rather pleased with myself for this idea.

I knock on the door, and Mark answers immediately. He's wearing jeans, a T-shirt, and an apron, which is the most casual I've ever seen him.

I open my mouth to greet him, but for some reason, the first thing that comes out is, "Where's your cat?"

The corner of his mouth kicks up. "No, 'Hello, Mark. I got you some wine'? Just demanding to see my cat?"

I shrug and suppress a smile. I hand over the wine and cherry pie, then step inside and slip off my shoes.

"For your information," he says, "she's shy. She doesn't like strangers. You probably won't see her for a while."

"What's her name?"

"You may learn her name when you meet her face-to-face."

"Here, kitty, kitty," I say in a high voice. "Here, kitty, kitty."

"Dear God," he mutters, but he still doesn't tell me her name.

Hmph. So much for that.

"Shall I open this now?" He holds up the bottle of wine.

"Whatever you like. Perhaps it doesn't go with what you have planned for dinner?"

"No, it's great."

He opens the bottle, and when he hands me a stemless wine-glass, our fingers brush, and for a split second, my attention is laser-focused on that point of contact.

Weird.

Then he returns to the counter and starts rolling out some dough. I think we're having pizza for dinner. I can't believe he's gone to all this effort for me.

"Did you make the dough yourself?" I ask.

"Yes. It's not that hard."

"I'm scared of anything involving yeast."

"There's nothing to be scared of."

Hmph. I decide I won't tell Mark about the Pineapple Bun

Incident of 2020. I also don't mention that it took me an hour to clean my oven thanks to the pie.

Instead I say, quite sensibly, "Ooh, you know what you should do? You should make sexy baking videos and post them online. I watched eight videos by this very hot Asian dude the other day."

I expected him to be appalled by this suggestion, and I think he is, but he doesn't say that.

"You think I'm sexy?" he asks.

Oh dear.

He steps away from the counter and approaches me. I gulp my wine. He's not all that close to me, yet it feels like he's getting in my personal space.

"I asked you a question, Emily," he says sternly.

Heat washes over me, and my skin prickles. I want him to come closer and . . .

No, I don't. This is *Mark*, the guy my mother picked out for me. Sure, I can appreciate that he's good-looking, but sexy? That's taking things too far. My face is flaming, but it's because I'm embarrassed by my words, nothing more.

"I'm sure *some* people would find them sexy," I say.

He folds his arms over his chest. "You still didn't answer the question."

I pour some wine down my throat.

He tugs the glass out of my hand and sets it on the table. "I don't need you getting lightheaded from drinking on an empty stomach again. Have some cheese." He motions to the small board on the coffee table.

I don't usually like when people boss me around, but he's insisting I eat cheese, so I can't complain. I take a seat on the couch and pop a piece in my mouth.

Oh my God.

That's certainly better than the cheap cheese I buy at the grocery store.

I cut off a small wedge of the soft cheese, place it on a cracker, add some fig jam—I think that's what this is?—and put it in my mouth next.

"Can I have my wine back?" I ask when I finish chewing.

Mark hands me the wineglass but doesn't return to the kitchen.

As I'm struggling to think of something to say, I hear a soft *meow.* A gray cat pokes its head around the side of the couch.

"Hello there," I coo, grateful for the distraction.

Mark mutters something under his breath.

"What's that?" I ask.

"I can't believe she's already graced you with her presence. I didn't expect her to come out at all while you were here."

"And then you would have avoided telling me her name, but you can't do that now."

He sighs and looks at the cat as though she's betrayed him. When he takes a seat next to me on the couch, she hops onto his lap.

"Ms. Muffins," he says seriously, "this is Emily."

"Your cat's name is Ms. Muffins?"

"What's wrong with that?"

"I expected her name to be, I don't know, Margaret. Maybe Barbara."

"So you think I'm the kind of guy who'd name his cat 'Margaret.'"

I don't know what kind of guy you are anymore.

"Uh, yeah," I say, scratching the side of my face. "Nice to meet you, Ms. Muffins." I hold out my hand.

She might have come out to see me, but she still appears deeply suspicious.

A moment later, she jumps off Mark's lap and disappears, and I dread what he'll say next. Will he return to asking if I think he's hot?

Fortunately, he takes mercy on me and goes back to the kitchen, where he washes his hands and continues with the pizza. I take the opportunity to help myself to more cheese before strolling around the room with my wineglass.

Mark's place is, unsurprisingly, neater than mine, and there's real framed art on the walls, which is certainly a step above my decor.

"This is nice." I gesture to a view of the Toronto skyline—as seen from the island, I think—in watercolor and pen. "Where did you get it?"

His place is open-plan, so I'm able to look over at him as he spreads tomato sauce on the pizza in the kitchen.

"I did that one myself," he says.

"Really?"

"Yes. Is that so surprising?"

I guess it never occurred to me that Mark had an artistic side.

"You're a man of many hidden talents," I say, then freeze.

Because suddenly, I'm thinking of what talents he might have with his mouth and his hands . . . on my body.

And I don't want to go there.

But I concede—in my own mind, not out loud—that Mark has grown on me, and the juxtaposition of his neat clothes and cat named Ms. Muffins is weirdly delightful.

Mark doesn't speak, his head bent over the counter, but it looks like he's blushing.

Nah. Probably my imagination. Or the heat of the kitchen.

"Do you paint a lot?" I ask.

"Not recently. I should do it more often."

I set down my wineglass. "Where's the washroom?"

He points me in the right direction, and the first thing I notice about the washroom is the small watercolor sunset on the wall. Similar in style to the skyline in the living room—I'm sure he did this one too.

On the way back, I pass a den that contains a desk and computer, as well as the most extravagant cat tree I've ever seen. Two eyes peak out from a round hole. Watching me. Judging me.

Unsettled, I return to the living area.

"It's almost ready," Mark says.

I grab my wineglass and take a seat as he brings a salad bowl and pizza over to the table.

"It smells delicious," I say, and this isn't a lie. I'm excited to scarf down all those carbs and cheese. The pizza is topped with roasted vegetables, mozzarella, and a little meat—prosciutto? I can't remember the last time I had pizza that wasn't from the discount pizza place down the street from my apartment.

When I try a bite, I'm happy to discover it's as good as it looks and smells.

"So," Mark says, "what's your goal?"

"Tonight? In life in general?"

"With writing, I mean. Do you wish to be able to quit your job at the coffee shop and write full-time?"

"Yes, but I don't see that happening anytime soon."

"No? You have a second book coming out this year, yes?"

"Are you ready for that three-hour lecture on publishing and the economics of being an author?"

"Perhaps a slightly shorter one, in the interest of time, but I'm curious."

"I suspect you'll take that back in ten minutes," I say, "but if you insist."

I don't know where to begin. By the time we've finished half the pizza, I've said a lot of jumbled-up words, though Mark seems to following along—as in, he looks appalled at the times he should look appalled.

"Anyway." I finish my wine. "That's a short introduction to the life of being an author."

"It's not at all like the movie I saw a few years ago. An editor rewarded an author with a vacation to Paris after finishing a book."

"I saw that movie too. Well, I saw the first half hour of it. I couldn't finish it. Apparently, her book was already in stores by the time she got back from that month-long trip."

I spear the last of the mixed salad greens with my fork and pop them into my mouth, then look longingly at the pizza. Mark immediately begins to serve me another piece.

"That's really not necessary," I say. "Save it for tomorrow."

When he doesn't listen and puts the slice of pizza on my plate, I don't protest any further. Who am I to decline home-made pizza?

After he clears the table and refuses my offers to help with dishes, he brings out the cherry pie, as well as two small servings of another dessert.

"I didn't know you were bringing dessert," he says, "so I made some panna cotta."

Each plate contains a perfect little dome, garnished with berries. Seriously, who is this guy? My pie is positively sad in comparison.

"Great!" I say, feeling a little inadequate. "More dessert for me."

"The cherry pie looks delicious."

Okay, I can't stand this. He doesn't need to lie.

"It looks like it survived multiple kitchen disasters."

"Is that so?" he murmurs. "I couldn't tell."

And then the unthinkable happens.

Mark winks at me.

I'm disoriented. Did that actually happen? Or did I imagine it? Must be the latter. I shake my head to clear it and focus on the dessert in front of me.

The panna cotta is amazing—as I knew it would be—and the pie is actually not too bad. It tastes better than it looks. Thank God. I don't feel embarrassed for bringing it to Mark's, even if it's clear I'm not going to win any kind of baking show. The piecrust isn't perfectly flaky, but it's a decent attempt.

Once I'm properly stuffed with food, I stagger to the couch.

"Thank you," I say. "That was amazing. But there's one more thing we need to do tonight."

"What's that?"

"I need pictures of us together. Couples usually have such photos on their phones. I figure I'll make one my lock screen."

I take out my phone and move closer to Mark, until my shoulder is brushing his arm. Being close to him like this . . . it actually feels quite nice, and if I tilt my head up . . .

What?

I jerk back.

His brow furrows. "Is something wrong?"

"Nope, nothing!" I say cheerfully.

I think the problem is that I'm starved for physical touch. It's been a while since I got physical with a guy. That kiss he brushed against my cheek last month is as far as I've gotten with a man in a few years, sadly.

I like Mark, sure, but not like that. As a friend, I suppose. A friend who I can acknowledge is attractive. This certainly isn't what I expected the first time we met, but I'll admit that he's not quite the stuck-up guy I thought he was, and maybe I enjoy the fact that he's a little starchier than I am.

I remind myself not to be affected by his proximity as I lean close to him once more and hold out my phone. I snap a few pictures of us, then take a look at them. They're not quite what I want.

"Let's try it again," I say, "but this time, try smiling. I know you can do it—I've seen it with my own eyes. You're handsome when you smile."

"First it was 'sexy,' " he murmurs, "and now 'handsome'?"

Crap. Another slip of my tongue.

"Yep," I say, with a breeziness I don't feel. "I'm really getting into my role as your fake girlfriend."

There's something odd in his expression, something I can't quite figure out.

Ah, well. We'll just try this again.

I hold up my phone and say, "Cheese!"

Mmm. Cheese.

When I see the photo, I laugh.

"That's why I don't try smiling in photographs," he says. "I look constipated."

"I wouldn't go that far, but it isn't your best look."

"Not 'sexy,' is it?"

"You really seem to enjoy saying that word." I tilt my head and put a finger to my lips. "Hmm. I think I'll have to tickle you to make you smile."

"Dear God, no."

"Which part of you is ticklish?"

"Emily," he says warningly.

Dammit. I shouldn't enjoy it when he says my name that way.

"Okay, fine," I say. "Just look stern and brooding for the photograph. I'll do the smiling."

I rest my head against his shoulder, he places a hand on my shoulder, and I take yet more pictures. These ones turn out better. Mark looks serious; I look happily in love.

"Could you send one to me?" he asks.

"Sure. Good idea for you to have one on your phone too." I send the photo, then hold up my phone again.

"Another picture? I thought we had enough."

"A funny face picture."

"Absolutely not. Well, you can make a funny face, but I won't."

I didn't expect him to agree; I just wanted to annoy him a little.

"It's fun to get on your nerves," I say.

"I'm sure it is. That doesn't mean you need to do it on a regular basis. There are other fun things to do in this world."

Oh God. Why am I thinking of sex?

"I'll, uh, be right back." I hurry to the washroom, where I lean against the door and put a hand to my forehead. I really am out of sorts today.

After taking several deep breaths, I head back to the couch, but I stop before I get there. Mark is talking quietly to someone, and I don't want to interrupt. I guess he's on the phone.

"I'm surprised you're out here," he says. "You usually don't show your face when I have a guest . . . yes, I know, it's been a while . . . but she's not so bad, right?"

Hold on.

Mark fucking Chan is talking to his cat.

Ms. Muffins is perched on the recliner, looking unimpressed with the world, and Mark is still on the couch.

Why does it feel like there's a mushy spot in my chest?

I clear my throat as I approach the couch. When I sit down again, Ms. Muffins scurries away. I open my mouth to make a comment about the conversation I overheard. I'm sure it's obvious I did hear, but maybe I shouldn't say anything. It might make Mark too self-conscious, and I want him to feel comfortable talking to his cat in my company again. I want him to feel he can say whatever he wants around me.

The whole perfect-Asian-son thing he has going on isn't the whole story when it comes to Mark, and perhaps it's armor to deal with the world.

Disconcerted, I say, "I should be going."

"You can stay a little longer if you like. It's not late."

"No? You're not the sort of person who goes to bed at eight thirty in your matching pajamas and nightcap?" I tease.

His lips twitch, and I wish I could have caught that in a photo.

"I saw you last Saturday after eight thirty, didn't I?" he says.

"And I assure you, I don't wear a nightcap to bed, even if you think I might look *handsome* in one."

His lips twitch again. It's distracting.

"I really should be going." I grab my purse and head toward the door. "There are lots of writing-related things I have to do tomorrow, so I need to get a good sleep."

After I put on my shoes, I straighten up, and Mark is right . . . there. I can feel the warmth emanating from his body.

"Thank you for coming over," he says.

"You're w-welcome," I stammer. I take a step to the side and feel like I can breathe again. "It was great to see your place and, uh, meet Ms. Muffins."

As soon as I say that, I look around for the cat. I don't expect to see her, but there she is, walking across the once-pristine tile floor, leaving red pawprints in her wake.

Oh no.

My gaze snaps to the partially eaten cherry pie, still sitting on the table. This is most definitely not what I wanted to happen when I baked a pie for my fake boyfriend. I wish I'd picked something that wasn't, well, almost the color of blood. Apple pie, perhaps.

"Not again," he mutters.

"Again? Does she often walk on the table?"

"It hasn't happened in a while. I'm usually careful about leaving food out, but . . ."

Ms. Muffins hurries across the floor, and Mark runs to catch her before she can make more of a mess.

I start to slip off my shoes. "I'll help—"

"No," he says, cat in his arms. "It's fine."

"Are you sure?"

"Positive."

I feel a little guilty, but I don't protest any further.

As I put my hand on the doorknob, something occurs to me. "Does Ms. Muffins have a first name?"

He hesitates. The cat wriggles in his arms, but fortunately, he's still wearing his apron, and she doesn't get cherry pie filling on his shirt.

"It's Margaret," he replies at last.

"Seriously?" I say.

"Seriously."

I laugh all the way home.

16

♡

*"I know I'll get hate for this, but I suspect burnout is a myth.
Like writer's block."*

—Tess Donovan

Any plans for the summer?" the doctor asks me.

"Uh . . ."

Look, I'm all for small talk in the right situations, but this isn't one of them. I'm naked from the waist down, covered in a flimsy paper sheet. I find it weird that she's asking about my summer while she shoves a speculum inside me.

"Maybe I'll go to Montreal for a few days?" The words come out as a question, and I grit my teeth. I'm lucky I don't experience a lot of pain—unlike Paige—when a doctor pokes around up there, but it's still unpleasant.

She tells me about a restaurant she likes in Montreal, and I squeeze my eyes shut and try to think of happier things, like the long list of stuff that people claim is being ruined by Millennials.

"All done," she says.

After she closes the curtain, I start putting my clothes back on.

I take transit home, but rather than going right to my apartment, I find myself heading to the new gelateria. Surely I deserve some gelato after a once-every-three-years pap smear. Besides, it's been a while since I had gelato.

Well, it's been only six days, but still. And, yes, I should be trying to cut costs because the amount of money in my savings account is lower than I'd like—in fact, it's rather close to zero—but it's just one cup of gelato.

"Good afternoon, Emily," says the woman behind the counter when I enter.

Okay, I do come here rather often.

"A small cup with two flavors," I say. "Stracciatella and Amarena." The latter reminds me of that unfortunate cherry pie I brought to Mark's.

Once she hands over my cup—the serving is extra generous, perhaps as a reward for being a loyal customer?—I take a seat by the window and spoon gelato into my mouth as I scroll through my phone.

I wonder if Mark has any social media accounts. I doubt he'd post pictures of himself, but he might still have an account somewhere.

Or maybe Ms. Margaret Muffins has one?

That seems like a stretch, but I have nothing better to do as I eat gelato, so I go to Instagram and see if I can find an account for his cat.

Ten seconds later, I put a hand over my mouth to muffle my laughter.

Ms. Muffins does indeed have a social media presence. She posts about once a week, and the text is all written in her point of view. In the most recent picture, there are red pawprints on the floor. The caption: *Marking my territory.* In the photo before that, she's standing imperiously on the couch. *Yes, I may be a small cat, but I need all this space to myself. Don't ask questions.*

I imagine Mark bent over his phone as he typed it, and I can't help sending him a text.

ME: I found Ms. Muffins online. Thank you for telling me her
    first name. I might not have found her otherwise.
MARK: Can't talk. I'm working.

Hmph.

Feeling impatient, I message Ms. Muffins from my author
Instagram account.

It was nice to meet you on Saturday!

A minute later, I get a text from Paige, saying we need to go
out tonight, because she's had it up to *here* with her boss, who's
complained, again, that she isn't a team player because she won't
go out for happy hour drinks off the clock.

However, seeing as it's a work night and I'm also trying to
save money after that very necessary gelato, I suggest we go out
for coffee instead of booze. Not at Coffee on College, though,
because that would feel like work.

She agrees, and I go back to my DMs.

Still nothing from Ms. Muffins. I suppose she's making use
of her very fancy cat tree.

At the coffee shop, I order a large coffee and take a seat at a table
near the back. Paige and Ashley enter a few minutes later and
order their drinks.

"You're having coffee?" Ashley gestures with her London Fog.
"It's six o'clock."

I shrug. "I've drunk coffee later. It's fine."

She looks skeptical, but whatever. I'm the expert on coffee;
I'm a writer (and barista).

I pick up my phone to turn the volume off—I won't let any

calls from my mother interrupt my time with my friends—and the picture of me and Mark pops up on the screen.

"Ooh, what's that?" Ashley asks.

"A picture of me and my 'boyfriend,' obviously."

Ashley and Paige look at each other.

"What?" I say. "I'm trying to sell this relationship. If I take out my phone when I'm around my mom . . ."

"You had a date with him this past Saturday, didn't you?" Ashley asks.

"Yeah, I went over to his place, and he made pizza. From scratch. Yeast and everything. And he prepared panna cotta for dessert."

Ashley and Paige share another look.

"What?" I turn to Paige. "I thought you wanted to vent about your job."

"Not anymore," she says. "This is much better. I still can't believe you went to his place."

"What's wrong with a date at home?"

"I thought the whole point of real fake dates—can't believe I'm saying those words—was in case people saw you out and about. But nobody will see you at his condo."

"They might see me going into his building," I say, "or on the elevator."

"Mm-hmm."

"And our pictures together? Those were taken in his living room. That adds to the credibility of our relationship."

Ashley drums her fingers on the table. "The fact that you're falling in love with him also adds to its credibility."

"What?" I cry. "I'm not falling in love with Mark. He's just not as terrible as I initially thought. He has a cat named Ms. Margaret Muffins. Isn't that adorable?" I bring up her social media account to show my friends.

"Now you're calling him adorable," Paige says. "Yep, you're definitely falling for him."

"I called his *cat* adorable." I gulp my coffee.

"That's not exactly what you said."

"I misspoke."

"Sure you did. You like this man and his homemade pizza and his old-lady cat."

A notification pops up on my phone. Ms. Margaret Muffins has messaged me back.

> It was nice to meet you as well, even if I spent most of the night hiding from you and stepped in your pie.

Why does Ms. Muffins have such terrible timing?

Paige grabs the phone out of my hands and starts typing a message.

> I think your owner has a cute butt.

I grab my phone back and quickly delete the words. Thank God she didn't get the chance to send them. "What the hell?"

"You don't think he has a cute butt?"

I hesitate for a split second.

"Ha!" Paige says. "You like him, don't you?"

"I hate you guys," I mutter.

"Why are you in denial?"

"I'm not in denial."

Ashley places a hand on my wrist. "We're just trying to help you acknowledge your feelings. You spent Saturday night on a 'date' with him, and it seems like you enjoyed yourself. And you're now messaging him."

"I'm messaging his cat."

"You know that cats can't actually type, right? No opposable thumbs."

I stick out my tongue at her.

"You're using it as an excuse to talk to him more," Ashley says.

"I bet you like having pictures of him on your phone, don't you? I get it—he is rather cute."

The image of him winking at me pops into my mind. Did that actually happen?

I need to stop thinking about Mark.

"Speaking of dates," I say. "How's it going with Jeremy, Paige?"

"That's the other reason I'm in a bad mood today." Paige sighs. "We had a minor disagreement."

"What did you disagree about?"

"Doesn't matter. But then he told his mom, and his mom called me—"

"He gave his mother your number?"

"Apparently, even though we'd only been dating for a month! She called me and got mad at me for not treating her son right, and I said she could tell Jeremy that our relationship was over and blocked them both. Better to be single than to put up with nonsense like that. I'm convinced she's the kind of mother who'd want to come on the honeymoon."

"Ugh," I say. "I'm sorry."

"Whatever. Better to find out now."

"So back to Mark," Ashley says.

My friends won't let this go.

"Why?" I ask. "There's nothing more to discuss."

"When are you going on your next so-called fake date?"

"I don't know. We didn't talk about it."

"You sound disappointed," Paige remarks.

"Well, it's important we keep up our act to convince my mother."

"Yeah, that was *so* convincing. You want to see him again, don't you?"

"When did you get so annoying?"

My phone buzzes again. Ms. Muffins has sent another message.

I apologize if I wasn't very friendly, but I'm not a dog. Also, I'm not used to strangers.

Paige takes my phone again and starts typing, somehow managing to dodge my attempts to grab it.

I think your owner has a cute butt.

I finally manage to get it back from her.

Unfortunately, in grabbing the phone, I also send the message.

"Shit," I say. "*Shit.*" I'm about to unsend her message when I notice he's already seen it. I nearly shriek in horror. "You can't send stuff like that to Mark!"

I begin typing.

Sorry, my friend took my phone. Ignore her. She's drunk.

I wait for a reply, heart hammering in my chest, but nothing appears, so I drown my sorrows in coffee. I'm not sure he'll believe me, since I blamed drunken texts on my roommate before, then later admitted I was lying.

"I can't believe you did that," I tell Paige.

"Hey, you're the one who sent it."

I try my best to channel Mark and level her with a severe glare.

"I'm not sure what you're doing with your face right now," she says.

"I'm glaring at you."

"You should be thankful to her," Ashley pipes up. "For revealing your love for Mark."

"Saying he has a cute butt doesn't mean she loves him," Paige says.

"Exactly," I agree.

"Just that she thinks his butt's cute."

"I—"

"Admit it," my roommate says. "You enjoy spending time with him."

"In a friendly sort of way."

"And you're attracted to him."

"Fine," I huff. "But that doesn't mean—"

Paige smirks. "You baked for the first time in years for Mark. I think that means something. And you're more than a little excited whenever you get a message from him—or his cat."

"No," I scoff reflexively.

But now I'm starting to—oh God—wonder if my friends are right. I do look forward to receiving messages from Mark and learning more about him. The real him, not the stories my mom spins. I might even be developing a slight—very slight—affection for sweater-vests.

However, I don't wish to discuss this startling revelation.

"I had a pap smear today."

Yep, I'm talking about my pap smear rather than discussing my fake boyfriend. I'm sure this is healthy.

I go to take a glug of my coffee, then realize I'm out.

Well, I guess I'll have to get another.

At one in the morning, I'm wide awake.

I know, I know, this is my own damn fault for having two coffees between 6 and 7:30 p.m. The second was a small one, but I think the coffee at that café was particularly strong. I'll have to remember that for next time.

What's pissing me off—well, one of the things pissing me off—is that if this were a few years ago, I'm positive I'd be fast asleep by now. But getting older means that some things affect me more than they used to.

After I changed the conversation to gynecological exams,

nobody asked about Mark again. When Paige and I returned to our apartment, I made myself a noddle bowl for dinner. My phone buzzed while I was eating, and I wanted to immediately leap for it and see if it was another message from Ms. Muffins, but Paige was there, and she might have seen that as a sign that I think Mark has a cute butt. So I took my time picking up my phone.

It was a text from Mark, telling me not to bother his cat, who has a very busy life.

I didn't reply.

And now that it's one in the morning, I can't help wondering about everything from Mark's perspective. What did he think of me before we met? What does he think now?

When he said, *You think I'm sexy?* was he flirting with me?

Nah, I doubt it. I suspect he simply enjoys making me squirm on occasion. You know, as a slightly annoying friend—like how Paige and Ashley teased me about Mark, even though it pissed me off.

Yeah, that's it.

I consider the fact that things went south with both Andrew and Clive on the first night we hung out, but I've seen Mark on more than one "date," and he hasn't made me feel like an ancient relic or tried to give me tons of unsolicited advice about publishing. Sure, I thought he was a bit judgmental when we first met, but we talked that out, and he never complained to his mother about my actions, unlike Jeremy. (I mean, it's possible he did, but that seems unlikely, and at least she hasn't called me.)

Given my unfortunate recent experiences with dating, I suspect this little crush on Mark is just my hormones acting out of desperation, and I won't do anything about it. For now we'll proceed as usual with our fake relationship.

Sighing, I climb out of bed to get a drink of water, and as I stand at the kitchen counter, I grab my phone and scroll through social media. Tess Donovan has a post about how burnout is fake, which makes me roll my eyes. Burnout is definitely real, and while it hasn't happened to me yet, it's happened to people I know.

Rather than read the many, many replies, I catch up on the latest publishing news. There's a recent deal announcement for another Nazi romance, plus a publisher who hasn't been paying royalties.

I put down my phone and try to think of something else. Unfortunately, the first thing that comes to mind is Mark Chan's ass.

Goddammit.

17

—♡—

*"Millennials think everything should be
handed to them on a silver platter."*
—Randy Cooperson

Writing isn't going well this morning, so I'm in a bad mood. After it takes me two hours to write 114 words, I give up and start washing my bedsheets instead.

When I return from the laundry room, I allow myself a few minutes for one of my favorite hobbies: looking at fancy furniture websites and dreaming about what I'll buy when I'm a rich and famous author. Teenage me would be horrified that this is what passes for fun in my life, but whatever.

Once I pick out a very nice sectional, a desk for my home office, and a few bookshelves, I go to a real estate website and dream about buying a house.

I find a detached house that's less than a ten-minute walk from the subway line and has a garage. Though I wouldn't call it a mansion, it's still larger than it needs to be. The six-million-dollar price tag, however, is the bigger problem.

Now this one is a little more reasonable. In size, that is; it's listed at over two million dollars. Three floors, four bedrooms. I imagine the third-floor bedroom, with its sloped ceiling and small window, could serve as my home office. I could watch the quiet residential street when taking a break from my writing, rather than looking at a brick wall, which is my current view.

Following another failed attempt at writing, I go to social media and find Randy Cooperson complaining about the entitlement of Millennials. There's so much wrong with his words, including the fact that he seems to think Millennials are Andrew's age, when the oldest are over forty.

I don't expect to be handed everything on a silver platter, like he says, but when my parents came to this country, they figured their kids would be able to start a career and buy a house—without parental assistance—by their early thirties, and look what happened. Sure, Allison and her husband own a house, but that's because his family is rich.

Randy Cooperson probably also complains about how people my age don't want to stick through the hard times in marriage. Women won't put up with the nonsense they once did . . . because there are more options these days! I don't want to be married for sixty years to a man who thinks that if he gets the oil in the car changed twice a year it excuses him from ever doing dishes.

I'm about to head back to the laundry room—it's time to put the sheets in the dryer—when my phone rings.

Hmm. I wonder why Allison is calling me.

"Auntie, you look so pretty today," Khloe tells me as we walk—well, she's skipping; I'm walking—to pick up Scarlett from kindergarten.

"Thank you, sweetie." I say.

Allison's nanny has a migraine, so Allison asked if I could watch the girls for a few hours until she gets home from work. Since she was in a bit of a bind, I agreed. In the event of situations like this, my name is on the list to pick up my niece from school.

Scarlett frowns when she sees me, though. "What are you doing here?"

"Your nanny has a migraine and had to go home."

"What's a migraine?"

"A very bad headache."

"Headaches aren't all that bad."

Just wait until your thirties, kid. You'll have pain in places you never expected.

But I've been blessed in some ways: I've never experienced a migraine.

"Auntie Emily, what's sex?"

"Uh . . ."

I can't think of a coherent answer for a five-year-old at the same moment as I'm trying to stop a three-year-old from running onto the road.

"Ask your mother when she gets home," I say, grabbing Khloe's hand. I think that's a reasonable answer. Best to let Allison make the call on what to tell her daughters.

Fortunately, Scarlett is immediately distracted by a dog and starts running toward it.

"May I pet your puppy, please?" she asks the owner sweetly.

The woman nods, then says to me, "Thank you for teaching your daughter to ask."

I'm about to tell her that the girls are my nieces, but then I figure that's too much of an explanation for a woman I'll never see again.

However, Scarlett doesn't let it go. "I'm not her daughter. Auntie Emily is my aunt." She pets the dog. "He's so fluffy!"

Eventually, I manage to get the girls away from the dog, but Khloe immediately starts chasing a squirrel. All in all, it takes twenty minutes to walk back, even though it would have been a five-minute walk if I were by myself.

After we have some fruit for snack, the girls want to draw,

which is fine by me. I can sit here and watch. Alas, that lasts about two seconds before Khloe insists that I draw too, so I grab a sheet of paper and a purple crayon.

"What are you drawing?" I ask Khloe.

"A dinosaur," she says.

"What about you?" I ask Scarlett. Her picture appears to involve people.

"It's you! You're getting married to your boyfriend." She giggles. "Auntie Emily and Mark! Sitting in a tree!" she sings.

"Who's that?" I point to a third figure in the picture.

"That's me," Scarlett says proudly. "I'm the flower girl."

"Right. Of course."

"Auntie Emily, your picture's not very good. I thought you were an author. How can you be an author if you can't draw?"

"I write the words in the book. Someone else draws the pictures."

"Oh! You do the easy part."

Hmph. It sure wasn't easy this morning. Depressing that even a five-year-old doesn't respect my career choice.

After my nieces lose interest in drawing, Khloe runs around shrieking for five minutes. Then we play hide-and-seek, which lasts a total of ten minutes, and Scarlett asks me what sex is again. I debate turning on the TV, but I know Allison likes to limit screen time, so instead we play with a children's tool set. The girls have a fight for reasons that are unclear to me, and I have to act as a mediator. Luckily, I broke up a lot of fights among my younger sisters when I was a preteen and teen, so I'm an expert on this. Sort of.

It feels like hours, but it's barely been forty-five minutes since we got home from school. I wonder if the girls would listen with rapt attention as I officiated a funeral for a doll or stuffed animal, but I suspect not.

By the time Allison returns, another forty-five minutes later,

I'm exhausted. For the fifty millionth time, I wonder why my parents had five kids and how they managed to survive it.

Scarlett grabs her drawing and runs to her mother before Allison has had time to take off her shoes. "Look! This is Auntie Emily getting married. I'm the flower girl."

"Yes, I can see that."

"This picture is for you, Auntie."

"Thank you," I say as she hands over the drawing.

"Why don't you two watch something on the tablet for a few minutes?" Allison says to her daughters.

The girls scurry away.

"Thank you for looking after them today." My sister gestures me into the kitchen. "You know, Scarlett will be brokenhearted when you don't end up marrying Mark."

"Well—"

"I know you're not actually together. You don't need to pretend otherwise with me."

"Why are you so sure?" I ask. "Because he's too good for me?"

"No!" She sounds offended that I assumed this was her reasoning. Huh. "It's just awful suspicious that Mom keeps pestering you to date this guy, you keep saying you're not interested . . . then suddenly, you're together. Doing exactly what Mom and Dad want you to do? That's not like you."

"Uh . . ."

"Besides, he's not your type."

I have a picture of him on my lock screen! I nearly shout, but instead, I say, "People change." I think of Mark, opening the door for me while wearing an apron, and the memory makes me slightly warm. "Plus, he's a little different from what I assumed, based on the things Mom said to me."

"Is that so?" Allison's voice is heavy with skepticism. She gives me that knowing big-sister look. I've been scared of this look since I was, well, Khloe's age.

I sigh. "Don't you dare tell Mom, okay?"

"How long are you going to keep up this little charade?"

"I've got it under control."

"How many pictures of your wedding will Scarlett draw before I have to tell her that it's not happening?"

"Dating someone doesn't mean I'm obligated to marry him," I say. "You can tell her that. Oh, by the way, she asked what sex was. Twice."

"What did you say?"

"I told her to ask you, of course." I pause. "You're not going to tell Mom about Mark, are you?"

She shakes her head, and I exhale in relief, though I remind myself not to be too relieved. Allison might still betray me, like she did in the Pocky Incident of 1998—not to be confused with the Pocky Incident of 1996.

I say goodbye to the girls, who take a break from the tablet long enough to give me enthusiastic hugs, then head home. I'm in the middle of cleaning up after dinner when my phone rings. My mother, of course.

Oh shit. Has Allison already gone back on her word? Does Mom know that Mark and I aren't actually together?

"Hi?" I say.

"Ah, Emily, why does your voice sound so weird?"

"I don't know what you're talking about. I sound normal."

Hmm. I think my voice was a bit squeaky there.

"Allison told me that you babysat today," Mom says.

"Yes." My heart hammers in my chest.

"I hear Scarlett gave you a picture of your wedding with Mark."

"She did."

"I hope that picture will become a reality soon, but you know, venues book up so far in advance . . ."

I exhale in relief. It appears Allison hasn't betrayed me. Yet. Also, Mom isn't asking if I'm pregnant, which is nice.

Yep, it's a sad day when I'm relieved my mom is talking about my wedding.

"I know it might not be *cool* to date a man your mother picked out for you," she says, "but I'm glad you gave him a chance."

"Yes. Me too." Hopefully that sounds believable. I can feel a headache coming on, but I'm sure it's nothing as bad as what Allison's nanny had. Nothing some ibuprofen won't fix.

Then my mom says something totally unexpected.

"I'm proud of you, Emily."

Huh? Did I just hear those mythical words that children of Asian immigrant parents long to hear but never do? I've dreamed of this moment before, but I never thought it would come. And when I imagined it happening, it was after I, say, won the Governor General's Award for my novel, not after I started dating the man of my mother's choice. Usually, she just expresses affection—not pride—by giving me food.

I thought this sort of thing only happened in books.

"Uh, thank you," I stammer. "I'm proud of you too."

I nearly smack myself in the head after I say that. *What the hell, Emily?*

"Thank you," I say again. I hope she didn't actually hear the other thing I said.

For once I seem to be in luck, and my mother ends the phone call within two minutes, which is unusual for her. Perhaps she's out of her element after saying those words to me.

Dear God. What if my mother, who's now proud of me, ever discovers the truth about my "relationship"?

I'm not sure I could survive it.

I try to do some writing, but I'm a bit out of sorts, unable to focus on the words on the page, so I look at real estate websites once more and avoid thinking about my family.

Perhaps I could move somewhere outside of Toronto, where the housing prices are lower and traffic isn't as terrible. Even towns a decent distance from Toronto are expensive, though, so it isn't long before I'm looking at property up north. A two-bedroom house on the outskirts of Sudbury is reasonably priced. Unfortunately, that's a long-ass way from my friends and family—though being far from my family could have its advantages—and it's cold up there, but it's tempting. I still don't have enough savings for the down payment, but at least it's a possibility in the next decade. A place that's *mine*. A proper home office for writing.

My phone buzzes.

MARK: When are you working tomorrow? I'll be in the area.
ME: 12-6:30. Later shift than usual because I switched with someone.
ME: What are you doing?
MARK: Buying some art supplies before I meet up with a friend.

Part of me deflates. He's just going to stop by and say hi, nothing more. I shouldn't be disappointed, but I am.

ME: My sister Allison guessed the truth, by the way.
ME: Also my niece gave me a picture of our wedding.

I snap a photo and send it to him.

MARK: What am I wearing on my head? Is that a family of snakes?
ME: I think it's a hat. Either that or a clown wig. She captures your energy perfectly.
MARK: I agree.

Before I can return to looking at real estate listings and/or a furniture website, there's a knock on the door to my room.

"Come in," I say.

Paige opens the door. "Want to go out for dumplings after your shift tomorrow?"

I hesitate.

"Do you already have plans?" she asks.

No, I was just thinking that I should save money so I can make a down payment on a house far away from Toronto. But it's not like cheap dumplings will interfere with that, right?

Besides, I'm not sure I'd survive the cold weather up north. Though I could probably get lots of writing done in the winter because I wouldn't want to venture outside . . . or I'd spend even more time looking at furniture websites and dreaming of tropical vacations.

"Emily?" Paige says.

"Nope, no plans. Dumplings sound great."

When she leaves, I realize, with horror, that I might be more excited about briefly seeing Mark tomorrow than I am about eating delicious dumplings.

Maybe my feelings for him really are more than hormonal desperation.

18

—♡—

"Here's my list of twenty-nine things to think about
when naming a character. Just kidding. When it comes to
character names, I'm all about vibes."

—H. A. Kim

It finally happened. I'm rich!

Okay, not really, but I got the next part of my advance for my second book. The money hit my bank account this morning, and later, I'll do something very rash, like ordering the most expensive dumplings on the menu tonight. I briefly consider getting that pricey cherry pie milkshake, then decide I'll save that for another occasion.

I make a decaf Americano for a woman who comes to Coffee on College semiregularly, and when I look up, my face splits into a grin.

I immediately scale back my reaction. I shouldn't be so happy about the appearance of my fake boyfriend. I try to tell myself I'm just pleased about the money in my account, but I know it's more than that.

"Hello, stranger," I say. "What can I get for you today?"

Mark's lips twitch. "One medium Earl Grey tea. To go."

I ring up his order and get out the tea bag. "How's your day going?"

"Not too bad." He pauses. "I was wondering . . ."

I set his cup in front of him.

"Thank you," he says. "I was wondering if you'd like to go out tomorrow. It seems to me that at this point in our relationship, we should be seeing each other every week."

"I agree." I try not to show how happy I am with this suggestion. "You paid last time, so I'll pay this time. I'll think of a restaurant and text you, okay?"

He nods. "Very well."

"How's Ms. Margaret Muffins? She hasn't posted any pictures lately."

"You've been keeping tabs on her account, have you?"

"I have," I reply. "Tell her that I'd like to see some more content."

"Ms. Muffins posts when the mood strikes her. She cannot be rushed."

"I understand. She's an *artiste*."

"Exactly."

We share a smile.

"By the way," I say, "how did she get her name? Did you spend hours poring over baby name websites, like I sometimes do?"

He frowns. "Why would you spend hours doing that?"

"For character names."

"Right. No, my sister named her after the main character in *North and South*, which is one of her favorite books. She was actually joking when she suggested 'Margaret,' but I went with it."

Okay, that's rather sweet. He seems to be close with his sister.

"And the surname?" I ask.

"Cassie said she needed a more catlike surname, and the alliteration appealed to me."

"You thought that 'Muffins' was more appropriate than 'Mousecatcher' or 'Meatloaf' or . . ." I'm struggling to think of other alternatives. " 'Meow-Meow'?"

The corner of his mouth tilts up. "I did."

Just then the door opens. I silently curse whoever has decided to patronize Coffee on College at this very moment.

"I should be going," Mark says, and I try not to feel disappointed. "See you tomorrow."

After another half hour of steady business, Andrew comes in.

"Hey, Emily," he says.

"The usual?"

"Yeah."

Luckily, things haven't been too weird between us since our not-so-spectacular date. He's been in a few times lately, and I'm glad about that; I'd hate if he stopped coming to the coffee shop because of me.

"Any plans for the weekend?" he asks.

"I have a date tomorrow."

I don't know why the truth pops out of my mouth. Well, it's not the full truth—the full truth is that I have a fake date with a guy I kind of like—though of course I wouldn't say that.

But by mentioning my date, am I rubbing it in Andrew's face?

"Yeah? That's cool. I'm going clubbing." I must grimace, because he says, "You don't like clubbing?"

"I enjoy dancing, but I'm not a fan of the whole club situation. And the places I remember . . . they didn't really get going until midnight, which is too late for me now."

There. More proof we're not compatible.

When he reaches for his drink, I can't help admiring the swell of his arm muscles, just the teeniest-tiniest bit, but I don't feel anything more than a little admiration—I'm certainly not lusting after him

He sits at a table near the front and pulls out his phone.

"We close in fifteen minutes," I remind him.

He salutes me with his cup.

There's a trickle of customers in the next fifteen minutes, including Paige.

"Ready for some dumplings?" she asks.

"I have to close up."

"Shit. I forgot about that. I'll be outside. Might pop into a few stores, but I'll be back in twenty minutes." Her gaze slides to the side. "Who's that?" she whispers.

"Andrew."

"The young guy you dated?"

"What other Andrew would he be?" I ask.

"Well, there's no shortage of Asian guys named Andrew."

"True."

She eyes him appreciatively.

"Want me to introduce you two?" I inquire.

"Uh . . . you don't mind?"

"If you don't mind the fact that he's twenty-four and might make you feel like a senior citizen, then no, I don't mind."

There are no new customers, so I come out from behind the counter and walk over to Andrew's table.

"This is my friend Paige," I say.

I'm not sure how to manage this introduction. *She thinks you're hot?* Nah, I can't actually say that. *She's curious about your workout routine?*

That's probably true. Paige enjoys talking about such things—and she sure as hell can't do it with me—but I'm not going to say that either.

Before I can think of anything to add, he says, "Hi, Paige. I'm Andrew."

They shake hands and seem to get lost in each other's eyes.

"Paige is waiting for me to finish up here," I say. "You two can, uh, talk on the patio. Or something. I'll just. Uh. Yeah."

They head outside together, and I lock the door. My manager and I begin closing up. I used to work later shifts and closed up all the time, but it's been a while.

At six thirty, I head out. I'm about to text Paige to see where she is, when she appears in front of me.

"I've got a date tomorrow," she says as we head to the dumpling restaurant.

"That's great."

"Are you sure it's not weird?"

"Andrew and I went on one date," I say, "and nothing happened. It's not as if you're going out with a man I dated for two years."

In fact, I feel rather pleased that *I'm* the reason they met. My brain is jumping ahead to fantasies of being Paige's maid of honor and making a speech at their wedding. Sometimes my imagination runs away with itself—nothing new there.

These thoughts are making me feel like my mother, though, which is disturbing.

"I'm going clubbing with him tomorrow," Paige says. "You'll have to help me pick out an outfit."

"I have a dinner date with Mark, so I'll probably be leaving home hours before you."

"That's okay. We can figure it out earlier. I'll help you find something to impress Mark—"

"I'm not trying to *impress* him."

She gives me a look.

"Okay, fine, maybe I like him a little," I admit. "I need to think of a restaurant, and it has to be affordable because I'm the one who's paying. My advance came through, but I can't spend that money recklessly. It's not like being an author pays me on a monthly basis."

Paige and I eat our delicious dumplings and spend a long time dissecting our relationships with our mothers—as one does— before we head home and I spend a few hours being productive. (I watch an episode of a C-drama and read a few chapters of a mystery by H. A. Kim, an author I like.)

I'm getting ready for bed when I receive a text from Mark.

I hear Ms. Muffins posted a new picture.

I immediately check it out. There is, indeed, a picture of Ms. Muffins lying on her back.

ME: Aww. She's cute.
MARK: She'll be disappointed to hear that. She was going for fierce.

I can't help chuckling as I type a response. I never would have thought, the first time my mother told me about Mark Chan, that I'd be texting him and laughing.

But how, exactly, does he feel about me?

19

—♡—

"She is tolerable, but I have no thoughts beyond friendship."
—Mark Chan, possibly

*"Who is the weird lady my owner invited
over the other weekend?"*
—Ms. Muffins, probably

One of the great things about novels is that you can get multiple points of view. Now, some books have only one point of view. *The Catcher in the Rye*, for example. I don't plan on ever writing a book like that because I've always enjoyed being able to see inside multiple people's heads. Or, in some cases, inside the "head" of an inanimate object, like a car. Yes, I recently read a book that had a few scenes from the point of view of a blue Corolla hatchback.

In *All Those Little Secrets*, one of the mothers is preparing to tell her daughter who her biological father really is, but it's not as much of a secret as she believes. Thanks to the time spent in the daughter's point of view, we're aware that she already knows the truth; both mother and daughter aren't aware of what the other knows.

I don't write romance novels, but I read them, and a romance with multiple points of view—how delicious is that? You know what everyone's thinking, unlike in real life.

Unless you can read minds. I'll admit, it's probably for the best that I can't. It would test my sanity. But sometimes, I really, really want to know what someone else is thinking.

Like, wild example here, Mark Chan. What does he think of me now? And what outfit would he most appreciate me wearing tonight?

I went to the effort of shaving my legs, but I've since decided I don't want to wear the dress I picked out earlier. To me, it says "trying too hard," especially since we're going somewhere casual for dinner, though possibly it would say something different to Mark.

"What do you think?" Paige enters my room wearing a tight, sleeveless red shirt.

"It looks great," I say. "When did you buy that? I don't remember it."

"You don't think it shows too much arm?"

"Too much arm? Is that a thing? Besides, your arms are amazing."

"Remember that date I had in March? The guy who was intimidated by my workouts? Plus, my mom keeps telling me that men don't—"

"I'm going to stop you right there," I say. "You know better than to listen to your mother about such things. You look amazing, and I'm sure Andrew will think so too."

She helps me pick out a purple shirt that she assures me is "cute" and "sexy in an understated way," as well as a necklace. Once I'm dressed, I do my makeup and check my hair in the mirror.

Hmm. Why does that single strand of hair look . . . oh my God, I have a white hair!

I immediately cut it, but I continue to feel disturbed. I'm too young for this, surely, although some frantic googling reveals that I'm really not. I remind myself that it's just a single hair, and it doesn't mean I'll be all be gray before my thirty-fourth birthday.

Still, it would have been nice *not* to find my first white hair the night before my real fake date with Mark. Did it happen because I'm stressed?

I'm about to leave when I get a text from Meghan. Timmy has an ear infection, and I feel guilty that Meghan is sleep-deprived and spending her Saturday night caring for a sick kid, while I'm preparing for a date and my roommate is going clubbing. It doesn't seem fair. I get to have fun . . . but I also feel like I'm not a proper adult in her thirties, despite that white hair.

With a sigh, I send Timmy my best wishes and head out.

By some miracle of the Toronto Transit Commission, I arrive at the sushi restaurant ten minutes early. The server shows me to my table, and even though I've been here several times and know what I like, I peruse the menu as I wait for Mark, feeling a mix of dread and anticipation. When I look up, I note a table of white ladies glancing in my direction. I wonder if they take the presence of me, an East Asian person, as a sign that this place is good and authentic.

Just as I'm starting to fear that Mark might be late for once, he sits down across from me.

"Sorry, there were problems on the subway." He was coming from a different direction than I was.

"You don't need to apologize for being exactly on time."

"I know, but I like to be early."

At one point, this exchange would have made me roll my eyes, but now I find it a little endearing. Same with his sweater-vest and neat haircut. I feel like my entire body is smiling.

"You look nice tonight," he says with a brisk nod.

I manage to stop myself from saying something stupid, like, *Oh, this old thing?*

I'm not usually awkward and nervous in situations like this, but the whole thing with Mark is way outside my experience. Is he saying I look nice because he genuinely thinks so? Or is it merely part of our act? Would he have said that if I'd shown up in my oldest hoodie, which is in such rough shape that I haven't worn it out of the apartment in two years, just because he felt like he ought to?

This is the perfect example of when it would be useful to have insight into someone else's mind. Fake relationships are very confusing.

My hand shakes a little as I reach for my water glass.

"Are you okay?" he asks.

"You look nice tonight too."

Hmm. I probably waited too long before I said that, and now it's weird. I'm not usually *this* awkward.

I slide over his menu, and my fingers brush his—a complete accident, of course. I swear I feel a prickle of electricity, but there's a 46.7 percent chance that's just my imagination.

Or maybe 87.8 percent. I don't know.

Fortunately, as we discuss the menu, I manage to sound more coherent. We order edamame, octopus balls—I'm determined not to laugh because I don't want Mark to think I'm juvenile—and a selection of maki and sashimi. He doesn't order any sake or the most expensive fish on the menu, which is very considerate, since I'm the one paying.

When I'm finally starting to relax, our edamame arrives, and as I watch him slide the beans out with his teeth, I lose my cool. There's something about him doing things with his mouth that, uh, turns me on.

I attempt to seductively eat an edamame bean, and instead, it goes down whole and I begin coughing. Great. Just great.

"You okay?" he asks.

"Yep," I croak, having flashbacks to the first time we met, at Hannah's wedding.

Hmph. Not a memory I want to have right now.

I want him to think I'm sexy and sophisticated, and I'm not pulling that off. At all. Should I make a joke about calculus being derivative? Would that make things better or worse?

Probably worse.

"I have a question about writing for you," Mark says.

There are a few beads of perspiration on his face. Is it hot in here? Or is he a little nervous too?

"Go ahead," I say, though I fear what he might ask. Like, does he want to know how I think of ideas, and I'll just have to be like, *I don't know, sometimes things come to me in the shower?*

"Do you read while you write? A while back, I read an article by a novelist who doesn't read at all when drafting. They're afraid they'd pick up the style of the book they were reading."

Phew. I can handle this. "That did happen to me a bit when I first started writing, but now that I've 'found my voice,' if you will, it's not really an issue."

"You do have a pretty distinctive . . ." He trails off.

Interesting.

"Did you read my book?" I ask.

"No," he replies quickly.

That was a terrible lie, and it's kind of adorable. I might have trouble figuring out his exact feelings toward me, but I know the truth here.

"Mark . . ." I say.

"When you realized your mother had read your book, you didn't take it well, but I was curious. I couldn't help it. So I read it and decided I'd never mention it to you."

"That's a little different. It's my mother, and she's pretty judgmental—"

"You thought I was quite judgmental when we met."

"True," I concede, "but had I known you'd read my novel when we first met—"

"I didn't read it until a few weeks ago."

"—at least I wouldn't have been worried about you asking if characters were based on you. I mean, it's a book with multiple important mother-daughter relationships, and one doesn't end well." I'm sure there are Asian women authors who don't write about mother-daughter relationships . . . but maybe not many. "Plus, there's something particularly awful about your mother reading a sex scene that you wrote."

My face heats as I look across the table at Mark. I do certainly feel *something* about knowing he read that scene. Something that I can't quite put into words.

In my nervousness, words start spewing out of my mouth at a much faster rate than usual. "I've heard from some romance and erotica writers that creepy men will ask if you need help with *research* for your book, so I guess that's worse. Maybe I should have written under a pen name and not told anyone in my family what it was, but I fear they might have assumed I was lying about the being-a-published-author business if they couldn't see a physical copy in their hands, so instead I'm lying about having a boyfriend and . . ."

"Emily."

"What?"

"I'm afraid you're forgetting to breathe."

Hmm. I do feel a bit lightheaded.

When the server puts the octopus balls on our table, I immediately reach for one.

Okay, self. Calm down. Act normal.

Of course, nothing stops me from acting normal quite like telling myself to act normal. I open my mouth to ask Mark if he's fantasized about being an octopus in the deep blue sea, but then his hand covers mine on top of the table, and I nearly forget to breathe again.

His touch feels wonderful.

"Is this all right?" he murmurs.

"Yes."

"Is something up today? You're a bit . . ." He puts down his chopsticks and makes a vague gesture with his other hand. "Wound up."

I suspect Mark never gets consumed with nervous energy quite like this. Or maybe he does, but he doesn't show it like I do.

Before, his serious-yet-calm demeanor got under my skin, but now I appreciate it.

"I'm okay," I say.

Because I am—he's still touching me, after all.

I'll do my best to enjoy this "date" and not obsess too much over where it's going. I'm sure I won't completely succeed, but if I get 78.4 percent of the way there, that's still pretty good.

For the rest of dinner, I enjoy the food—not a surprise, since it's my favorite sushi restaurant in the city—and I refrain from any scatterbrained monologues. I take a couple of pictures as content for my social media, and Mark and I discuss, among other things, the use of terms like "content creators." He has a much younger cousin who wants to be an influencer when she grows up, much to the consternation of her parents, and that makes me feel old. Influencers weren't a thing that existed, at least not in that form, when I was her age (thirteen).

When the bill comes, Mark offers to split it, but I insist on paying, and he doesn't fight it. I appreciate that I don't have to resort to any of the tactics I learned from my mother and aunties at dim sum when I was younger.

"So," he says, as I tuck my credit card back into my wallet, "what would you like to do now? I could walk you to the subway, or . . ."

"Or what?"

"Well." He clears his throat. "There's a new gelato place near here."

I hesitate. "Sounds good."

He reads into that unfortunate hesitation. "You shouldn't feel obligated to spend more time with me."

I lean toward him so I can lower my voice, in case an acquaintance of my mother's is here. "We need to sell this. If a date were going well, would we just have dinner and nothing else?"

There's an odd expression on his face. Is he disappointed I'm bringing up the fact that this is an act? Or is that wishful thinking on my part?

I told myself I wouldn't obsess about it too much, but I'm failing now.

He leans forward infinitesimally. "A good point, but we don't have to do gelato."

"I like gelato. The problem is . . ." Okay, this is embarrassing. "I've been, uh, having a lot of gelato lately. There's a new place near my apartment, and I try not to go too often, but some weeks I still go twice."

"You live near Little Italy. Is it a more traditional Italian gelateria?"

"Yes."

He leans even closer, like he's about to tell me a secret. I can feel his breath on my neck, and I swear I'm breaking out in goose bumps.

"This one is different," he says. "They have flavors like Hong Kong milk tea and ube and Vietnamese coffee. Spiced persimmon. Mango lassi. Jasmine tea."

There's something sexy about Mark listing off gelato flavors for me.

"I see your point," I say. "It's different from what I usually have. I should try it. To expand my horizons."

"Exactly. You could call it research for one of your books."

"I like the way you think."

We leave the restaurant and start walking. After a few minutes of debate, I link my arm with his.

"Part of our act," I murmur.

"Right. Yes. Very sensible of you."

"I'm always sensible," I say, and to his credit, he doesn't snort.

It's not long before we arrive at the gelato shop—well, the line for it. This is quite the happening place. It's early June now, and I hate to think of what the line might be like in the middle of summer.

We stand close to each other and look at the menu online as we wait. It's another seven minutes before it's our turn to order, but to be honest, it takes me all of those seven minutes to decide what I want. I mean, to narrow it down to two flavors. You'd think, given my experience with living near a gelato shop, I'd be used to making such decisions, but I still struggle with it.

I ask for a cup with rosewater cardamom—I can't turn down anything with cardamom—and Hong Kong milk tea. Mark orders ube and Vietnamese coffee before pulling out his credit card, and I let him pay.

There's nowhere to sit inside the shop—the one table is full—and the two benches outside are taken. But the advantage of it not being hot and sunny? You can walk a little without your gelato melting, which is how we end up on a bench about a block away. I sit closer to Mark than I need to as I spoon gelato into my mouth, taking delicate bites with the little spoon.

"What's your expert opinion?" he asks.

"It's very good," I say, "but I'll need to return to make a full assessment of the menu."

"Naturally."

There's a beat of charged silence.

Distantly, I hear a siren. A horn honking. People laughing.

I'm aware of the noises of the city, but they don't really matter, not now.

It's just us.

I want to have many, many more dates like this. I want to try all the flavors . . . with him.

I certainly didn't expect to feel this way about a man of my mother's choosing. Not when she first started talking about him, and not when I finally met him at Hannah's wedding. But there it is. I've gotten to know Mark over the course of our pretend relationship, and I've discovered he's actually a great guy.

I scoop up the last of the rosewater cardamom gelato with my spoon and slide it into my mouth, appreciating that it's cool and refreshing—a contrast to my flushed skin.

When I put my cup down on the bench, he does the same. His gaze locks on mine. I feel like I'm pinned here, in this moment.

Then he places a hand on my cheek and slides it into my hair.

"Can I kiss you?" he asks.

"Yes," I whisper.

As he leans closer, it feels like everything is in slow motion, and then his lips—cool from the gelato—brush mine. His kiss is careful, controlled . . . until he sinks his hand deeper into my hair and emits a low growl.

Now he's *really* kissing me. The kiss of someone who rarely lets go but is allowing himself that luxury now. I feel consumed, in the best possible way.

Plus, there's the elation of knowing it's not just me. This fake relationship has become more to him too.

He pulls back slightly and rests his forehead against mine, and out of the corner of my eye, I see a familiar face. I swear I'm imagining it—that can't be Auntie Sharon—but I turn to take a closer look, just in case.

It's her.

Wait a second. Is *that* why Mark kissed me? Because he saw someone we knew and was trying to sell our relationship?

Oh God.

It didn't actually mean anything to him after all. My heart plummets.

Auntie Sharon disappears with her companion—thankfully, she didn't try to talk to us—and I take a moment to steady my breath.

And then I run.

MARK: What happened? What did I do wrong?

MARK: Are you ok?

MARK: If you don't want to talk to me, that's fine, but can you at least tell me you've gotten home safely?

PART TWO

The Invincible Emily Hung

20

—♡—

Mark

Wearily, I sit down on the recliner in my living room.
Ms. Muffins approaches and gives me a judgmental
look. I expect her to wander off a moment later, but she climbs
onto my lap and nuzzles my hand, which is most unlike her. Does
my cat sense that I need comfort?

I scrub a hand over my face and sigh. That was not how I wanted
my first kiss with Emily Hung to go. Not at all. I'd hoped . . .

Well, I'd hoped she wouldn't run away from me.

Did I like Emily when I first met her at her sister's wedding?
No. No, I did not.

I thought she was pretty, but she quickly showed that she was
even more judgmental than Ms. Muffins, which is quite a feat,
and had a lot of preconceived notions about me. I had the sense
that her parents—or at the very least, her mother—had spoken a
lot about me, even before she confirmed it. It's alarming to realize
that much has been said about you when you weren't there, especially when you get the impression that it wasn't entirely accurate.
(It was a little different with my mom. Yes, she'd like to see me
"settled down," and she mentioned Emily on a couple of occa-
sions, but that's it.)

After our unfortunate first meeting, I figured nothing would
come of it. But then her mother persuaded me that actually,

Emily would like to see me again and doesn't do well in group situations—a date, just the two of us, would go much better. I wasn't entirely convinced, but the memory of Emily, gorgeous and laughing at something with her sister, was enough to make me agree. Besides, as I said, her mother is rather scary, and I would disobey her only with very good reason, especially since she's a friend of my parents'.

When we met up at Lily's Kitchen, it quickly became clear that Emily hadn't wanted to see me again; it had all been a setup by her devious mom. I suppose I should have known. We ate our brunch, and although Emily still didn't seem thrilled with me, I was a little intrigued.

So when she suggested the fake-dating scheme, I agreed. In part because it seemed like the only way to get to know her better, despite being a completely outrageous idea—and I'm not prone to going along with outrageous ideas.

Thankfully, the fact that her mother seems to know half the city of Toronto—definitely scary—resulted in us needing to go on actual dates rather than spewing lies. It felt like Emily was starting to see me in a different light. She seemed delighted by my paintings and my cat . . . and my cat's name. She also seemed to delight in irritating me, and I rather delighted in being irritated, though I tried not to let it show. Occasionally, I even irritated her back.

I thought we might have that elusive thing called "chemistry," and I found myself thinking inappropriate thoughts about her at the most inappropriate moments, like during an important Zoom meeting. I spent an inordinate amount of time searching for restaurants and other places I thought she'd enjoy for our "dates." That gelato place, for example? I made a list of six options for dessert, then did a deep dive into the reviews.

I wish I were joking. Why did I spend so much time trying to please this woman who initially hated me?

Ah, yes. Because I've long fancied women who are very different from me, and because of that so-called chemistry. I value stability—I like a nine-to-five (well, more like eight-to-six) job, thank you very much—and I wouldn't be able to live Emily's life, but I admire her for having the guts to do it, for knowing exactly who she is. I can't imagine putting myself on the page like that. I'd feel so . . . exposed, and I'm a private person.

When I set out a few hours ago, I thought tonight might be the night that *something* finally happened. Perhaps she'd make an aggravating comment, I'd kiss her, and she'd beg me to take her home.

And we did kiss. A good, solid kiss, and there was a delightful amount of enthusiasm on her part.

Then it was over, and she bolted.

I still don't know what happened.

Now, I did see her looking at an older woman who seemed vaguely familiar—a friend of her mother's? Was Emily ashamed to be kissing someone in public? It's not the sort of thing I usually do, but I wouldn't think she'd be too bothered, especially since we're supposedly dating.

I pick up my phone. She still hasn't seen my texts, and it's been well over an hour.

I think back to the night she told me she was on a shitty date and I—internally—freaked out, worried what might have happened. I need to know that she's okay.

Finally, she replies. Yes, I'm home.

I release a shaky exhale and stare at the screen for another couple of minutes, but I don't get any more texts. She doesn't tell me why she left.

I set my phone aside and consider having a drink. The problem, however, is that I'm what you'd call a social drinker. I never drink alone and thus don't have anything appropriate. Sure, there are a couple of wine bottles in the cupboard, but I'm not going to open a whole bottle of wine just because a woman kissed me then ran away.

Instead, I pet my cat—it's rare for her to let me do this for more than a minute or two—and try not to think of the way Emily laughed when I told her my cat's first name.

Why does she look so luminous when she laughs? It's most unfair.

Dammit, I wish I knew what she was thinking. To be honest, I'm rather terrified to know what goes on in her head half the time, but right now I'd give quite a bit just to have a clue. I don't think she had an issue with my kissing *technique*, such as it was, and she kissed me back quite eagerly. But maybe she couldn't believe she was kissing *me*, the "proper" guy her mother wants her to date.

I snort. Some of the thoughts I've been having about her certainly haven't been proper.

I hope she'd like them; I hope she's had similar thoughts, but I just don't *know*. I consider pouring my heart out—by which I mean, sending a few additional text messages to hint at my feelings—but I'm too embarrassed to do it.

"She ran away," I say. I suppose I'm talking to Ms. Muffins.

My cat is silent, likely disturbed by my outburst, but she remains in my lap. I think she's concerned about my state of mind.

What I need is a plan of attack. Plans are good. I consider asking Cassie for advice, but then I'd have to explain that I've gotten myself embroiled in a fake relationship and my sister would spend half an hour laughing at me. I'm not sure I need that right now.

No, I have to ask Emily why she ran. In person. Then, depending on what she says, I'll admit that I'd be interested in some not-so-fake dating, and hopefully she won't think that's ridiculous.

Okay. I can do this.

But I'll wait until tomorrow before texting her again. Give her time to talk to her roommate about me—there's no doubt in my mind that she'll do that, and I wish I could be a fly on the wall or an Elf on the Shelf to hear that conversation.

Alas, I'm only human.

I can't help thinking back to earlier in the evening, to when I arrived at the restaurant and she talked faster than usual and seemed a bit wound up. What was happening then? Does that have something to do with why she ran?

I chuckle wryly as I remember how I tried to lie about not reading her book. She didn't buy it, of course.

And then, because I can't help myself, I recall that kiss once more.

21

—♡—

Emily

"The Human is behaving oddly."

—Ms. Biscuits, my imaginary cat

I plod up to my apartment building. My adrenaline has faded, and I'm not looking forward to being alone. But when I open the door, the lights are on. Both Paige and Ashley are here.

"You haven't left yet?" I ask Paige.

"I've still got half an hour."

I turn to Ashley. "Are you going clubbing with her?"

My friend isn't dressed for clubbing, though. She's wearing old jeans and a T-shirt.

"Frank and I had a fight," Ashley says. "About laundry."

"Oh no," I say. "Is he one of those idiots who doesn't know how to do laundry at all? Did he shrink a wool sweater in the dryer?"

She shakes her head. "We've been doing our laundry separately, and he thought we should combine it because it would be more efficient. He promised we'd alternate doing loads, but somehow the idea of our laundry commingling freaked me out, and I became convinced the 'alternating' wouldn't last long and . . . I left. Paige said I could stay the night. We didn't want to disturb you on your date."

"What happened, Emily?" Paige asks. "You look awful."

"Thank you," I mutter.

"Did something go wrong? What did he do? You're back earlier than I expected."

"We kissed." I get myself a glass of water.

"And then?" Paige gestures for me to continue.

"I ran away!" I cry.

"Why? I thought you liked him. Who kissed who?"

"He asked if he could kiss me; I said yes."

"Was it terrible?"

"No, it was a very good kiss." I'm not in the mood to wax poetic about it now, but, yes, it was good.

Ashley frowns. "So what happened?"

"The kiss . . . we were sitting on a bench, and then I saw my auntie."

"Oh my God," Paige says. "Your auntie saw you tonguing your fake boyfriend?"

"We were not *tonguing*." I pause. "Okay, maybe there was a little tongue. Anyway, when I saw her, I realized he was probably just kissing me for our act. He must have seen her first."

I pull out my phone and tell him that I've returned to my apartment, but I don't reply to his other questions. I still don't know what to say.

He didn't do anything *wrong*. He committed to our act, precisely like I wanted him to do. He told me once that he was good at pretending, and he's proven that to be true. I shouldn't complain, but I *am* complaining about it.

"Uh," Paige says, "it sounds like this was more than a peck on the cheek or a brush of lips. You really think he kissed you like that for your *act*?"

"Yes!"

Paige and Ashley share a look. I hate when they do that.

"You said it was a great kiss." Paige speaks slowly.

"When Mark sets his mind to something," I say, "he does a good job of it. You know, high-achieving Asian son."

Paige shuts her eyes briefly, as if my words have caused her great pain. "I think he likes you too. I'm pretty sure that's why he kissed you."

My chest is buoyant with hope for a few lovely seconds. Then it comes crashing down. "I doubt it."

"Emily, come on."

I smack a hand against my forehead. "I can't believe that *Mark Chan* has me so mixed up. I don't normally like the things—or people—my mother wants me to like! If I were a character in a book, readers would complain that I'm inconsistent."

"I can't believe you just ran," Paige says. "Why didn't you ask about his feelings, rather than assuming?"

"I couldn't think straight, and I didn't want to stay a second longer. I had to get out."

"Text him now and ask. Or call him."

I'm appalled by her reasonable suggestion. I can't do that. It's too scary. Even if he kissed me because he likes me, do I have space in my life for a real relationship? I already have three jobs.

I look at Ashley. She's spending the night away from her boyfriend because of laundry. Is that what I want?

My mom thinks I should get married and have kids, but there's more than one template for a woman's life. I don't need a man.

"I should get going," Paige says. "You two have fun without me."

After she leaves, Ashley and I decide that fictional men would be a nice change from reality, so we make some popcorn, open a bottle of wine, and start a movie.

When I wake up on Sunday morning, there's another person in my bed.

It isn't for sexual and/or romantic reasons. No, I told Ashley she could sleep in my bed—I have a queen—since it's more comfortable than the couch, and she took me up on that offer.

I haven't shared a bed in a very long time. At one point, Ashley called me "Frank" and tried to snuggle me, and it took me a while to get back to sleep after that.

I get up carefully, so as not to wake my bedmate, and head to the kitchen, where I start some coffee. I check my phone. I have a text, sent at 2 a.m., from Paige, saying she's heading to Andrew's and won't be home for the night.

Well, good for her.

Once the coffee is ready, I pour myself a large mug and pull up the advice column that I sometimes read when I'm sad about being single. It's always good at reminding me that relationships just aren't worth it. The column is filled with people who have mothers-in-law from hell and husbands who refuse to change a single diaper or cook a single meal. The husband might sleep with the letter writer's best friend and tell his wife that it's all her fault for "letting herself go," i.e., not fitting into her wedding dress a month after birthing triplets.

Okay, some of the letters are probably fake, though some of them must be real because of the whole truth-is-stranger-than-fiction thing. The ridiculous comment sections are truly spectacular and satisfy my need for drama. Filled with righteous anger, I wish I had the opportunity to give these men a piece of my mind.

"Hey." Ashley stumbles out of my bedroom.

If my friend asks to stay another few nights or, hell, move in with us permanently, I'll say yes—after talking to Paige, of course. I don't want Ashley to go through any of the nonsense in these letters.

Maybe I can suggest that the three of us buy a house in Sudbury and get a couple of cats. If we pool our resources, we could probably afford something nice up there.

"Thanks for letting me crash here," Ashley says. "Can I help myself to the coffee? I'll get out of your hair after that."

"No need. Stay as long as you want."

"I realized the argument was stupid. It was all my fault, and really, I was just remembering a bad fight my parents had, not long before they got divorced, and freaking out about how serious we are. But we're thirty-three! If I can't manage a serious relationship now, when will I ever be ready?"

"Romantic relationships aren't for everyone. If they're not for you, that's totally fine—"

Ashley frowns. "No, no, that's not it. I just have way too much baggage."

We chat for a few more minutes before she heads home to Frank, and I empty the bucket under the leaking bathroom sink. Then I start looking at real estate in Newfoundland, in case it's cheaper than Sudbury. I find some houses for under two hundred thousand, which is mind-blowing. All you could buy in Toronto for that would be . . . I don't know. A bus shelter?

I imagine getting a cat—Ms. Biscuits—for my house in Newfoundland. She'll sit in front of the window in my home office and snuggle me when I get stuck. Then Mark will bring me a fresh cup of tea . . . Okay, this domestic fantasy is getting out of control.

"Hello!" My roommate enters the apartment in yesterday's clothes. She looks positively drunk on sex.

It's a bit depressing when everyone is getting laid but you, but I'm happy for her.

"Have a good night?" I ask, already knowing the answer.

"Yep, it was great."

"I can't believe you stayed out so late. I would have been practically comatose at two in the morning. Andrew didn't ask you to do any, like, weird Gen Z stuff in the bedroom?"

"What have you been reading? What weird stuff does a Gen Zer do in bed?"

I don't know, actually. I just remember how old I felt on that date.

She slips off her shoes and comes over to me. "Are you sure it doesn't bother you that I'm seeing him?"

"Nah, it's all good." I have zero interest in Andrew, even if I can admit he has nice muscles. Instead, I've been mooning over my fake boyfriend.

Who, as it turns out, is texting me.

We should schedule our next date.

My heart leaps in excitement before falling. He's just dedicated to our act. He's given me no real reason to think otherwise, other than the way he kissed me . . .

"Is it Mark?" Paige asks.

"Yep," I reply. "He wants to schedule our next fake date."

"Of course he does." She smirks.

I can't trust her opinion right now, because her brain has been addled by sex. I return to my phone.

MARK: How's next Saturday?
ME: Sounds good.
MARK: It's my turn to pay. Shall I think of a place for us to eat dinner?

I read his text messages over and over, trying to see between the lines. How, exactly, does he feel about me?

"Come on," Paige groans. "Just tell him now."

"If he says no, it'll ruin my mood and I won't be able to write. I can't do that today. I have stuff I need to get done. Sometimes it's better to be unsure than to know the truth."

She rolls her eyes and heads to the washroom, while I debate having popcorn for breakfast, then eventually settle on toast and a lot more coffee.

Just a few more minutes of reading the comments on this advice column, and then I'll get down to work. I hope.

Dammit, where did that last hour go?

Okay, I'm going to start writing. For real now.

22

—♡—

Mark

For our next date—real or fake? I'm not sure—I select a restaurant near Chinatown that has reviews criticizing the "unfriendly" service. I suspect this is a good sign about the quality of the food. I make sure I arrive several minutes early, and I study the extensive numbered menu as I wait for Emily.

It's not long before she sits down across from me. She's wearing a summery dress, and she might be slightly overdressed for the surroundings, but I'm not complaining—she looks lovely.

Rather than telling her this, I say, "Hello."

"Hey."

There's a beat of silence, and I take the opportunity to pour us some tea. Then we spend a few minutes discussing the food options.

After an unsmiling server takes our order, I consider saying something about last weekend. *Why did you run away? Do you think I'm just some Goody Two-shoes that your mother wants you to marry?*

However, I fear these questions might be awkward, and I wish to enjoy the meal.

Hmm. Perhaps I should have suggested a coffee date instead.

I read a review of a novel—not Emily's—recently that complained the book could have been two hundred pages shorter if people just *talked* to each other. I admit I found the book tedious at times, but saying what you want to say can be difficult.

"Any plans for this week?" I ask.

"One of my writing friends is coming to Toronto, on vacation with her wife. We're having dinner on Tuesday."

"Where do they live?"

"Texas. They've never been to Canada before, and they're going to Toronto and Montreal. Paige and Ashley are my closest friends, but there are some things they just don't get. The other day, I was trying to explain a scandal involving a literary agent who ranted about—"

"Why did you run away?" I won't let this date end like the last one.

I want answers. I'm going to get them.

"What did you say?" she asks.

"Last Saturday. We kissed—"

"Yes, I know. I was there."

"And then you ran. I want to know why."

"Well, I didn't understand why we were kissing."

I'm not quite sure what to do with that, but I still want this beautiful, amusing, frustrating woman.

"You didn't understand *why* we were kissing," I repeat slowly. "Please explain. Surely you're aware of why two people usually kiss."

"But I've never kissed someone while in a fake relationship before."

"I see."

She looks away. "I saw Auntie Sharon, and I assumed you kissed me as part of our act. To make it believable."

Ah. Now I'm getting somewhere. "I wouldn't have kissed you like *that* just to fool your auntie."

"Yes, perhaps the tongue was overkill."

Comments like this are why I find Emily Hung delightful.

"When I kiss my other fake girlfriends," I say, "I never use tongue."

She shakes her head. "I'm ninety-eight-point-five percent sure you're joking, but sometimes I'm not sure with you."

"Which is why you bolted." I lean closer to her. "You wanted the kiss to be because I liked you, but you weren't sure that was the case."

She looks away again. "Yes."

And there it is.

On the inside, I'm elated, but I simply give her a faint smile. I put my hand on her warm cheek and turn her head back to look at me. "I assure you, Emily," I say, very seriously, "that I kissed you because I wanted to. And you kissed me back."

"Yes. I can't believe I started falling for the man my mom wanted me to date."

"Is that the only thing that bothers you? That your mother actually approves of me?"

"Well, it's definitely a strike against you. I don't trust her judgment, at least not when it comes to my personal life."

"Shall I quit my job and get a neck tattoo, in the hopes that she'd like me less?"

She makes a strange snort-laugh that I find disturbingly adorable.

"Though I admit," she says, composing herself, "that I don't think my mom really knows who you are. I'm the one who's actually spent time with you."

"I'm glad I improved, in your opinion, the better you got to know me." I pause. "Is there anything else that's troubling you?"

"You're also quite different from the guys I usually date, not that I've done a great deal of dating in the past few years. It hasn't been a priority in my life, and the experiences that many women have . . . they don't exactly inspire confidence. In fact, the stories

I've heard make me a little unsure about having a relationship at all—a real one, I mean." She fiddles with her paper napkin. "There were a lot of things going through my head last weekend and . . ."

She trails off as the server returns with our food, and I inwardly curse him for the quick service. Emily reaches for the rice, and for the next several minutes, there's little conversation, aside from her murmuring her approval. She's particularly taken with the tofu dish.

As we eat, there's an odd crackle of awareness. She now knows exactly why I kissed her. I wish she'd given me the opportunity to explain a week ago, and she seems a bit unsure about making it real, but it's a start.

After dinner, we amble along the city streets. I haven't kissed her yet today, even though I've imagined it many, many times since last weekend. When I can stand it no longer, I tug her around the side of a building.

"If I kiss you now," I say, "will you promise not to run away?"

"Yes."

As soon as she says that, I set my lips to hers.

The kiss is as electrifying as the one last weekend. It feels like she's melting against me, and my ability to make her react like that . . . it makes me feel powerful. But while her body seems to go slack, her mouth is needy, and she kisses me . . . well, I don't know how to describe it. She's the writer. And although I'm usually very much in my head, right now it all feels *physical*. Nerve endings I didn't even know I had are springing to life. Pulsing with want.

It's been a long, long time since I've felt anything like this.

She pulls back, and while she promised me she wouldn't run, a frisson of fear skates up my spine.

But she stays.

"So now what?" she asks.

Come home with me.

I wouldn't usually say that to a woman I've kissed twice, but there's nothing "usual" about this situation.

"I suppose we start going on *real* real dates," I say. "As opposed to real fake dates, as you called them. How about next weekend?" I'd suggest an earlier date, but she mentioned she has a friend visiting, and besides, I don't usually go out on weeknights.

Yet I'll need to learn to be a bit flexible, since Emily doesn't work the same hours as me.

"Sure," she says, "but I don't want to rush into anything. It's been a while since I had a relationship—one that isn't pretend, I mean—and I want to take it slow. See if we're compatible. I also don't know what to do about my sister."

"Which one?"

"Allison, the oldest, who figured out it was fake, and hopefully hasn't told my parents."

"Right." This is definitely more complicated than my normal relationships. "For now, how about bubble tea? After all, we were supposed to have a bubble tea on our second post-brunch date. We should have it together at some point."

"Okay," she says. "Bubble tea."

I take her arm, and we discuss which of the many options nearby would be best—there's no shortage of bubble tea in downtown Toronto.

Afterward, we walk around some more, and when she says she should be heading home, I hide my disappointment. But I get to kiss her goodbye, and this time, when I arrive home after my date, I don't feel the need to start drinking.

"We're going on an actual date next weekend," I say to Ms. Muffins, even if she's presently hiding from me.

As I step under the spray of the shower, I think of Emily's lips on mine. I think of slipping the straps of that pretty dress down her shoulders and baring her breasts to my gaze. My mouth.

What will it be like, when I have her in my bed?

Can I really turn this fake relationship into a real one?

23

—♡—

Emily

"You think publishing is a meritocracy? Ha!"
—H. A. Kim

"Okay, if you believe publishing used to be a meritocracy,
back in the good old days, but isn't anymore just because a
few queer POC are getting opportunities . . . well, fuck you."
—H. A. Kim, ten minutes later

Tuesday after my shift, all is well with the world.

I'm sitting at my computer, reviewing copyedits on my second book before having dinner with Julia Liang. (Not her real name; I don't know her legal name. That might sound weird, but it happens with writing friends sometimes—you only know their pen name.)

Mark Chan likes me.

My mother is proud of me.

There's some money in my bank account, and I felt so rich at the grocery store that I bought expensive cheese. Well, not actually expensive, but I didn't buy the cheapest stuff.

I suppose there's one small problem: I'm not getting much actual writing done. I keep daydreaming about Mark. I imagine telling Emily-from-two-months-ago about this curious development. Former me would have laughed her ass off.

My phone pings, and I jump on it. A real excuse not to write! It's an email from my editor.

Oh shit.

My editor is leaving. She's not just leaving the imprint; no, she's leaving publishing completely, probably for something with better pay. She assures me that my new editor will do a great job with my third book.

I, however, am skeptical.

My current editor acquired me. Would this new editor have done so, if given the chance? Will she like my voice? I've heard horror stories about this exact situation.

And will she be interested in buying another book from me?

My first book, as far as I can tell, sold okay, but not well enough that the publisher will bend over backward to keep me, and without my editor . . .

I can't help wondering if this is the reason why my third book was pushed back.

God, trying to make a living in this business is ridiculous. Why did I think I could do it?

Most advances, especially when you consider that they're split over multiple years, aren't all that huge. Part of the problem with the shit pay in publishing—and I'm not just talking about authors—is that it can be difficult for people who aren't rich to pursue careers in it. And when you do the job of your dreams, you're expected to tolerate the crappy pay because you love it, and you feel like you can't complain. Plus, some people think that everything is a perfect meritocracy, though how they can believe that in this day and age is a mystery to me. If you're not making more money, they say it's obviously because you're not good enough.

I email my agent to ask if we can speak on the phone later

this week. Then I give up on pretending to review copyedits and amuse myself with cute animal videos. I watch five in a row of my favorite donkey. Yes, I have a favorite donkey.

On the plus side, I'm meeting Julia tonight, which is perfect timing. She'll understand the situation.

I release a sound of frustration, and fortunately, Paige and her great hearing aren't around. She's at the gym, working off her annoyance with her incompetent new colleague.

I briefly wonder whether I should start going to the gym to express my frustrations with the publishing industry, then dismiss the idea because it involves, well, going to the gym. I also suspect that I'd have to train for a triathlon—probably the Ironman—to get it all out of my system, and that isn't happening.

Besides, the last thing I need is the expense of a gym membership.

I snap a picture of us with our cocktails and upload it to Instagram. Julia doesn't do the same, since she's taking a social media break. A few weeks ago, she had a post go viral and someone accused her of being a spy for the Chinese government—which, given the circumstances under which her family left (escaped) the country, was particularly upsetting—and she started getting death threats.

I wish I were joking, but unfortunately, there are some terrible people in the world.

But Julia has, as she will readily admit, been lucky in some ways. Her first book sold at auction, and she got a reasonably large advance and marketing push. I'm a little envious on occasion, but mostly I'm just happy for her.

This is the first time we've met in person, but it's not weird at all. I mean, it was weird for about three seconds, but now, after having hot pot for dinner—the same place where I had that ill-fated double date—we're at a literature-themed cocktail bar. I ordered a drink called North and South because it reminded me of Ms. Margaret Muffins . . . and her owner. Julia has insisted on paying.

Julia Liang is one of those people who ooze sophistication, even in Zoom calls. I can't imagine her walking around her home in a threadbare concert T-shirt and pajama pants with holes, although maybe she does sometimes. But today she's perfectly put together, and I'm glad I put a little extra effort into my makeup.

I've never been to this bar before. It feels like I'm drinking in a library—which seems so wrong—and there are a couple of cool vintage chandeliers. Some people might find this space a bit pretentious, but I like it.

I also appreciate not having to explain publishing. Julia doesn't say things like "can't you just . . ." and proceed to describe something that's completely counter to how the entire industry works. We discuss a recent plagiarism scandal, then a rejection letter with more than a couple of racist comments—it's been making the rounds on social media. We also discuss some remarks from a publishing executive who seems to know absolutely nothing about how books are sold.

"How's the domestic thriller coming along?" Julia asks.

"I'm almost ready to send the proposal to my agent."

"Want me to take a look at it for you?"

"That would be great. Thank you."

"Did your editor—the first one—suggest you go in this direction?"

"No. The thriller would be under a different name, and my option clause isn't too broad. My hope is that, between the two names, I could have two releases a year." I pause. "But what if I can never sell another book?"

She takes a dainty sip of her cocktail. "I wish I could tell you that would never happen because you're a brilliant writer . . ."

Hearing people compliment me is still weird. Perhaps because I grew up in a family where everything I did was never quite right.

". . . but unfortunately, it doesn't always work like that. There are lots of things you could try, though. You could self-publish. Or write in different genres. Ghostwrite—I know someone who's doing reasonably well as a ghostwriter right now."

"I once thought if I could get one book published, I'd have it made." I shake my head.

"Yeah, I know what that's like." She pauses. "Or if it's not what you want anymore—"

"No. It is. But I wish I wanted to do something easier with my life. Like being a doctor."

"Uh—"

"I'm kidding! I wouldn't survive residency, and I didn't even take grade-eleven biology. But sometimes I dream about having a career that wouldn't lead to arguments with my parents." Although, come to think of it, my mother hasn't been giving me much grief about my career lately. She's just been talking about Mark. Hmm.

Julia laughs. "When my mother goes to bookstores, she accosts the poor employees if my books aren't on the shelves. If they do have my books, she turns them so that the cover is facing outward. Tries to give them better placement. She also told everyone to put a hold on my book at the library so they'd have to order more copies. She tells me it's so that I get rich and famous and have enough money to support her in her old age."

We stay at the bar until ten thirty. When I get home, I feel better than I did before I left, and it's not just because of the two (very) strong drinks I consumed.

Tomorrow is another day, and I will make this career work . . . somehow.

Wednesday morning, I'm about to return to copyedits when my mother calls.

"Hi, Mom." I try not to sigh. Why does she have to call at the most awkward times?

For a split second, I'm tempted to brag about the fact that I'm now dating Mark for real, but my mother isn't supposed to know it was ever *not* real. That would defeat the entire purpose of this fake relationship.

"I have great news," she says.

"What is it?" I ask cautiously, concerned about what she might consider "great" news.

"We're going away for a long weekend."

"You and Dad? Oh, that's good. You should do it more often."

"No, all of us. The whole family! Probably not Meghan because she doesn't want to travel with a baby, but everyone else."

Oh no. What has she gotten me into?

"I got a great deal on a set of rooms up north," she says. "Well, they're actually individual cabins, and I've booked six of them for three nights. You'll bring Mark, of course?"

I search for my ibuprofen, convinced I'm about to get a killer headache. This situation is nothing short of horrifying.

"Mom," I say calmly, trying to channel Mark, "I work on Fridays and Saturdays."

"You never take vacations. Surely you can switch shifts? Thursday to Sunday."

"I don't know if Mark can get the time off."

"I'm sure he can manage. Plus, there's Wi-Fi, so he can work if needed."

"You're really okay with us sharing a cabin?" I ask.

When I was in university, my boyfriend stayed at our house for a night. My parents insisted he sleep on the couch, even though we'd been together for over a year.

She clucks her tongue. "At your age, I already had three kids. I know you're having s—"

"Mom!"

Dear God. I don't need to hear that phrase come out of her mouth.

I'm not sure why I bothered asking if she was okay with Mark and me sleeping in the same room. She thought I might be pregnant at Wayne's party, and she didn't sound angry at all. Since I'm old now, things are different.

"Look," I say, "I can't afford a vacation."

"I'll pay half of it and Mark can pay the rest."

I flop down on my bed. "Don't volunteer him to pay for things."

"Ah, I'm sure he can manage, and it'll be a great opportunity for us all to get to know each other better."

I don't know how a new boyfriend—*is* he my boyfriend?— can be expected to survive a long weekend away with my family. That's too much. He'll never see me again after this, and that's not what Mom wants, right?

As I'm thinking of how to explain all this to her, she drops another bombshell.

"If Meghan can't come, I'll ask Mark's parents to stay in that cabin instead."

"You *what?*"

"Why are you screaming?" she asks.

"This could be a complete disaster."

"It'll be fine."

"Mark has a cat," I say, grasping at straws. "I doubt the cabins are pet-friendly, and he can't leave her alone for four days." I don't know much about cats, but that seems a bit long.

"I'm sure he can work something out. He can have someone check on her."

I don't know what to say. My mother isn't going to listen to any protests. She always thinks she knows what's best.

And, okay, fine, she had a point about Mark, but that's an exception.

"I just checked," she says. "The cabins allow pets."

My headache is officially here.

"All right, I'll discuss it with him," I say weakly, "but right now I need to write."

She doesn't take this seriously and continues talking for ten more minutes.

At long last, I get off the phone. I put it on the bedside table and, in dramatic fashion, press the back of my hand to my forehead.

How is this my life?

This isn't what I thought my thirties would be like. I'm living with a roommate, working a dead-end job at a coffee shop, and sure, I have a book published, but I don't know what's happening with my writing career. My impossible dreams? Having a comprehensive dental plan and affording a small house in Toronto.

I pick up my phone and search for a distraction, but a headline about a billionaire casually losing three hundred million dollars nearly makes my head explode. Then there's the "feel good" story about the eighty-seven-year-old who works as a pizza delivery driver.

I wouldn't consider myself a pessimist by nature, but being cheerfully optimistic doesn't feel right at the moment.

I get a notification on my phone. A new email from my mother . . . with the recipe for Mark's favorite meal, which I'm supposed to make for him. She must have asked his parents for this. His parents, who might go on vacation with my family.

How is this my life? Seriously, how?

And why is my mom quite so keen about Mark Chan? Her single-minded determination to get us together is a little much, even for her. I chalked it up to the fact that she *really* wanted to see all her kids married.

But I suddenly can't shake the doubt that she has other motives too.

Now, this could be because I'm working on a thriller and I've become suspicious of everyone. Maybe it's also because I have an overactive imagination . . . and the mother turned out to be the killer in the last movie I watched.

Yet I still can't help wondering if something else is going on.

I don't think she's killed anyone, though I wouldn't put it past her. No, it's more that she used to criticize my career choices, but now it's all about the relationship, to the extent that I felt like I had to get a fake boyfriend. She doesn't mention my jobs anymore. Is that because I'm a "legitimate" writer who now has a book on the shelves?

With these thoughts weighing heavily on my mind, as well as that harrowing phone call, there's no way I'm going to finish copyedits—or drafting my proposal—today. Instead, I'll be productive in a, well, less productive way.

I think the next book I write should involve lots of cool food, so that I can stuff my face and call it work. I make a note to investigate whether I can claim said food as a business expense.

But for now I'll watch a K-drama to study story arcs.

Thursday is similarly productive. I read about criminal procedure and abnormal psychology. I talk to my agent. I spend a few hours reading a novel. All very important stuff.

However, I should also be doing actual writing and I'm not . . . aside from the text messages I send to Mark.

ME: My mother wants us to go up north with the whole family
    in a few weeks. She might even invite your parents if Meghan
    can't come.
MARK: Sure.
ME: Really??? That's OK with you?
MARK: If you want me to go on vacation with your family, it's no
    problem.

From this baffling exchange, there are several possible con-
clusions.

First, this man is absolutely gone for me and it has impaired
his good judgment. He's so in love with me that he would do literally anything for me. This causes a flutter in my heart, but it seems
unlikely. After all, we still haven't had our first *real* real date.

The second is that he's scared to disobey my mother.

The third is that he and my mother have something up their
sleeves, and I don't have a full handle on the situation.

The fourth is that there is something very, very wrong with his
brain. Perhaps carbon monoxide poisoning?

Hmm. Better do some research on that later.

ME: By the way, the cabins are pet-friendly. You may bring
    Ms. Muffins.
MARK: Margaret will stay home. She doesn't like car rides. I'll ask
    my neighbor to check on her once a day.
ME: You're on a first name basis with your cat now?
MARK: No, she calls me Mr. Chan, alas.

I find this funnier than I should.

Unfortunately, I'm still not in the right headspace for writing.
Maybe I'll watch something for inspiration instead. Or I could
attempt to tackle copyedits again, but that will likely just lead to
me obsessing over a single comma for half an hour and question-

ing everything I ever learned about punctuation, grammar, and life in general.

After my shift on Saturday, I tell myself not to be tempted by the gelateria. Nope, I'll head right home, do a few chores, then prepare for my date with Mark.

Yes. Good plan.

But when I go to my bedroom, I look out my window and all of a sudden . . . I've got it! I know what has to happen, that little detail that will make everything hang together in my thriller.

I fire up my computer, and my fingers fly across the keyboard in a way they haven't done in weeks. In less than two hours, I write almost 2,500 words—the final chapter I need for the proposal, and when that's finished, I'm still itching to do more.

So I start on the synopsis. Now, I hate synopses, despite being a plotter, but right now I feel like I can conquer this. I begin typing, and two double-spaced pages later . . .

Oh shit. Is it really that late?

I text Mark.

I'm sorry. I know we're supposed to meet in half an hour but I lost track of time while writing. I'll start getting ready right away, but the earliest I can get there is 45 min from now.

I hurry to my closet. To be honest, I don't exactly want to go on this date, even though I've been looking forward to it. The end of this synopsis is in sight, and I know I could finish it, but I promised him . . .

24

—♡—

Mark

I fully admit that I'm not great with changing plans and going with the flow, so when I get Emily's text right after I exit the subway, I freak out for about ten seconds. Then I start thinking of alternatives and text her back.

How about I get takeout and bring it to you instead?

I figure she still has to eat, and we can have a meal together. If she kicks me out afterward, so be it. But perhaps I can stay for a while, and then we'll . . . you know.

Emily agrees to my plan. The only problem is that the restaurant where I made reservations . . . well, I don't think the food will make great takeout, so I call them and cancel. After a frenzy of googling and reading restaurant reviews, I find a Thai place not far from where she lives. I order a few curries, mango salad, and rice, then get back on the TTC. This woman has me changing my plans and running around the city.

I arrive at her apartment, food in hand, an hour after she texted me. She's wearing yoga pants that hug her thighs and a T-shirt that has seen better days. There's something intimate about the fact that she's letting me see her like this.

She takes the plastic bag from my hand. "Oh my God, you're the best."

The first time I met Emily Hung, I never imagined she'd say a sentence like that to me.

"If we hadn't had plans," she says, "I probably would have forgotten to eat until ten, then polished off a bag of ketchup chips."

I follow her to the kitchen. "Is your roommate here? There's probably enough for her too."

"Nah, she's out."

"I'll stick around and read on my phone while you work, if that's okay. How much longer do you think you'll write?"

"Like an hour or two? You don't have to stay—"

"I want to." I hold her gaze for a moment.

After dinner, she makes us each a cup of tea and says I can read on her bed or on the couch while she works. I pick the bed so I can be closer to her. My attention keeps straying to where she's seated in an incomprehensible position on a deteriorating office chair, fingers tapping away. Then she pauses and makes a face before continuing to type some more.

Fascinating.

At ten o'clock, she flops down beside me.

"Finished?" I ask.

"Yeah."

"How often do you write like that?"

"Once a month at most. I promise I won't flake out on you on a regular basis. I've had a tough time writing lately, so it was exciting to actually be in a good flow today." She looks at the clock. "Do you want to stay over?"

Certain parts of my body get a bit too excited at her words.

"A platonic sleepover," she emphasizes.

"Platonic?"

"I mean, we can kiss, but I'm too zonked for anything more."

"Of course I wasn't thinking of 'anything more.' I'm a gentleman."

"I'm sure you are."

I appreciate the note of sarcasm in her voice.

"There's an extra toothbrush under the sink," she says.

"Thank God. It wouldn't feel right to go to bed without brushing my teeth. Not sure I could have managed that." I'm not joking. I'm very serious about oral hygiene.

"And yes, I'm aware there's a leak. The super knows, but it still hasn't been fixed."

I wash up and return to the bedroom.

"Would it be okay if I took some clothes off?" I ask. "Not all of them, but—"

"Yes, yes, you can strip down to your boxers or whatever you like."

Emily, I note, has changed into a different pair of pajama pants and a different T-shirt.

As she takes her turn in the washroom, I hear an odd sound— the door opening? I'm instantly on alert, and then I remember her roommate.

Actually, I hear two voices. It sounds like her roommate has a guest.

Well, that will make tomorrow interesting.

Emily comes back, shuts the bedroom door, and climbs into bed with me. I roll onto my side, and tentatively, I hold her.

She sighs. In pleasure, I think.

And then she says, "You seriously don't mind going up north with my family?"

"Why would I? It's a weekend away."

"The thing is . . . I can't really afford a weekend away. I have money in my account, but it needs to last because it'll be a while before I get paid by my publisher again. My mother volunteered to pay half and said you'd pay the other half."

"That's fine."

"Mark, I don't think you understand. You'd be paying to spend a long weekend with my family."

"We'll have our own cabin, won't we?"

"Yes." Her gaze slides down to my crotch. My erection is pressing against her thigh.

I start to move away, but she pulls me back.

Dear God. I'm not going to survive this so-called platonic sleepover. Emily's long, dark hair is fanned out on the pillow, and the blankets are pushed down to our waists. I can just make out the outline of her areola through the thin T-shirt. If I sucked that nipple into my mouth . . .

I shut my eyes, but this doesn't have the intended effect, as I'm now imagining her naked. I try not to express the pain I'm feeling, although it's clear I've failed at that when Emily says, "Is something wrong?"

"Nope, nothing."

"I'm sorry about tonight. I'll make it up to you tomorrow." She speaks the words very, very close to my ear, her breath tickling my skin.

"Now I really won't be able to sleep."

Indeed, when her breathing changes several minutes later, I'm wide awake.

25

———♡———

Emily

"There's nothing quite like a good writing session."
—Julia Liang

I wake up feeling invincible, which is an unusual feeling for me. Normally, I feel very much, well, vincible.

Did you know "vincible" is a real word? I didn't know that until a few days ago. Odd that "invincible" is so common, yet "vincible" isn't.

Anyway, I usually feel like I could easily be struck down, by a phone call from my mother or too many emails in my inbox.

But not today.

Guess who wrote a whole synopsis yesterday?

Guess whose very sweet date brought dinner and let her continue writing?

This is a perk to dating I've never experienced before. I was discouraged when it came to relationships; I feared dating would take up precious time and get in the way of what I want in life, but I don't feel that way now.

I look over at Mark and smile. Then I take off my shirt and start shimmying out of my pajama pants so he'll wake up to a mostly naked Emily in bed.

Unfortunately, I accidentally kick him in the shin while removing my pants, which isn't quite the sexy wake-up I had planned.

"Good morning," he murmurs. "Did you just kick me?"

"Uh. Yeah. Sorry about that."

He scrubs a hand over his face, and there's something adorable about seeing him mussed up in bed first thing in the morning.

I'm suddenly rather nervous.

Mark and I haven't slept together yet, despite what my mother thinks—ha!—and I intend to change that very soon. Based on last night, I'm pretty sure he'll be into it.

But what if the sex is terrible? The kissing was good, but that isn't a guarantee we're compatible in the bedroom.

So much for feeling invincible.

Before I can work myself up even more, he kisses me, nice and slow, and I sink into the mattress as he rolls on top of me.

"Did you sleep well?" I ask.

"Not great. New surroundings, woman in bed with me. Plus, you hogged the blankets."

"I did not," I say indignantly, but I don't know why I'm protesting. I was asleep, and I may very well have stolen all the blankets. "Sorry. You could have pulled them back."

"I tried, but you swore at me and held them tighter."

How embarrassing. "Then you should have woken me up. I wouldn't have minded. Actually, I probably would have minded, but if you couldn't sleep, it would only be fair to—"

He kisses me again, and my words die on my lips.

"I've wanted to do that for a long time," he says, mouth curving upward.

"Kiss me? You kissed me half a minute ago."

"Kiss you to shut you up."

Before I can express my outrage—or tell him that I've wanted to do the same thing—he's kissing me yet again, and his hand drifts down to my naked breasts.

"When did you take off your shirt?" he asks.

"Right before I kicked you in the shin."

His chuckle rumbles in my ear, and I swear it also vibrates between my legs. Then he dips his head and takes one of my nipples into his mouth. "Hmm."

He toys with the waistband of my underwear, and when I nod, he slips his hand underneath the fabric. Before he's even touched me *there*, I know.

I know this isn't going to disappoint.

He murmurs his approval when he slips a finger inside me and discovers just how wet I am for him.

"I should punish you, you know." He speaks matter-of-factly, belying the fact that his erection is pressing against my thigh. His ability to be serious right now . . . it turns me on even more.

"For what?" I ask.

"For kicking me, stealing the blankets, forgetting about our date, hating me the first time we met, and—"

"Okay, okay, I get the point. How will you punish me?"

"Orgasms," he says solemnly. "So many orgasms that you lose the ability to speak."

Never before have I dated a guy who could sound quite as stern as Mark, and now that seems like a mistake. It's so delicious when he talks to me like this.

He slips a second finger inside me, and I gasp but accommodate him easily.

"Good girl," he murmurs.

He strokes me with his fingers, his thumb moving to my clit, and I don't know how he's doing what he's doing, but . . .

I jerk my head to the side and release a totally undignified noise into the pillow.

He slides down my body, stopping to lick my breasts again before moving between my legs. But he doesn't immediately set his tongue to me.

"Mark," I groan.

"Is there something you want?" he asks pleasantly.

I attempt to glare at him, but it's rather difficult to glare a mere minute after having an orgasm—and one wasn't enough. Fortunately, I don't have to wait long before his mouth is on me, and . . .

Ohhhhh.

My breath comes faster. I stifle my cry as I buck against his face and come again.

"Was that acceptable to you?" he asks.

I nod as I reach into my bedside table and pull out a foil packet.

He sheds the rest of his clothes, takes the condom, and rolls it on. I spread my legs, eager to feel him inside me. When he nudges at my entrance, I moan, but rather than pushing inside, he kisses my lips, and I'm a ball of need and desire.

God, it's been so long since I've had a man inside me, and even though I've already had two orgasms, I need more, more, more.

He pulls back and places a hand on my cheek, looking at me like . . . I don't know how to describe it. I'm not sure I fully understand what I see in his expression. It's severe and hot, but fond at the same time.

Then he pushes inside, and I can't contain my gasp.

"How's that?" He sifts his fingers through my hair. "Okay?"

I nod again, and he starts moving within me.

I can do nothing but wrap my legs around him and hold on as he thrusts in and out, bringing me to the brink before he slows down, and then . . . and then . . .

He growls as he finishes, and somehow, that spurs me to a third orgasm.

As he flops on his back next to me, I try to find words of some kind, but I'm unable to make anything coherent come out of my mouth.

I start laughing. That son of a bitch was right—he made me orgasm until I lost the ability to speak.

I laugh harder, then kick him—gently—in the shin again.

I'd forgotten how wonderful the post-sex haze feels. This is the problem with self-induced orgasms—at least for me. It's more like scratching an itch, then I go about my day.

But this is different.

We laze in bed for a while, and it's a luxury to see Mark languid and sprawled out. I'd have difficulty imagining it if I couldn't see it with my own eyes.

Eventually, the smell of coffee beckons, and we get dressed and leave my cozy room.

"Good morning." Paige waggles her eyebrows when I enter the kitchen and grab two mugs from the cabinet. "Sleep well?"

I wonder how much she heard with her elephant/bat ears.

I glance at Andrew. Maybe she wasn't paying attention at all.

Well, this is a weird situation. Four of us in the apartment first thing in the morning. Yes, it's ten o'clock, but I figure that can count as "first thing" since it's a Sunday.

"Good morning," Mark says.

"This is my roommate, Paige," I say, realizing they haven't met, even if Paige has heard quite a bit about him. "And this is Andrew."

I don't mention that we once went on a date.

Introductions are completed. Coffee is poured. We crowd around our small table, which isn't used to this much activity. Mark looks vaguely uncomfortable with the fact that the other people here know exactly what we were doing.

I often enjoy having a roommate. It's nice to have someone to talk to at the end of the day, someone to watch movies with if I have no other plans. But at moments like this, I curse the

Toronto rental market for preventing me from living on my own. It's not just that I don't have the down payment to buy a little house; no, even the average rent for a one-bedroom apartment is crazy now. In fact, simply the idea of trying to find a better two-bedroom—it would be nice to have a bigger unit in a place where things actually get fixed—is nearly enough to make me break out in hives.

I push those thoughts aside.

"What are your plans for the day?" I ask.

"I have to go home soon to see Ms. Muffins," Mark says.

Andrew sips his black coffee. "Ms. Muffins?"

"My cat. What about you, Emily?"

I'll review everything I wrote yesterday in that frenzy of inspiration and—

"Oh shit!" I cry. I can't believe I forgot. I guess this is what happens when I have a writing marathon, followed by a good night's sleep, followed by excellent sex.

Mark's eyebrows draw together. "What's the problem?"

"Family dim sum!" I dash toward my room and rummage through my closet for proper clothes. Something nicer than pajama pants and a hoodie. Jeans and a blouse? That'll have to do.

Mark leans in the doorway. The sleeves of his shirt are rolled up. One hand is in his pocket; the other is holding his mug.

Distracted by his good looks, I momentarily consider telling my mom I have a horrible headache that necessitates staying home (and having more sex), but I already did that once this year, and besides, I totally want dim sum.

"Would you like me to come with you?" he asks.

"No, I made excuses for you the other day."

"What did you say?"

I pull on the blouse. "I'll tell you on the way to the subway."

26

—♡—

Emily

"Why are people telling lies about me?
I refuse to be dragged into this human nonsense."
—Ms. Muffins, perhaps

B y the time I arrive, my after-sex glow has evaporated thanks
to a frustrating trip on the TTC. My family is already seated,
but there's no food on the table yet. I sit on the only empty chair
at the large table, in between Scarlett and Meghan, who has
Timmy in her lap.

"You're late," Scarlett says.

"I am. I'm sorry." I look around the table, and rather than
saying I was busy fucking my boyfriend, I use the excuse "Transit
was slow." It isn't even a lie.

"Hmph." Scarlett sounds much older than her five years.

"Where's May?" I ask.

"She has to work," Dad says.

Since May is a pharmacist, this is considered a good excuse.
I had to cover someone's shift at the coffee shop or *I'm struggling
to meet a deadline but was too blocked to write all week and for
some reason the words started flowing today* would not be looked
on the same way.

"Where's Mark?" Allison asks.

"Taking his cat to the vet," I reply. That's what I told Mom on the phone the other day.

"The vet is open on Sundays?"

It feels like Allison—the only person here who knows the truth—wants me to admit the lie to the rest of the family.

Except now Mark and I are actually dating.

"Some vets have to be open," I say. "What about emergencies?"

"Is it an emergency?"

"Uh, no. He made the appointment a few days ago." I hope she doesn't ask what the appointment is for. Having never had a pet of my own, I have no idea about such things.

"What's the cat's name?" Khloe asks.

"Ms. Margaret Muffins."

She giggles. "That's a funny name."

"You want to see a picture?" I take out my phone and bring up Ms. Muffins's social media account. I show it to Scarlett and Khloe.

"Mommy, can we get a cat?" Khloe asks.

"No," Allison says.

"Pleeease?"

The next few minutes are focused on the can-we-get-a-cat conversation rather than Mark Chan, for which I am thankful.

As the girls are begging for a cat and arguing over what they'll call him—Khloe wants to name him Melon Ball and Scarlett is pushing for Kitty—I turn to Meghan.

"Are you sure you won't come up north with us?" I ask. "Mom's going to invite Mark's parents, and that's the last thing I need right now."

"Why's that, Emily?" Allison inquires in faux innocence.

Ugh. I thought I was speaking more quietly.

"It will make the trip extra stressful for me," I say. It has nothing to do with the lies Mark and I were telling before. Whether the relationship is real or fake, it's not something I'd want.

"I'm really sorry," Meghan says, "but leaving the apartment for dim sum is enough of a struggle. Timmy cried the entire way here. Didn't you, baby?"

He giggles.

Food starts arriving in bamboo steamers, thank God. It's a good distraction from the horror of going on a trip with my parents and Mark's parents, although having a cabin all alone with Mark could be fun . . .

"You're spacing out, Emily," Mom says. "Are you thinking about the book you're writing? Or mooning over your boyfriend?"

Allison rolls her eyes. "Are you two really going to share a cabin?"

"Yup!" I say cheerfully.

"Ah, Allison," Mom says. "Are you judging because they're not married yet? She's thirty-three. It's fine. I don't care. In fact—"

"Could I have the siu mai?" Hannah asks in a rush, probably afraid of what Mom will say if she finishes that sentence.

Mom passes the bamboo steamer. "I'm sure Emily is already doing it—"

"Mom!" my sisters and I all shout at once.

"What's 'it'?" Scarlett asks.

"Checkers," Allison says without missing a beat.

Meghan reaches for a piece of char siu bao, and Timmy smacks her arm. The food falls from her chopsticks and hits him on the shoulder. He starts crying.

"Shh, it's okay. Mommy's sorry," Meghan murmurs, rocking him back and forth.

"He's such a baby." Scarlett does not sound impressed. She reaches across me, and I block her before she can touch Timmy.

"You were a baby once too," I tell her.

"I was never like that," she says indignantly.

"Mommy, can we get Melon Ball today?" Khloe asks.

"No, stupid, that's a silly name for a cat." Scarlett crosses her arms over her chest.

"Don't call your sister names," Allison says.

"Ahhhh," Timmy cries, and Meghan stands up and takes him outside.

Believe it or not, we aren't the loudest family in the restaurant. At the table next to us, there's a very, *very* loud fight over the bill.

I help myself to lots more food, figuring that the least I deserve for putting up with this is a generous amount of siu mai and char siu bao. Besides, Dad and Allison's husband have been quietly demolishing a lot of the food, so I need to make sure I get my share.

"I joined a book club," Mom says.

"Good for you, Mom." I stack the empty bamboo steamers.

"I convinced them to read *All Those Little Secrets* next."

I manage not to choke on my siu mai. "Is that so?"

"You'll get the royalty money, right?"

"It'll count against my advance, yes."

I'm not sure who's in this book club, but I imagine a bunch of Asian women in their sixties sitting around a table, discussing my book—and yes, in theory, I want people to read my novel, but that image makes me slightly queasy.

"Did you tell them I wrote it?" I ask.

"Of course. I said you'd come to the book club meeting to discuss it with us. You told me you've done book clubs before."

I have. Most of them were associated with libraries; all of them were virtual.

None involved my mother.

"Nobody else has met a *real live author* before," Mom says, "and I gave birth to one."

As if I popped out of the womb with a pen and pretty notebook in my hand.

I'm rather conflicted. Mom said she was proud of me the other week—but that had to do with me dating Mark—and now she seems at least a little proud that I have a book in bookstores. I shouldn't care about what she thinks, as long as I'm happy with my path in life, yet I still haven't been able to stop yearning for it. At the same time, I'm utterly appalled that my mother wants to discuss this book with other people.

"I'll, uh, think about it," I say. "You can send me the date. I'll see if I'm free."

"We're flexible," Mom says.

Of course they are.

"Can I read your book, Auntie Emily?" Scarlett asks.

"No, it's for grown-ups," I tell her.

She scowls. "You should write a book that I can read."

"Maybe one day."

"Write a book about dragons."

"No," Khloe says. "A book about cats!"

"Don't be a stupid-face."

"Girls," Allison scolds.

Just then Meghan returns with Timmy, who grabs a chopstick and nearly pokes himself in the eye, and in a moment of desperation, I consider poking my own eye to get out of this situation. In fact, if real life is anything like the book I'm currently reading, it might cause me to travel back in time, and time traveling sounds pretty good right about now.

We're standing outside the restaurant later when Allison says, "I need you to babysit on Wednesday afternoon."

I grit my teeth. "Sorry, I have to work."

"You don't work on Wednesdays."

Well, I do write, which is a job, even if many people don't see it that way, but . . . "I picked up an extra shift this week."

Allison's eyes narrow. "Is that just another convenient lie?"

"You can come by Coffee on College and see. I'll be working."

"I can't visit you at work," she says icily, "because I have my own job and I need to find someone to take care of my kids because my sister won't do it."

I feel a flicker of guilt. We're family. We're supposed to help each other. But she can't just assume I'll be free, and besides, I do help her sometimes; it's not like I'm never there for her.

Dad comes over. "What time do you need babysitting? I can leave work early—"

"You don't have to do that. I'll find someone."

Yep, there she goes, telling Dad not to go to the trouble of leaving early but expecting me to rearrange my schedule.

"But if you can't, let me know tomorrow, yes?" He pats her shoulder, then turns to me. "Would you like a ride to the subway, Emily?"

That would be nice, but . . . "It's out of your way."

"Then why don't you do us a favor first? Our printer stopped working."

So this was his ploy all along. Mention giving me a ride before sneaking in the printer business. I'm not thrilled at the idea, but . . .

"Sure," I say, feeling like I can't say no to another request from my family.

Ten minutes later, I'm in the back of my parents' car. My mom keeps going on about the trip up north and how wonderful it is that I'm dating Mark. I keep thinking about the three orgasms he gave me this morning, which isn't the sort of thought I want to be having here.

"You know," I say, "if you really want Mark and me to stay together, maybe inviting his parents along on this trip isn't the best idea."

"Why not? Everyone will get to know each other."

"Sometimes there's a bit of family drama when we're all together," I say diplomatically. "Perhaps that will put him and his
parents off."

I recall briefly talking to Terrence Chan at Wayne's party. He
seemed a bit like Mark, both in appearance and temperament.
I wonder if, like Mark, he's actually quite kind, but I don't wish
to get better acquainted while on vacation. I'd prefer to start with
an uncomfortable dinner. There are fewer things that could go
wrong in such a situation.

"Ah, what are you talking about?" Mom asks. "Is there something wrong with our family? Are you ashamed of us? I thought
you got over that when you were a teenager."

I sigh. "I'm not ashamed. I just . . . never mind."

Mom, who's in the front passenger seat, turns back to look at
me. "Is there something you're not telling me? Do *you* have any
little secrets?"

Oh boy. Where to start with that one?

"Nope," I say. "Of course not."

Mom stares at me for a long moment, and just when I think
she's suddenly developed the power to know every lie I've ever
told, she turns forward again.

Back in my old childhood bedroom, it takes me only a few
minutes to fix the printer—a hard reset resolves the issue. I'm a
bit annoyed that I came here for this, though it's better than an
hour of frustration.

The drawer in the computer desk is open a crack, and as I'm
about to shut it, a piece of paper catches my eye. Specifically, a
circled name.

Mark Chan

I freeze.

After listening to make sure no one is approaching, I remove
the paper with unsteady hands. It's a list of sixteen names in my

mother's handwriting. Twelve are crossed out, some of them rather . . . aggressively. The remaining four names are familiar to me: they're all thirtysomething men whom Mom has mentioned at one point or another. Mark's name is the only one that's circled.

Holy shit. I found my mother's matchmaking list.

It's not labeled as such, though. At the top of the list are the words "Project Pen." Weird.

"Did you fix it?" my mother calls.

I shove the list in the drawer and close it.

"I did," I say with cheerful innocence as she enters the room. I show her what I printed.

The course of true love never did run smooth.

Mom frowns. "Are you having trouble with Mark?"

"It's a quote from Shakespeare. A *Midsummer Night's Dream.* Just what came to mind."

"Because you're having problems with love?"

"No! I assure you, Mark and I are fine."

My heart beats quickly as I wait to see if she buys this.

Finally, she nods, and I exhale in relief.

"Your father will drive you to the subway now," she says.

When I get home, I turn on my computer. Time to review the chapter and synopsis I wrote yesterday. I'm pretty sure they're brilliant—okay, maybe not brilliant, but at least reasonably good—because the words were flowing so easily, but I bet there are a few typos here and there. Maybe a couple of sentences that lack clarity.

Unfortunately, I soon conclude that there are more problems than a handful of typos. The synopsis isn't bad, but there's one plot point that isn't quite working, and I start brainstorming how to fix that.

However, I get distracted when I look over at the bed, where I woke up with my once-fake boyfriend this morning and kicked him in the shin as I tried to quietly disrobe.

I wonder what Mark's doing right now.

And how long was my mother working on that list?

27

—♡—

Mark

"Let me get this straight," Cody says, laughing, "you agreed to a fake relationship because you liked this woman, even though she kinda hated you—"

"Yes," I say, my voiced clipped. "I don't know why you feel the need to repeat what I just told you."

"—and now you're fucking?"

My eyes dart around the coffee shop. "Could you lower your voice and remind me again why we're friends?"

"Because I'm friends with everyone."

He has a point.

I've known Cody since I was eighteen. I suppose you could say he was my first friend in university—we met during frosh week. Although he has his annoying moments, he's not a bad guy. Most of the time.

"What's her name?" he asks.

"Emily." I sip my coffee. "I'm afraid I might be more into her than the other way around. For our last date, I brought takeout to her place because she was on a roll with writing."

"You know, I've always wanted to write a book," Cody says.

"Is that so?"

"Yeah." He pauses. "Aren't you going to ask what I'd write about?"

I gesture for him to continue.

"An epic fantasy with anteaters," he says.

"Anteaters?" I repeat, hoping I've heard incorrectly, but I'm pretty sure I didn't.

"Dragons are overdone, so in this kingdom, everyone worships the mighty anteater. They're large anteaters. Like, the size of a hippo."

"That's your whole idea?"

"You sound skeptical, but don't you think someone would pay me a cut—like ten percent—for the concept? I know the actual writing is the hard part, but it still has to be worth something."

"Uh. I'm pretty sure most writers have lots of ideas."

He better not expect me to tell Emily about his idea and offer to split profits. I doubt he would, but you never know.

"So, where are you taking her next?" Cody asks.

"We're having dinner together this weekend, and the weekend after that, we're going on a trip with her family. My mom and dad are also invited."

His eyes practically bug out of his head.

"I'm sure it'll be fine," I say, partly to reassure myself.

I've always done well with parents, which might be the reason Emily's mom fixated on me as the person who should date her daughter. Not because I'm charming, but because I'm serious and have a stable job. I'm son-in-law material.

Which is kind of amusing, given my own father isn't particularly impressed with me.

"Your *dad* is going?" Cody asks.

"I highly doubt it. He won't want to be away from the office that long." That's why I wasn't too stressed about my parents being invited—it's hard to imagine anything would come of that.

"Still, I think you should beg off," Cody tells me. "Say you're sick. This is too much pressure for a new relationship. An over-

night trip?" He shakes his head. "Why couldn't you meet someone the normal way?"

"Like?"

"At a bar."

"I rarely go to bars."

"On an app. There are lots of options."

Apps are appealing, in a way. You can say exactly what you're
looking for, and if a person's on an app, you know they're also
looking. Cassie met her husband on an app, but sometimes, they
can be a bit of a cesspool, and I know a couple of women who've
had terrible experiences.

"I'm not going to fake an illness to get out of it," I say. "I
wouldn't do that to her."

"Is she worth all this fuss?"

I think of waking up to her kicking my shin . . . and a few
minutes later, kissing my way down her body . . .

Cody snickers. "You're thinking about—"

"Shut it." I glare at him with what I hope are murderous eyes.
"And yes, she's worth it."

Though I do worry about my ability to keep her. I've always
liked women who were quite different from me, going back to my
first crush, a girl at day camp one summer. She was loud and kept
getting in trouble, something I did my best to avoid. While nothing ever came of it—I'm not sure she knew I existed—it's been a
trend that has followed me ever since, typically with poor results.

The women I date usually want to change me, and not in
ways that I'd consider reasonable. Some men have a disturbing
lack of knowledge when it comes to basic chores, and if someone
wants you to change from a man whose mother does his laundry
to one who does his own laundry—well, I consider that a reasonable change.

But women normally want me to be more free-spirited and
nonsense like that.

Now, I'm not my father, but I do take after him in some ways, and "free-spirited" is the last word anyone would use to describe him.

My last girlfriend, a few years ago now, decided to spend a year in Australia and wanted me to come with her . . . with one week's notice. When I said no, she complained I wasn't spontaneous enough.

Will Emily expect such things of me one day?

I'm good at tweaking the image I present to the world—it was a necessary survival skill when I was younger—but I won't completely change who I am.

"Are you sure?" Cody asks, more serious now, and I know he's just looking out for me. He's seen me postbreakup, when I wasn't at my best.

He might be a bit of a nuisance at times, but he's a kind and genuine nuisance.

"Absolutely," I say.

"I can't wait to meet her."

"When you do, promise me you won't mention the anteaters, okay?"

"I promise," he says.

On Wednesday after work, I'm about to start my laundry when my phone rings.

"Hi, Ma," I say, abandoning my laundry and settling in on the couch.

"Judy invited us to come up north with her family, but we're not going." She chuckles. "The idea of your father taking a long weekend! I said she should ask someone else. It was silly of her to make a nonrefundable booking."

I murmur my agreement.

I expected this, but it's still a relief to hear that my parents won't be there. Emily will be pleased with this development.

"I talked to Cassie before I called you," Ma says.

My sister and mother don't speak often—but they do talk to each other. Cassie doesn't speak to our father, though.

"How is she?" I say.

"I mentioned your girlfriend, and she was shocked! I assumed you'd told her."

I scrub a hand over my face. I suspect I'll get a text from Cassie soon.

Sure enough, a few minutes after I start my laundry, a message from my sister arrives.

CASSIE: You've had a girlfriend for MONTHS and you didn't
   tell me?
ME: There were extenuating circumstances.
CASSIE: UM.
ME: We were only pretending to date at the beginning. Her mother
   was eager for us to get together, and Ma liked the idea too.

Ugh. It sounds so ridiculous when I actually see the words on the screen. But I feel like I have to tell my sister the truth, or she'll be hurt that she didn't know earlier.

CASSIE: Are you serious??
ME: But now we're dating for real.
ME: Don't tell Ma that it was fake at the beginning, of course.

I trust Cassie. But outside of Cassie and Cody, no one else needs to know the truth.

On Saturday, Emily and I go out on our first proper date since we decided we could be something "real" to each other. We have dinner at a midpriced Italian restaurant and amble down the streets afterward.

We come across a bakery that, to our surprise, is still open. When we step inside, Emily points at the cherry pie, and we cover our mouths and laugh as the man behind the counter looks on in bemusement. We end up getting the pecan pie instead.

Full of dessert, we return to my condo, where Ms. Muffins is asleep in one of her weird contorted positions. I prefer my place to Emily's because I don't have a roommate.

When she falls asleep beside me, I can't help thinking that in less than a week, we'll be sharing a bed in a little cabin . . . with her family right around the corner.

I hope it goes better than she fears.

28

—♡—

Emily

*"If a book is good, it will sell, no matter how big
its marketing budget. Don't let people tell you otherwise.
Cream rises to the top."*

—Randy Cooperson

When we set out on Thursday morning, it's cold and rainy, because of course it is.

"The weather hates me," I tell Mark as we're stuck in traffic.

"It doesn't hate you," he says, his eyes on the road. We're taking his car because, well, I don't have a car. "I'm sure it doesn't know of your existence."

I roll my eyes. "Thanks."

"We can spend more time alone in the cabin." There's zero innuendo in his voice, but a smile plays on his lips.

"Hmm. Good point. We can spend lots of time . . . reading." I do want to read on this trip; I stayed up late last night because I was engrossed in a fantasy novel by a new author, Oz Delgado, and I'm itching to get back to it. I love the feeling of being swept away by a book.

Alas, it looks like this book isn't getting the attention it deserves. "Good books"—however you define them—don't always succeed. Spend a little time in publishing, and that should become obvious. Randy Cooperson claims otherwise, of course, and when I read his post earlier today, it was the push I needed to finally block him on all social media. Better for my mental health this way.

I doze as Mark listens to a podcast. When I wake up, I check my phone.

"Ms. Muffins just posted," I say.

"Oh, did she?"

"Mm-hmm. She's having a party with all her friends."

"Her friends," Mark repeats. "Ms. Muffins doesn't have friends."

"Aren't you her friend?"

"She tolerates me."

"Po-tay-to, po-tah-to."

"You have very low standards for friendship," he says.

"I . . . ooh!"

"What is it?"

I finish reading the email. "There's serious interest in the film rights for my book."

"Yeah? Which one?"

"The next one, out at the end of the year."

"That's great news, Emily."

If I shared this with, say, Clive, he'd probably be jealous more than anything else, but Mark is happy for me. He expresses it in a restrained way, but he sounds genuinely pleased.

I spend the rest of the drive daydreaming about what might happen if my book is made into a movie. Who'd be cast. What I'd wear to the premiere.

When we arrive at the cabins, it isn't raining, though everything is wet and it's cool for mid-June. We spend half an hour arguing about what to do. And by "we," I mean most members of my family, but not Mark. He doesn't partake in the arguing, and I suspect he's wondering what the hell he got himself into. His parents aren't here—thank God—but Auntie Sharon and Uncle Wayne will be joining us later tonight.

Eventually, we decide to eat an early dinner, seeing as all we had for lunch was a quick stop at Tim Hortons. Then we spend another half hour arguing about where to go for dinner, ultimately selecting a chain restaurant fifteen minutes away that luckily has enough space to accommodate us all.

I end up seated next to Mark and across from my mother.

"You look very happy today," she observes.

"Why wouldn't I be happy?" I ask. "I'm on vacation for once." I pause, debating whether to tell my mom. What the hell. "Someone wants to buy the film rights for my next book."

"Ah, really? How exciting! Who's going to play me?"

I'm already regretting my decision. "Mom, you're not a character in the book."

She frowns. "There was a character who was an awful lot like me. I meant to ask you—"

"This is for my second book, not the one that's already out."

"The one with the murders?"

"No, that's the one I'm writing now."

"When will the murder book be out?"

"I don't even know if it will be published. I'll send the proposal to my agent soon, but even if we get an offer quickly once we go on submission, it could be two years until release." I pause. "And selling film rights doesn't mean it will ever go into production." And if it does, a streaming service could still decide not to release it for tax write-off purposes or . . . something.

"You know which actor I like?" Mom names three. "You should email them and get them interested. Then the movie will be made."

"Um, I don't have those kinds of connections."

"You should bring me as your date to the premiere."

See, it's fun to daydream about these things, but as I listen to my mother talk about it, I realize I set myself up for failure. She'll keep asking about it, then be disappointed in me when nothing happens, which is likely.

"Maybe I'd like to bring Mark to the premiere," I say.

"I'm sure he'd understand." She looks at Mark, and he nods, perhaps terrified into agreement, seeing as he's spending three nights on vacation with her.

"Mom . . ."

"Fine. You can bring Mark. Unless Tony Leung is in the movie, then I get to come."

The waiter arrives. "Can I take your orders?"

Oh dear. Nobody has opened their menus yet.

"Just give us five minutes," I say optimistically.

The next day is nicer, thankfully, and we go to the beach. It's pleasantly warm, but not hot, and the beach isn't crowded, perhaps also thanks to the fact that it's Friday morning. I wear shorts and a T-shirt over my bathing suit. Scarlett and Khloe conscript me to help them build a sandcastle.

"This is the tower for the pincess!" Khloe says, dripping wet sand onto the dry sand.

"Yeah?" I say. "What does the princess do in her tower?"

"Wait for the pince!"

"What does she do while she's waiting?" I wonder if I should say something about how the princess should have her own dreams and goals in life that don't involve a man. Hmm.

Khloe thinks about this for a moment. "Plays with her dollies and blocks."

"Princesses don't play with dollies," Scarlett says as she fills a star-shaped toy with sand.

"Why not? Pincesses can do whatever they want, and mine wants to play with dollies."

"Don't say stupid things. It will bite you in the ass."

I look around to see if the girls' parents can help me with this situation, but they're out in the water, as is May. Mom is talking to Auntie Sharon. Dad and Uncle Wayne are snoozing. Mark is carefully applying sunscreen to his legs. Like me, he's wearing a T-shirt.

"What did you say?" I ask Scarlett.

"Stupid things will come back to bite you in the ass."

"Where did you learn that?"

"Mommy! I came downstairs because I couldn't sleep, and she was talking to Daddy. She said, 'Emily's lies will come back to bite her in the ass.'"

Um . . .

"What lies are these?" I ask.

Scarlett frowns as she continues filling her star with sand. "Something about markers?"

Yep, she heard "bite her in the ass" clearly but not "Mark." She knows what's important.

"I'll bite you in the ass!" Khloe exclaims.

Oh dear.

"You shouldn't say bad words like that," I tell my nieces.

"But Mommy said it," Scarlett protests.

"Sometimes grown-ups can say things that kids can't. In certain situations."

"It's not fair."

"You're right. It's not."

"Can I say 'bite you in the bum-bum'?"

"Uh . . ."

Scarlett stares at me in a rather frightening way, like she's a little girl in a horror movie. Right when I think her eyes are going to turn red, she says, "So what did you do? Did you leave the caps off the markers?"

"Yes, that's exactly what I did."

"You're not supposed to do that. They dry out."

"I know. It was an accident."

"Like when I wet the bed?"

For the next few moments, the girls are occupied with their sandcastle. I try to help Khloe drip the sand, but apparently, I'm "doing it all wrong"—she says this with great forcefulness—so I give up and just watch.

Then, out of nowhere, Scarlett announces, "Mark isn't really your boyfriend."

I try to remain calm. "Why do you say that?"

"I heard it from Mommy. She didn't know I was listening."

A different time from when she heard the biting-in-the-ass business? I consider a mini-lecture on eavesdropping, but before I can string two coherent words together in my head, Scarlett continues.

"I don't understand," she says. "He came with you to the beach. He must be your boyfriend."

"Yep, that's how it works."

I wonder if I should tell Scarlett not to repeat this conversation in front of anyone, especially not her po po. Alas, I fear that might make her more likely to say something, and it would end with me bribing a five-year-old with candy.

For reasons beyond my comprehension, Khloe suddenly hits Scarlett, and before I can say anything, Hannah and Allison come over. Hannah, in an attempt at distraction, asks the girls what they're making. Scarlett says something about a fire station— appropriate because looking after kids can feel like putting out endless fires—and Khloe's princess tower is apparently now a "very big boat with a cool playground."

"You know," Hannah says, "when I was little like you, Auntie Emily used to tell me lots of stories. Maybe she could tell you a story about your boat." She looks at me and smiles.

"Right," I say. "There once was a very big boat. It traveled all over the world." I have no idea where I'm going with this. My oral storytelling skills are a bit rusty. "When it went to Antarctica, a bunch of penguins came aboard to play on the cool playground. Then it went to Australia, where it picked up some kangaroos. In India, it picked up two tigers."

"Did the tigers eat the penguins?" Scarlett asks.

"Noooooo!" Khloe cries.

"They were nice tigers," I say. "No one got eaten."

Allison snorts.

Since I'm unable to reassure Khloe that the penguins would be safe, story time comes to an end. Young Hannah probably would have enjoyed hearing about the tigers tearing other creatures limb from limb, followed by a funeral, but Khloe is different.

Fortunately, Hannah gets the girls interested in some other sand toys.

Now that I'm no longer in charge of the kids, I turn toward Mark, who's reading in a folding chair. He's removed his shirt. There's something delicious about a man who's usually a touch buttoned-up not wearing a shirt, and I spend several seconds admiring him.

Allison pulls my arm and leads me a few paces away from everyone else.

"You're taking this fake-relationship thing a little far," she says, "don't you think? Bringing your so-called boyfriend on a family vacation? Making a point of looking in his direction so people think you're smitten?"

"It's not fake," I tell her.

She rolls her eyes. "You admitted it to me before. Why are you pretending now?"

"I'm not pretending. Yes, Mark and I went on a few dates so I could get Mom off my back about the whole single-in-my-thirties thing, but now we're dating for real."

"You and Mark Chan. Really. You once told me, after Mom

bugged you about him yet again, that you'd never, ever go out with him."

Hmm. Yes, I suppose I did say that. I was slightly intoxicated at the time. I'm not usually prone to confessing anything to my big sister.

"People change," I say defensively.

"Not you."

"What's that supposed to mean?"

She gives me that scary Big Sister look. "You were always the artsy one, who didn't take the classes you were supposed to take in high school."

"Mm-hmm. You mean I didn't take biology. I took multiple math classes and physics in my final year. Was I not supposed to take those?"

"You quit your job after only a few years."

Yeah, the one job she considered "real." I would tell her that I was so, so miserable, but she knows that, and I don't think she cares.

"You kept breaking curfew," she says.

"Like, four times. And it was fifteen years ago."

"It's just so frustrating . . . When will you ever grow up? You're thirty-three and you're faking a relationship?" My big sister has always thought it was her duty to judge me and give me advice.

"Not anymore."

She rolls her eyes again. "But you still did it. I can't believe he went along with it."

"Neither can I, to be honest, but he did."

Movement out of the corner of my eye catches my attention. Mark has put aside his e-reader and is heading to the water.

Ooh. I watch as he wades through the shallow water before turning back to my sister.

"There's not only one way to be an adult," I say. "Just because

I don't have a husband and kids—that doesn't mean I haven't grown up." Sure, sometimes I have trouble believing I'm allowed to call myself an adult, but I won't admit that to her. "It's not like it affects you; it's not like I'm expecting you to give me anything. I still take care of myself."

Yes, sometimes I start a C-drama episode at 11 p.m. and call it being "productive"—I know Allison never makes choices like that—but whatever. I like my life. I mean, I'd prefer if I made more money, and I *ought* to be able to make more money doing exactly what I'm doing, but I can't easily change that.

"Mommy!" Khloe runs toward us. "The sand is stuck on my skin!"

As Khloe asks Allison why sand can't be less sandy, I look out at the water, where Mark is swimming back to shore. I can't imagine going in a lake at this time of year. True, this one is orders of magnitude smaller than the Great Lakes—which can be ice buckets in June—but still.

I'm glad he went swimming, though, because now he's emerging from the lake, water sliding over his bare chest.

I grab his towel and go to meet him.

"Hey, you," I say. "Have a nice swim?"

"Yeah, but it was cold. I'm not sure how May's still in there."

At that moment, there's a shriek. I look over to see Scarlett dipping her toes into the water.

"It's freezing!" she exclaims.

"As I was saying," Mark says dryly. "You going in?"

"No, thank you. I don't like getting wet."

"Pardon me?"

Oops.

I just realized what I said. And his response was "pardon me."

I love this guy.

Well, not like *that*. I'm not in love with him—it hasn't been long enough for such feelings—but I do like him quite a bit.

"I don't enjoy going in bodies of water," I amend. I might have made a dirtier comment if we weren't so close to my family.

"What about a bath?"

"That's different. It's warm. But . . ." My voice trails off as I watch a water droplet trail down his chest. Mmm.

Yeah, it really is too bad that my family is around.

"You going to read more?" I ask.

"I was thinking about it."

"I'll join you."

I lie down on my towel and start reading, but I've read a grand total of one page when my mother walks over, her face protected from the sun by a ginormous visor.

"I've given more thought to the casting for your movie," she says.

I close the cover on my e-reader. "You haven't even read the book."

"I'm thinking of casting for the first book. You know who I think is hot?"

Next to me, Mark chuckles softly.

"Look, Mom." I need to end this conversation before it goes in places I really, really do not want. However, I'm not sure exactly how to prevent this. "I—"

"Do you think they will cut the sex scene when they film it? To make it PG?"

OMG. I can't believe this is happening. I put a hand to my head, feeling nauseous.

"I'm never writing a sex scene again," I mutter.

"Why not?" she asks. "I thought it was well-written."

I *cannot* with this conversation. I suppose it's nice that my mom is complimenting my writing, but if she could mention something other than the sex scene, it would be nice. Though knowing my luck, the next compliment I get will be about how well I write murders and serial killers.

"I'm serious," she says.

"Uh, thank you."

"I think it should be in the movie. There isn't enough sex in movies these days."

"I . . ."

I can hear Mark trying his best not to laugh. Bastard.

"Mom," I say. "Like I told you, it's for the second book, and even if we sell the rights, there's no guarantee anything will ever get made, and there's no sex scene in that one."

She looks rather disappointed. "What if—"

"I'm sorry, Judy," Mark says. "I have something important I need to talk to Emily about, okay? I'll let you finish this conversation later, don't worry."

My mother wanders off, tests the water, and yelps before going back to her chair under the umbrella.

"You could have saved me sooner," I say to Mark.

"Next time," he promises.

I playfully give him the middle finger, then attempt to return to my book. However, given the anxiety I feel over Scarlett or Allison revealing how my relationship started—and, equally, the anxiety I feel over my mother talking about sex scenes again—I find it hard to concentrate.

"Can I ask you something?" I say, when Mark and I are decompressing later in our cabin. It's been a long day with my family, and it's nice that it's just the two of us now.

"Go ahead," he says.

"Do you think I'm a real adult? Allison asked me when I'm ever going to grow up."

"You look plenty grown-up to me," he murmurs, stroking his hand over my breast.

This is a side of Mark I didn't see until recently, and I enjoy it.

I bat his hand away. "Be serious."

"I'm always serious," he says . . . seriously. "You're an adult. You don't need to have a mortgage and kids to be a real adult."

"That's what I tried to tell her. Besides, even if you *want* a mortgage and kids, it can be hard to do those things, even in your thirties. Day care is so expensive. Property is so expensive." I pause. "But you're more like Allison. Your life . . . is more like what our parents want for us."

Allison believes I don't care, at all, about our parents' expectations. The problem is that I do still care. I know it wasn't easy for them to move to the other side of the world. I feel like I owe them something, and I can't seem to shake my desire for their approval. Which, I suppose, is part of the reason for the fake relationship, the one that my sister refuses to believe is now real.

"I don't think there's anything wrong with you," he says. "Except . . ."

"Except what?"

"You're wearing clothes. That's a rather unfortunate situation."

"Is it? What are you going to do about it?"

"I have some ideas. You know, I was very disappointed when you didn't take your T-shirt off on the beach."

"It wasn't warm enough," I say, "and I didn't want my mother to critique my body."

"I promise to say only very, very complimentary things." He kisses my neck.

Mmm. The first full day of vacation is coming to a nice end.

But I still have to survive tomorrow.

29

❤

Mark

Saturday morning is rainy, but I'm not complaining. It's an improvement over having to spend a torturous few hours on the beach with Emily and her family. Yes, she never revealed her bathing suit, but I knew what it looked like because I'd seen it beforehand. And those shorts were . . . very short. I had to swim in the cold lake just to douse my desire for her. Trust me, I didn't enjoy that swim.

But this morning, there's no beach because there's a thunderstorm. Some of the Hungs are playing Monopoly, but Emily says she'd rather stay here with me. She also says that seeing her family play Monopoly would probably scare me off, and that would be awkward because I'm her ride home.

After we have sex, Emily decides to do some work. She pulls out her laptop and sets it up on the small table in the cabin, but she hesitates before turning it on.

"Do you mind?" she asks. "You can read, or—"

"Not at all," I assure her. "Actually, I'm going to paint, if you could spare a tiny bit of space." I nod at the table.

She smiles at me. "No problem."

I take out my watercolors, which I impulsively tossed into my bag before leaving, and decide I'll do a small painting of the view out the window. We work in silence for a while, the only noise in the cabin the pattering of the rain and the clack of fingers on the keyboard.

"Do you want some coffee?"

I nearly startle at her voice.

"If you're making some," I say.

Several minutes later, she sets a mug down in front of me, but after I thank her, I find it hard to return to my painting. I can't stop myself from watching Emily, just on the other side of the small table, brow furrowed in concentration. I've never been much for painting or sketching people, but the window scene now seems like a mistake.

She glances up. "This is nice. Working next to each other like this." She doesn't seem aware that my paintbrush hasn't touched the paper in a while. "When I went on that unfortunate date with Clive, I briefly imagined writing together, but this is better."

She reaches over to touch my cheek, and I'm about to plant a kiss on her lips—a quick one, so I don't interrupt her work— when someone raps on the door of the cabin.

"Shit," she mutters. "I guess we have to get that."

I walk to the door, open it up, and look down . . . and down . . .

"Where's Auntie Emily?" asks the smaller of the two girls. Her name is Khloe, I recall.

"She's writing." I gesture inside.

The other girl, Scarlett, frowns. "Mommy told us to play with Auntie Emily."

"Auntie Emily is busy." I hesitate. "But you can play with me?"

I don't have nieces or nephews, and I never babysat when I was younger. I know nothing about kids, though surely I can handle this. I want Emily to be able to write. Her sister might not respect her time, but I do, and it's more important for her to keep working than for me to return to painting.

"I have to ask Mommy if that's okay," Scarlett says.

"All right, you do that."

Scarlett and Khloe run to their family's cabin, and I finish my coffee in a few gulps.

"Are you sure about this?" Emily asks.

"Yeah," I say, with more confidence than I feel. "It's no problem."

The girls return to the door a couple of minutes later.

"Mommy says it's okay!" Scarlett says. "She says we can play Mud Puddles!"

"What's that?" I ask.

"It's when you jump in mud puddles and try to make the biggest splash." She jumps up and down. She's wearing rain boots with polka dots.

"Somehow, I doubt your mother said that."

Scarlett giggles. "She did!"

Hmm. If the girls go into the cabin, I doubt Emily will get anything done, even if I'm the one "playing" with them. Better not to let them in. Besides, it's not thundering anymore, and the rain has slowed down.

"We'll stay outside," I say, "but we're not playing Mud Puddles."

"What will we do?" Scarlett asks.

"Horsey!" Khloe shouts.

Oh no. I can only assume it involves small children riding on my back, and I'm not doing that outside in the mud.

I shake my head. "Some other time."

I hope they don't remember that.

"Wormies!" Khloe shouts.

Does this mean lying down and slithering in the mud? Before I can inquire, Khloe grabs a stick, and it appears she's looking for worms.

Well, I suppose I can manage.

———

An hour later, Scarlett and Khloe are still engrossed in looking at worms and picking them up with sticks. My shoes—since I don't have cool polka-dot rain boots—are soaked.

"Ah, Mark," Judy says as I'm bending over to examine a worm that may or may not be dead—Khloe wants my expert opinion. "Where's Emily?"

"She's working."

"This is a vacation. She should be spending time with her family."

"Well, when she has time off from the coffee shop, she tries to spend some of it writing. I'm sure she'll be finished soon, though."

Judy nods. "I'm very happy you're here."

"I'm glad I could make it work," I say as I stand there in my wet shoes, which are doubtless smeared with worm guts, and Khloe accidentally (or purposely?) pokes me in the knee with a stick. I think longingly of my half-finished watercolor.

"Po Po, do you want worm soup?" Khloe giggles.

"Not now, maybe later." Judy turns her attention back to me. She's wearing a bright green raincoat that's rather big on her. "I'm so glad she's finally dating you. I've been trying to find someone for Emily for years. It's been a long time since she's had a relationship."

The way her family sees her . . . it bothers me.

"You know," I say carefully, "Emily doesn't *need* to get married."

"Aiyah! I'm not that old-fashioned, but I think it's nice to have a life partner, yes? Besides . . ."

Judy looks away, and maybe I'm paranoid after hearing Emily talk about her domestic thriller, but I suddenly wonder whether Emily's mom has secrets. Perhaps there's more going on here than I thought.

"She's never shown any interest in women, to my knowledge,"

Judy continues. "That's why I picked out a man, even though I have a friend with a very nice lesbian daughter. But if Emily did like women, would she tell me? I don't know. I think there is a lot she doesn't say."

I try to keep my face neutral. Luckily, I'm saved by a screech.

"Khloe is killing the worms!" Scarlett cries. "Stop her."

Khloe responds by picking up some worm guts on the end of a stick and holding them to Scarlett's face.

"Ew, stop it," Scarlett says. "It will bite you in the ass!"

"Ah, what are you saying?" Judy asks. "Why are you using those words?"

"Mommy said it. She didn't know I was listening, but I was."

Khloe bursts into tears.

"What's wrong?" I try to sound warm and nurturing, but my lack of experience with crying children makes this difficult. I am, frankly, a little scared, especially since Judy might be judging how I handle this interaction. She seems fond of me, and I don't want her to change her mind.

"My stick isn't *sticky* enough," Khloe says.

"What's wrong with you?" Scarlett says. "You're being a baby."

"I'm not a baby!"

The thing about small children is that you can't win them over with rational arguments. They're rather like Ms. Muffins in that respect. I have no idea what's wrong with the stick that Khloe has been happily carrying and using to pick up worms for the past hour, but I don't try to understand. I recognize that would be a fruitless endeavor, so I go into problem-solving mode.

"How about we get you a new stick?" I suggest. "There are lots of sticks on the ground."

"I don't want one from the ground."

Khloe's lower lip trembles, and just when I think Judy is going to jump in and save me, she says, "I will leave you to it. It looks like you're doing a good job." How she came to this conclusion is a mystery to me.

Scarlett runs off to follow her grandmother, deciding that hanging out with Po Po is more fun than me and her little sister.

It's not long before Khloe cheers up. Alas, she cheers up only because she discovers that she enjoys jumping in mud puddles and splattering me with mud.

When I return to our cabin, Emily is putting her laptop back in its case. She looks up at me, and her mouth drops open. "Oh my God. What happened to you?"

"Khloe decided mud puddles were fun," I say. "She was okay playing with worms and sticks for a while, but ultimately, those mud puddles proved too alluring."

Emily walks over to me, and after I remove my rain jacket, she reaches for the hem of my T-shirt and pulls it over my head. Fortunately, it got only the tiniest bit of mud on it, but my pants are another matter. She makes quick work of those too.

"Thank you," she murmurs, standing on her toes and kissing me. "I got lots of work done, and for the rest of the day, I'm yours."

"Are we avoiding your family all day?"

"Don't mention them now." She strips off her own shirt and pajama pants. She's not wearing a bra, and her breasts are now bare, the peaks of her nipples tightening. She leads me to the small washroom, where she removes our underwear.

I'm certainly not complaining about this development.

She's far too beautiful for this small, basic washroom—I wish we had a luxurious hotel suite instead, but this will have to do for today. I appreciate the view as she leans over the tub to turn on the tap, and once she likes the temperature, she starts the shower and steps in.

"Aren't you coming?" she asks.

"Yes," I croak. It's hard to get my feet moving when I'm overwhelmed by how beautiful she is, the water sliding over her skin. It was disappointing that she didn't go into the lake yesterday, although I couldn't blame her—it was damn cold.

But I want to touch her, so I join her under the spray and close the curtain.

This is why I was happy to go away with her for a weekend, even if it involved going to the beach with her family and playing with worms. Not that I predicted the worm part, of course.

I cup her ass and bring her flush against me. She feels magnificent. The corner of her mouth tips up and she looks down at my hardening length. The next thing I know, she's on her knees, and as soon as her mouth is on me, I'm fully erect.

There's a grab bar in the shower, thank God, because I need it to keep myself stable. One of my hands clutches it while the other glides through her wet hair.

"If you keep going . . ." I warn.

Her pretty eyes gaze up at me for a moment, but then she's looking down again, continuing to suck me off, and I can barely breathe. Fuck.

"Emily, I . . ."

I can't speak properly anymore. I'm consumed by what she's doing to me, under the spray of the water.

And then I explode in her mouth.

She licks her lips as she stands up, and fuck, I need to touch her. I slip my fingers between her legs, and she releases a shaky breath as soon as I penetrate her, her head tipping back. I wrap my other arm around her shoulders, sensing that she needs extra support to stay upright. My thumb circles her clit.

"You feel so good," I tell her, adding another finger.

"Mark . . ."

She shudders in my arms. I lean over and kiss her; her movements are sloppy and inelegant, and I love that I did this to her.

We soap each other up and wash our hair, and as soon as we step out of the shower, I wrap her in a towel, which isn't fluffy enough for my liking—she deserves better—but it'll have to do for now. She uses another towel to dry her hair, and when we walk out of the washroom, the air is cooler and less humid; goose bumps pebble on her skin, but she doesn't seem to care.

She kisses me and walks me backward to the bed, where she pushes me onto the mattress, then crawls on top of me. She's not sated yet, and I'm certainly not complaining.

"Thank you," she says. "For taking my work, the fact that I wanted to get some writing done . . . for taking that seriously."

A little light is filtering through the worn curtains—I think the sun might be coming out—but for now, I just want to stay here. She slides up my body and kisses me, her thighs spread across my lower belly; I can feel her wetness on my skin. I pick her up and shift her until she's sitting on my face. She grips the headboard as I give her a long, slow lick.

"Oh fuck," she mutters.

I do it again.

"I need you," she says desperately. "I need you inside me."

I flip her over, sheath myself, and slide into her.

She orgasms on my first thrust, her body shaking, her mouth open, and though I've seen her come before, every time feels new and special, and I know I'll never tire of it. We move together, as one, and I can't help kissing her again and again . . . and then I pull back so I can see her, flushed and lovely beneath me.

I find my release for the second time, and after I clean myself up, I return to bed and hold her. For now, everything feels right with the world.

When I was in grade one, I started getting bullied. It was led by this kid, Jacob Foo, whose face I can still picture clearly. I guess it had something to do with me being small and nerdy and whatever passes for uncool when you're six.

Eventually, I told my dad. I knew not to trouble my mother—my grandma had been very sick, and Ma had too much to worry about—but I had to tell someone.

My father blamed me, and then he gave me some advice that stuck.

Nobody wants the real you.

Ever since, I've become good at adjusting how I present myself. The way I act has changed over the years, but it's almost always an act, to some extent.

I hide who I really am, at least a little. I'm a private person; it's a form of protection. When another person doesn't like someone who isn't the real you—it doesn't hurt as much. Sure, people might see me as a bit aloof, but I can deal.

But the result is that sometimes, I'm not sure even I know myself. Not fully. Do I naturally take after my father . . . or do people comment on the similarity in our expressions, our mannerisms, because I patterned myself after him when I was young and in awe of the man whose attention I craved?

In some ways, as I've gotten older, I've made sure I didn't become my father—he's married to his work more than anything else—but in other ways, I'm unsure of who I am. I'm very used to hiding; I'm so used to protecting myself that I've lost sight of what I'm protecting.

With Emily, though, I think I could find out who I am.

She isn't like me. Nobody would call her aloof. She's always herself, in such a brilliant way, regardless of what others think. I like that; I respect it. She might be a little uneasy with her parents reading her book, but she's able to put something of herself on those pages and show them to the world.

"My dad got mad at me for being bullied in school." The words are out of my mouth before I realize I've said them—which is most unlike me.

She turns over in bed to face me. "What? Did he tell you to man up or some shit like that?"

"Yeah. He later apologized to me—the only time he's ever apologized—after my mom got angry at him, but it's a formative memory, I guess you'd call it."

"I'm sorry. That's fucked-up."

I chuckle without humor. "It is."

She doesn't say anything more for a while, just burrows against me. In this moment, my guard is down . . . and I feel safe.

She likes me as I am. I might be too rigid for some people, yet never enough for my dad, but she doesn't want me to change. I'll always be a bit private—and that's okay. I just want to know that I can open myself up around her.

"I think it's sunny now," she murmurs eventually. "We should probably go out."

"We should."

Neither of us moves. I don't want to leave our little cocoon.

Then someone knocks on the door, and I jolt up.

"Auntie Emily!" Scarlett shouts through the door. "Mommy says you need to come out!"

"Auntie Em-i-lyyyyy!" Khloe sings.

Although nobody can see us, I feel embarrassed by my current nudity. I feel exposed, in more ways than one.

"I'll be out in five minutes!" Emily calls.

"There's a rainbow," Scarlett says. "You have to come now."

Emily and I exchange a glance, and then we quickly start getting dressed. I open the door two minutes later to see the girls standing outside with their mother, who gives me a strange look. I wonder what Allison assumes we were doing, given she doesn't seem to think Emily and I are actually together.

I tense, prepared to say something to that effect, but then Khloe says, "Where's all the mud? You were muddy before."

"I had a shower," I say.

"Thank you." Allison gives me an awkward smile. "For playing with them earlier."

"No problem."

She opens her mouth again, and for a split second, I wonder whether she's going to question our relationship. This situation is such a mess—and I'm not fond of messes.

But then Emily joins me, patting my shoulder before stepping outside into the sunshine, the rainbow fading in the distance, and I think . . .

It's worth it.

I hope she feels the same way.

30

—♡—

Emily

*"Fortunately, you don't need to have an interesting life
to write interesting books. My life is the opposite of glamorous
and exciting. I promise I know nothing about pretending to be
my twin sister and sneaking onto a billionaire's yacht."*

—Tess Donovan

Today has been full of highs and lows.

There was the high of waking up in bed with my fake-turned-real boyfriend, then feeling inspired to write . . . and actually being able to write all morning because Mark offered to play with my nieces.

The change in setting helped. Some writers go on "retreats" and get lots of work done away from their everyday life, but I can't afford that. The most I can do for a different setting is a coffee shop or library, which has never worked particularly well for me.

I was touched that he seemed to understand how important it was to me, and he also kept my nieces out of our cabin without complaint.

Getting off in the shower? That was definitely a high point too.

But then my family showed up at the door . . . and I feel like I'm running on borrowed time. Eventually, someone will have to say something.

It might be better if I ended things soon. After all, there are lots of other men out there, right?

Men like Clive, who'd be jealous of any success I have.

Men like Andrew, who was born in a different century from me.

Men who sit on their ass and expect the woman to do all the housework and all the childcare and have a full-time job.

Men who send unsolicited dick pics.

Men who claim they can't be racist because they once dated an Asian woman.

Look, there are good men out there, but the dating market is a bit grim, and Mark has turned out to be surprisingly wonderful, despite my first impression of him.

I think of how it felt when he kissed me as he buried himself inside me. I don't want to give that up. I want to know him better; I want to peel back the layers.

I want to be righteously angry when people harm him—like how I felt following our conversation this morning.

After lunch, we all went on a hike. Going on a hike with such a big group of people and two small kids—after a heavy rain— probably wasn't the best idea. Mark admitted that he'd never gone on a hike with so much yelling before, and I laughed more than I should have.

The hike ended in a beautiful waterfall though, so that was nice. Another high.

Once we returned to the cabin, I checked my email and discovered that I'd been invited to speak at a conference. They can't afford to pay my travel expenses, but they'd generously waive half of my conference registration fee, and wouldn't it be great "exposure"?

Hmph. I can't afford to do something like that for exposure.

After dinner, Mark finished his painting, and then we joined everyone around a campfire and made s'mores. That was a good part of the day too. I was sandwiched between Mark and

Hannah, and nobody asked about the sex scene in my book, or whether I have doubts about the identity of my bio dad. Nobody questioned whether Mark is really my boyfriend.

Well, I've survived the trip. Tomorrow morning we'll drive back to Toronto. I'm glad the weekend is almost over, but at the same time, I'm not particularly looking forward to returning to my regular life.

"I'm so glad you came," Mom says to me, while Mark puts the suitcases into his car. "I could tell you were skeptical at first, when I told you about the cabins, but you had a good time, didn't you?"

"Yes," I say. For the most part, it's true.

But then she gives me an odd look, and my skin chills. For a split second, I feel like she's onto me. She knows about the lie. Has Allison told her? Have I accidentally given myself away?

Then her expression clears and she says, "I hope the traffic isn't too bad."

"Yes," I manage to say as my anxiety fades. "I hope not."

She hugs me goodbye and turns her attention to Hannah.

In the car, I doze on and off. I know I'm not going to get any writing done for the rest of the day, so as we approach the city — traffic isn't great, but it could be worse — I say to Mark, "Rather than dropping me off, how about we go to your place for a few hours? I don't feel like heading home yet." When he doesn't immediately answer, I continue, "But if you have things to do . . ."

"I just need to give the neglected Ms. Muffins some attention. You're welcome to keep me company for the rest of the day."

"Ms. *Margaret* Muffins. She's recently decided that she prefers her full name."

"I have it on good authority that she doesn't care."

"What good authority?" I ask.

"The fact that I've spent much, much more time with her than you have."

"But Ms. *Margaret* Muffins and I have a special bond."

"I'm sure you do."

"She's unhappy with her social media presence. She thinks you should post videos of her tapping piano keys or playing with string."

His lips twitch. "My cat would probably swallow the string, and unlike some of the other cats you seem to follow online, she has never been introduced to a musical instrument."

When we arrive at Mark's condo, Ms. Muffins eyes me with deep suspicion—she seems ignorant of our special bond, alas—and I wonder if she's been talking to Allison. Or Scarlett.

Is this what it's like when you commit a murder? You think everyone seems suspicious, even people (or animals) who have no way of knowing what you did. Anyone could spill your secret at any moment . . .

Ooh. This could be useful for my book.

"Is something wrong?" Mark asks while I'm paused in the entryway of his condo, my right shoe halfway off.

"You know the saying 'write what you know'?"

"Yes, I've heard it before."

"If taken too literally, no one would write about aliens, and nobody alive today could write about the Renaissance, and people would be extremely afraid of anyone who wrote a book about a serial killer. But the feelings you've experienced can inform your writing . . ."

"I'm sorry, I'm not sure where you're going with this," he says.

"The way I'm afraid about my parents finding out the truth about how our relationship started . . . I imagine it's similar to how my character feels about the murder she committed."

"Mm-hmm."

"Not that I'm using you to learn what telling a falsehood feels like, and it's not like I've never lied to my parents before." I finish removing my shoes. "That was just on my mind, for some reason."

I stand on my toes and kiss him. He tastes like Tim Hortons coffee, which he drank to stay awake on the drive.

Me, on the other hand? I imagine I taste like a Tim Hortons donut.

Although we had a decent amount of alone time during our long weekend away, I'm somehow in the mood again. I don't know what it is about Mark, but I can't seem to keep my hands off him. His hands slip underneath my tank top, and his fingers toy with the waistband of my pants. I—

I hear a knock, and I jump back as if he's a hot stove that burned me.

"What's that?" I ask.

"I believe it's the door," he murmurs. He looks at me, as if to assure himself that I'm decent, before opening it.

The next thing I know, I'm face-to-face with his parents.

Shoot me now.

Mark is just as surprised by his parents' appearance as I am; clearly, this wasn't a planned visit that he failed to mention to me.

His mom claims they decided to stop in since they were in the area, but I wonder if they were actually in the neighborhood or if that's just an excuse. Perhaps they wanted to see him after the trip and were afraid that if they texted, he'd say no or brush them off. Not that Mark seems like the type to "brush off" his parents, but what do I know?

So rather than having sex, I'm now sitting at Mark's table, having tea with his parents. I'm struggling not to glare at his father, particularly after what I learned yesterday. But I know Mark wouldn't want me to bring up any of that, so I don't. Before, I wondered if Terrence was a kind person behind his cold exterior, but now I suspect the answer is no. He's much different from his wife.

"I hear your book is going to be made into a movie," Cilla says.

"Where did you hear that?" I ask.

"Your mother told me."

For fuck's sake. I shouldn't have told Mom anything until there was an article online about the rights being sold, but then she'd get mad about learning the news at the same time as everyone else. At the very least, I'd have to tell her the day before it became public knowledge.

I remind myself that things could always be worse. For example, I'm not literally being eaten by a tiger at this moment. Nor am I literally in Hell; I just *feel* like I'm in Hell.

Well, that's not much comfort.

"I'm looking forward to when you come speak to our book club," Cilla says.

Wait a second. Mark's mother is in this book club?

That's it. My life cannot continue. Right now, being a marshmallow that gets burned to a crisp over a campfire sounds like a preferable fate to living through the next five minutes. Even being eaten by a tiger sounds not too bad.

Okay, maybe I'm a bit dramatic, but this is more than I can bear.

"Me too," I squeak to Cilla, as the reality of this whole situation finally hits me.

Our mothers are friends. If my mom ever finds out the truth about the beginning of our relationship, I'm sure she'll share it with Mark's family. There's no way around it. If our parents didn't know each other, such a fate could be avoided, but alas . . .

The whole reason I know Mark is because my mother set me

up with him. The whole reason she knows him is because she knows his mother.

I put a hand to my head.

"Are you okay?" Mark asks.

"Sorry, I have a headache. Long car ride. I need to lie down." I turn to his parents. "It was so nice to see you again. Sorry you couldn't come up north with us."

I hurry to Mark's bedroom, flop onto the bed, and wonder why on earth I decided to tell that "innocent" little lie about dating him.

It was meant to be a small thing, just to get my mother off my back. It was only supposed to be slightly bigger than the lie I told my mom when I was sixteen: I said I was spending the evening watching movies at my best friend's, when I was actually on a date. Ah, how things have changed—this year I was lying about going on dates instead of lying about *not* going on dates.

I wasn't even supposed to spend much time with Mark, but then I did . . . and I'm glad.

Except this is all too much.

Perhaps I should have dated the guy who made me feel like a history book instead. Truly, Andrew was all right—his main fault was being too young for me.

And now he's dating my roommate.

I bite back a moan of frustration. Why is everything all twisted up?

It's better for the drama to be in my imagination, not in real life. I'd rather be writing what I *don't* know, thank you very much.

Several minutes later, Mark enters the bedroom. "How's your head?"

"Not great," I say.

He lies behind me and holds me, and . . . mmm. This is nice.

Yet it also feels bittersweet, and my tears softly fall onto the pillow. One of them must fall on Mark's hand because he says, "What's wrong?"

"I can't help feeling like this can't last. Like, the longer we stay together, the longer we risk everything blowing up."

"What's the worst that could happen?" he asks.

"My mother finds out the truth. And if she does, that means everyone else does too, including your parents."

"That's not ideal, but would it really be so terrible?"

"Yes," I say. "All my life, I've been not quite right. I told my mother that I wanted to be a writer when I was eight, and she looked utterly horrified. So I tried to put that aside, but I couldn't. I couldn't be the daughter my parents wanted."

"Your mother brags about you to my mother all the time. Didn't you hear my mom talking about the movie?"

"Which will probably never be made. Plus, the way my mom talks to other people is not an indication of how she feels. She wants to put up a good front."

"I don't think it's just that."

"But I can't let her find out the truth about us." I press my hands to my eyes. "I just can't. She'll lose whatever shred of respect she has for me, and I don't want to care what she thinks at all, but . . . I do."

I want my mother to be proud of me without doing the things that I know would make her proud. But I *did* date Mark, the thing that she wanted me to do, for real.

I can't bear for her to know how it started. The mere thought of Allison telling her, of Scarlett accidentally spilling the beans . . . it makes me break into a cold sweat. I can't even consider what happens after that. My brain refuses to go there.

Maybe I should end the relationship before Mom learns the truth, but the truth could still come out afterward.

"My dad is disappointed in me," Mark says quietly.

That snaps me out of my reflections.

"Disappointed?" I say. "In *you*? You're, like, the perfect Asian son."

"Sure, I have a respectable career path, but that feels like a compromise. He hoped I would take over his business one day. When I wasn't interested, he accused me of being soft and lazy."

"Well, I'm glad you're a little 'soft,' in his opinion, and not a workaholic."

"Yeah, me too. I think I'm better this way." The corner of his mouth lifts. "It was worse with Cassie. She doesn't talk to him anymore. She was a friendly, affectionate kid, and they were always at odds."

"Oh dear."

He trails his fingers over my arm. "So, I know what it's like to not live up to parental expectations, though I suspect your mother isn't nearly as disappointed in you as you assume. That's not what I've observed, from spending time with your mom. She's not at all like my father. I know you feel the pressure to have a certain kind of life, as many children of immigrants do, but I think you can let some of it go."

I admit I'm not convinced, but as I roll over and look at Mark, a wave of fondness overtakes me. His expression is serious, and I reach out to smooth the notch between his eyebrows. Yes, we got off on the wrong foot, and, yes, he is very different from me . . . but we fit together. He's very supportive, in a quiet way, and I want to support him too. I no longer feel like he doesn't respect the choices I've made, and I admire that he's done his best to separate his self-worth from what his father thinks of him. I'm sure Terrence would be utterly appalled if he ever finds out that this relationship was initially pretend, but Mark isn't letting that get to him. I can't say the same for myself.

I shut my eyes, and something tickles my foot.

"Ms. Muffins," Mark says, "we've talked about this. You're not allowed in the bed."

He's speaking in a different tone from usual—the voice he uses to speak to his cat when no one's around. The last time he did this, he didn't know I was listening. But this time, he knows, and he's doing it anyway. He's not modifying his behavior in front of me. It causes a strange sensation in my chest, the way he can let his guard down around me now.

Ms. Muffins doesn't obey Mark. She stays on my foot, and I don't mind. I rather like it, actually.

If only I could keep all of this, but I'm not sure I can.

31

—♡—

Emily

*"It is a truth universally acknowledged that if you wear a
new white shirt, you will spill turmeric and/or tomatoes on it."*
—Me, aka non-bestselling author Emily Hung

It's 2 a.m., and I'm obsessing over my earlier cooking incident—
I was wearing an apron, yet still managed to spill crushed tomatoes on my shirt—before bouncing to another topic.

Thanks to my active mind, I can't sleep.

The other day, I learned that not everyone has an internal
monologue, which is fascinating to me. I can't imagine not having an internal monologue. I wonder if those people are less likely
to suffer from insomnia. Hmm.

I also learned that not everyone pictures what's happening in
a book as they're reading. Isn't that interesting? I don't picture
things in elaborate detail and bright colors, but there's always a
picture in my mind. I wonder what reading's like without that.

The older I get, the more I realize how different everyone's
brain is.

I think that's part of the beauty of a novel. What we see—or
don't see—in our minds, our pasts . . . a single novel can be such
a different experience for everyone who reads it.

After ruminating on books and brains and stains, my thoughts drift to sleep hygiene. The last time I was wide awake at 2 a.m., I read an article that said you should use your bedroom only for sleeping and sex, which was genuinely hilarious to me. It's not like I'll be able to afford a place with a home office in the foreseeable future. Our living room isn't big enough for my desk, and even if it were, I wouldn't want to put my desk there. Ugh.

What if that tomato stain doesn't fully come out?

What if Mom learns about my fake relationship?

Insomnia sucks.

I slept only four hours last night, and I'm hyped up on caffeine now, but I've done it! I've sent my proposal to my agent. I think it's amazing, and she's going to love it, and when I go on submission, I'll have multiple offers within a week. The book will go to auction and get me a huge advance. Then it'll spend six months on the *New York Times* bestseller list, and I'll actually be able to afford real estate in Toronto.

Yes! I'm brilliant.

Hmm. I haven't heard from my agent. It's been an hour.

What if it's terrible?

What if she drops me as a client?

What if I never sell another book?

Oh God.

It's been two hours.

I need to stop obsessively checking my email. It's after 5 p.m., so my agent is unlikely to respond today, knowing her. I need to think about something else.

Like how my mom is going to discover my lie and everything

will unravel and I'll have to move to Newfoundland because not only is real estate cheaper there but I'm too embarrassed to show my face in Toronto again, especially since my mother seems to know everyone . . .

Okay, not that.

To calm this roller coaster of emotions, I should do something productive, like watch a show. Yes. Good idea.

I head out of my bedroom just as Paige sets a bag of dirty clothes by her door.

"Another washing machine is broken," she says. "The functioning ones were all in use, so I'll have to try again later."

Ugh. I'm going to have to start doing laundry in the middle of the night when I can't sleep. We're not supposed to do laundry after 10 p.m., but nobody pays much attention to the laundry room hours—how can we, when there are so many people and so few machines?

"How was your trip?" Paige asks. "I haven't seen you since you got back." She was staying at Andrew's.

"How's it going with Andrew? Did he ask what it was like to travel by horse and buggy?"

Paige gives me a look. "He's very sweet. We've started going to the gym together."

"You don't get distracted by him lifting weights and grunting . . . or whatever people do at the gym?"

"Well, maybe a little . . ." She pauses. "You still didn't answer my question."

"It was a great trip. I mean, Mark was lovely. My mom asked me what would happen if they made a movie of my first book and whether they would keep the sex scene, and Allison and I had an argument, and then his parents showed up at his place within minutes of us getting back. Mark's mom is in the book club and his dad is apparently an asshole and—"

"Sorry, I don't think I caught all of that."

"Yeah. Well. That's okay," I say. "Do you think I should break up with Mark?"

"*What?* I thought everything was going great. You just said he was lovely on the trip."

"I'm convinced this will end badly. It's too complicated with him and my family. I've been having trouble sleeping."

"You're going to throw away a decent relationship because of that? Yesterday, one of my friends went out with a guy who got mad that she didn't put out after he bought her a turkey sandwich. He also bragged that he hadn't used soap since 2020. The dating pool isn't great, Em."

"I know, I know. If it weren't for Mark, I wouldn't be dating at all." I shake my head. "Burying a dead body wasn't supposed to be so complicated."

"Excuse me?"

"Sorry, I was thinking of my book. *Faking a relationship* wasn't supposed to be so complicated. Don't worry, I haven't killed anyone. Yet." I release a slightly unhinged laugh.

Paige puts a hand on my shoulder. "You're worried your mom will find out the truth?"

"Yeah."

"She picked out a great guy for you. She could be more understanding than you think. I know it's a bit far-fetched, but it's possible."

I recall what Mark said to me . . . but still. My hands get clammy at the thought.

As I'm debating which noodle bowl to have for dinner, I get a text from my mother. Rare for her to text instead of call.

Don't forget Timmy's birthday party on Sunday.

I scrub a hand over my face. Right. My nephew is turning one. I still need to buy him a present. I'll probably stick with books.

I assume you and Mark will come together?

I shut my eyes. Mark just devoted a long weekend to my family. He doesn't need to attend more events. Except, knowing my mother, she's already invited him as well as his parents.

A second later, my phone rings.

"Emily!" Mom barks. "Why haven't you replied to my texts? Have you been kidnapped?"

"You literally just sent them," I say. "I haven't had a chance to reply."

She clucks her tongue. "I don't like this texting business. Much faster to call you and get an answer."

"Did you already invite Mark?"

"Yes. He said he could come."

Of course he did.

"We'll probably come together, then," I say.

"Cilla and Terrence will be there too."

Yep, just as I suspected. "Okay."

When she doesn't immediately speak, my heart rate starts to speed up. Has she heard the truth from Allison? Have I accidentally given myself away? Has she suddenly developed the ability to read minds?

God, I'm not meant for this.

"Is everything all right?" she asks.

"Uh, yes! I'm great, thank you for asking. Gotta go now. Still haven't had dinner yet and it's getting late. Very late."

"It's only six o'clock."

"Bye!"

Yep, great job not sounding suspicious.

"One more quick question," Mom says before I have a chance to end the call. "Will you make and decorate a cake to show off your cake-decorating skills?"

I'm about to ask what on earth she's talking about when I remember the class that I supposedly took with Mark.

"Sorry, I don't have time this week," I say. "Plus, I took a two-hour class, that's all. My decorating skills aren't that impressive."

When I set my phone down and massage my temples, Paige laughs at me.

"Shut up," I mutter.

"I didn't say anything. Hey, you want to get falafels for dinner? They have a new special on Wednesdays. Buy one, get one half price."

Before I can answer, my phone buzzes. It's not my mother this time, but Mark.

> Did you send your proposal to your agent today?
> And should I buy a birthday present for your nephew?

He's so on top of things. I'll probably end up rushing to Indigo the morning of the party and buying the first books that catch my eye.

Ugh. I feel overwhelmed.

And for the first time, *he's too good for me* starts to burrow itself into my brain. Allison claims that's not the reason she didn't believe my lie, but I can't help hearing the words in my big sister's voice.

"You know what we should do tonight?" I turn to Paige. "Let's get drunk. After falafels, we'll stop at the liquor store and buy some wine."

"I have to work tomorrow," she says.

"It's still early, and we're not going to get so wasted that we're hungover."

"You make a compelling argument."

At the liquor store, we select a bottle of wine based on one very important factor: price. The cheaper the better. Then we head home, change into comfier clothes, pull out our plastic wineglasses (very classy), and start up a K-drama that we've been meaning to watch for ages.

See? This is the great thing about being in your thirties, child-less, and living with a roommate. You can do things like this, whereas Allison is probably wrangling her children into bed, try-ing to reason with them about monsters under the bed or similar.

This might not be the life that my parents imagined for their kids when they moved to Canada, but whatever. I'm a strong, in-dependent woman . . . who's currently wearing a unicorn onesie.

"That guy is hot." Paige gestures at the screen with her wine-glass.

"Nah, he's too young. The other one's better."

"You mean the hero's *father*?"

"What's wrong with that?" I ask.

"He's too old."

"I bet he's only, like, forty-five. That's not old." As soon as I say it, I start laughing in horror. Once upon a time, forty-five would have sounded terribly old to me, but those days have passed.

I wonder what I'll be doing when I'm forty-five. To be honest, I'm not sure I want to think about it too much. Maybe I'll be hid-ing in shame because of that one time, back when I was young and thirty-three, I pretended to date my mom's friend's son.

Hmph. I have some more wine.

After the first episode, I take a break to see what's happening online. I seem to have missed some drama about a fanfic writer faking her own death, an author stalking someone who gave her a bad review, and a racist politician getting a huge advance for his book. Also, a Black author I know got dropped by her publisher because her sales weren't high enough, and that was somehow all her fault rather than the publisher's fault for doing nothing to promote her book.

A normal day in publishing.

Then I see an article with some grim news on climate change, and, yes, climate change is very concerning . . . but I'm here in my moderately overpriced apartment in my unicorn onesie with my friend, and this show is helping me forget about all the problems out there.

Just like books do. Books can help people forget but also help them cope at the same time, and what I do is *important*, dammit. Even if you write something dark and twisted, it can help readers escape to another world. Or it can show them that other people are experiencing the same feelings that they are, maybe under different circumstances, but similar nonetheless. It can make you feel not alone when you're lonely, or it can simply entertain you when you're bored. There are so many things that fiction can do, and that's what I want: to be a part of the magic.

"Are you okay?" Paige asks. We're seated at opposite sides of the broken-down couch, but she shifts closer to me. "You're crying."

"I love you," I say. "Platonically, I mean."

"How drunk are you?"

"Only a little."

She looks skeptical but returns to her side of the couch and starts the show again.

We watch two more episodes, at which point the subtitles get a bit fuzzy and the bottle of wine is finished.

"I'm going to write the best book in the whole world and buy a house!" I say.

"I'm going to smack John in the face the next time he steals my lunch!" Paige holds up her empty wineglass and clinks it against mine.

Okay, maybe I'm a little hungover, but just a little.

I pick up my phone after I get out of bed. Oops, I forgot to text Mark back yesterday.

And ooh, there's an email from my agent.

32

—♡—

Mark

Lately, things with Emily have been a little off. Ever since we returned to Toronto, her texting has been sporadic. Sometimes she'll respond right away; other times she won't respond for over twenty-four hours. I asked if she wanted to come over Saturday evening, stay the night, then proceed to her parents' house together on Sunday, but she said she'd meet me at the subway station and we'd go from there.

"What's going on with Emily?" I ask Ms. Muffins on Saturday after dinner, as I get out my watercolors. "Is it something I did? Is it something I said? Is it just because she's worried about her mom finding out that we were initially faking a relationship?"

Ms. Muffins responds by licking herself.

Alas, this isn't an acceptable way to reply to questions if you're human, but she can get away with it because she's a cat.

I've started doing watercolors of mundane objects and food. The other day, I did one of a mug of coffee, a few coffee beans scattered on the surface of the table. This evening, after I clean the litter box, I decide to paint bok choy. But as I work on my little painting, my mind strays to Emily. I've been inspired by her dedication to writing to work on my own art—though unlike her, I have no desire to make money from it—and I also feel like she appreciates this side of me.

Goddammit, I really hope she hasn't decided this is over. I admit I don't love the idea of everyone learning the truth about our relationship either—it's the sort of mess I prefer to avoid in my life—but if I was given the choice between everyone knowing and breaking up, I'd pick the former, no question about it.

I want to wake up in her bed again and again.

I want to make her breakfast and coffee while she taps away on her laptop or cleans the living room to avoid writing.

I want to eat dinner with her as she rants about one thing or another, her hands moving every which way in excitement.

I want to sink inside her and make love to her as many times as I can.

I don't show a lot of what I feel on my face; the intensity of my emotions is often hidden. It's been that way since I was a kid—it's what my father expected of me—but I've become more open with Emily, and I do feel deeply for her. I want to build a life together. I don't know exactly what form that would take, because I'm not sure what she wants, but I wish for the opportunity to try.

Yet I'm not sure I'll get it.

I go to sleep alone, make breakfast and coffee alone, and after doing my chores for the day and having an early lunch, I drive to the subway station to pick up Emily. She's wearing jeans and a loose shirt that flutters in the breeze. In her arms, she's carrying a few packages wrapped in giraffe paper.

"Hey," I say as she slides into the car.

She presses a perfunctory kiss to my cheek before buckling her seat belt. "Hey, yourself."

As I begin driving, I'm painfully, excruciatingly aware of the silence between us. The silence that she'd often fill.

"Did you hear from your agent about your proposal?" I ask at last.

"Yeah, she says she'll get to it early next week. This week now, I guess, since it's Sunday."

"Anything more about the film rights? I'm sure your mom will ask."

"I'm sure she will. I might not hear anything else for a while. Who knows."

After that, we lapse back into silence. There are lots of things I want to ask her, but I feel like now isn't the time, not before her nephew's birthday party.

Maybe afterward.

By the time we get to the party, most people are already here. Huh. I didn't think we were late. Emily immediately leaves my side to help herself to some wine.

The fence has been strung with blue and purple streamers, and there are bunches of balloons throughout the yard. The birthday boy is wearing a conical hat, as is his mother. I dearly hope I won't be expected to wear one of those. Sometimes, I'm very conscious of the image I present, afraid of looking silly—especially when I know my father will be here later—but I could handle it. However, the elastic band that goes under the chin looks horribly uncomfortable.

"Mark!" Judy says. "So glad you could come."

"Mark!" Khloe runs up and hugs my leg. "Let's go find worms."

"I don't think there are any worms out today."

Apparently, this is the wrong thing to say. She starts crying, and I wonder if I should have offered to make her a worm out of construction paper—not that I have any paper with me—instead.

Allison comes over to soothe her daughter, and when Emily returns to my side, Allison says, "You can babysit for me Tuesday afternoon, right?"

"Uh . . ." It's somewhat unlike Emily to be at a loss for words, but she sips her wine rather than saying anything more.

"Emily has to work on Tuesday," I say.

Allison rolls her eyes. "Right."

"I've traded enough shifts lately," Emily says. "I'm not going to do it again, especially with such short notice."

"Right, because your job is so important."

"Earning enough money to keep my apartment is very important, yes."

Emily's tense, her shoulders hiking up toward her ears. I put my arm around her.

Allison gives Emily a look before following Khloe toward the food table, where Khloe nearly takes down a bowl of chips.

"Maybe I should have agreed to babysit," Emily says to me.

"Why?" I ask.

She looks around, as if making sure no one can overhear. "She could tell Mom how our relationship started."

"You think she'd snitch because you didn't babysit?"

"I don't know. It's possible."

"You're in your thirties. Isn't that a bit old for such things?"

"Yes, well. She thinks I'm too old to be living the life I have. You know, the roommate, the shitty day job. Yesterday, someone yelled at me because I made him the latte he ordered."

"Why?"

"It seemed he was expecting a cappuccino."

"But he ordered a latte."

"Yeah."

I can't imagine doing what she does, but if this is the job that allows her to write, then I support it. I want her to pursue her dreams.

A middle-aged woman approaches us. "Emily! I haven't seen you in a while."

She looks vaguely familiar—I think I remember her from Hannah's wedding.

"This is my mom's younger sister, Carmen," Emily says. "Auntie Carmen, this is Mark."

Her eyebrows rise. "Are you together now?"

"We are."

"But at Hannah's wedding . . ."

"I came to realize that my mother does know best. Some of the time."

Carmen chuckles before holding out her hand. "It's nice to meet you, Mark."

As soon as I shake her hand, I feel a tap on my leg. I turn around and see the birthday boy, crawling on the grass. He looks up at me with a goobery grin.

Meghan hurries toward us and picks him up. "He's getting so fast."

"Have you gone back to work, after your mat leave?" Carmen asks.

"Yes." Meghan sighs. "It's hard to be away from him all day and hard to get back into the swing of work, but I'll adjust. Eventually."

"Can I hold him?" Emily asks as she hands me her glass.

Meghan passes him over.

"Look at you in your little hat!" Emily says. "Very handsome."

"Mamamamama."

"Yes, Mama's right there. Let me turn you so you can see her, okay?"

I rather like the sight of Emily holding a baby. I'm not sure if she wants kids herself, though. I suppose I should ask her—assuming she isn't on the road to breaking up with me. The recent awkwardness has me worried, but she allowed me to keep my arm around her earlier, which I take as a good sign.

I'd like to have kids, but if she doesn't want them . . . I'd be okay with that.

I want her, however I can have her, and the thought that I don't exactly know where I stand right now . . . it causes a heaviness in my chest.

Which is immediately followed by someone hitting my hand.

I look down to see Khloe, who's holding a tiny stick. She giggles.

"No hitting," Allison says, from a few feet away.

Khloe giggles again. "Let's play horsey, Mark! You said we could do it another time, and it's another time."

Crap. She actually remembered that.

"A different day," I say, hoping she'll accept this. I don't want her to cry again.

To my surprise, she's not upset.

"Do you want to find sticks with me?" she asks.

"Sure," I say.

"Maybe we'll find a worm. Or a snake." Khloe doesn't seem alarmed by this possibility. Thankfully the only snakes I've ever seen around here are garter snakes.

We go to the path of interlocking bricks at the side of the house. There's a decent-sized tree up front, and there are a few small sticks here, which is enough to satisfy Khloe. I hand her all the sticks I find, and she puts them in a pile.

"We're getting lots of sticks so we can build a house," she says.

"Like the second little pig?"

Khloe doesn't answer. She's focused on looking for sticks. Just as I'm about to pick up another one, I hear a voice.

"I can't believe her, and I can't believe Mom's falling for it. Emily's still lying about her relationship? Seriously?"

I freeze, then slowly look up. Allison and her husband, Duncan, are speaking by the corner of the house. They don't see me.

"What's wrong with her?" Allison asks. "Does she think she's living in one of her books? Why can't she grow up?"

Duncan murmurs something, but I can't hear it.

"Why aren't you looking?" Khloe demands. "We need lots of sticks."

"Sorry, sorry." I say.

"Look at this one! Isn't it a weird stick?"

"I think that's a piece of plastic. You can put it back."

Of course, that just makes her more interested in it, but my attention is diverted once again by Emily's sister.

"Honestly," Allison continues, "why does she think we'll all believe that she's dating Mark? He's sensible and not her type at all, as she's made abundantly clear."

There's a sound behind me. I turn my head. It's one of Emily's parents' friends, walking up the brick path. Janie, if I remember correctly. Her hand is covering her mouth and her eyes are wide.

I'm pretty sure she heard every word.

33

— ♡ —

Emily

*"It is a truth universally acknowledged that if you
fake a relationship, the person you most want to fool
will find out the truth eventually."*

—Me, with reluctance

There's a shriek from the side of the house, and the birthday
boy starts crying.

"That must be Auntie Janie," Meghan says.

"I wonder what happened this time," I say.

Auntie Janie tends to have dramatic reactions. It is entirely
possibly that she chipped a nail or saw a mosquito.

Meghan reaches for Timmy. "It's okay. Mama's here."

Auntie Janie appears from the side of the house, and as soon
as she opens her mouth, I somehow know she didn't chip a nail.
No, she heard the truth. I'm not sure where from, but I can feel
it in my bones. And since it's Auntie Janie, she'll announce it to
everyone, and there's nothing I can do to stop it.

Auntie Sharon, on the other hand, would never embarrass us
like that. She might tell my parents privately, but not in public;
she wouldn't want us to lose face.

Well, this is rotten luck.

"They're not really together!" Janie points at me, and it seems so childish.

"What are you talking about?" Mom walks over to her. "Who's not together?"

"Mark and Emily."

"Why would you say that? Aiyah! Don't be silly."

"It's true." Allison approaches Mom.

"No, it's not," I say instinctively. "Mark and I are in a relationship."

Which isn't a lie, but . . .

"You told me it was a ruse," Allison said. "Are you going to deny you said that?"

I want to, but I don't think that will work. My older sister won't let this go.

"It was a ruse at the beginning," I admit, "but not anymore. Like I told you at the beach."

Allison rolls her eyes. "Be serious for once. Grow up."

"Did you tell Auntie Janie just because you were pissed that I wouldn't babysit for you? You're the one who needs to grow up. Not me."

"I didn't tell anyone except Duncan."

Timmy lets out a high-pitched wail.

Yeah, I understand, Timmy. I want to do that too.

This is a goddamn nightmare.

Mark comes over and puts a hand on my shoulder, and I flinch. I don't know why—I like when he touches me, and I usually find it comforting—but right now it's more than I can bear.

"You see?" Allison says.

I feel like we're kids again.

Indeed, our mother goes into Mom Mode, grabbing our hands and marching us into the house before I know what's happening.

Inside the back door, we both instinctively slip off our sandals. Dad is in the kitchen, taking out the most elaborate birthday cake I've ever seen, far fancier than anything I could have done even if I'd taken weeks of cake-decorating classes.

Allison and I share a look. We both know that twenty years ago, Mom and Dad would have considered this excessive.

Then we remember that we don't like each other and look in opposite directions.

"What happened?" Dad asks, turning his attention away from the cake.

"Apparently, Emily's relationship with Mark isn't real," Mom says. "I don't understand."

"It's real," I protest. "Now."

"She told me it wasn't," Allison says.

Mom gives me her scariest look, one I haven't seen in years because she deploys it sparingly. She could make entire armies crumble; I don't stand a chance.

"I didn't want to date Mark," I tell her. "I met him at Hannah's wedding and didn't like him, and then you tricked us into a date at Lily's Kitchen." I sigh. "I was just so tired. Of how you think I'm a failure because I don't have a proper profession and I'm not married."

"Aiyah!" Mom says. "I don't think you're a failure. I brag about you all the time."

"You won't say how you really feel in front of your friends. And you kept going on and on about Mark. You were clearly desperate to see me in a serious relationship. I don't understand why—it's the twenty-first century! I don't need a man, and you've already got four married daughters and three grandkids. But you wouldn't quit, so I suggested that we pretend to date to get you off my back. We weren't going on real dates at first, just saying we did, but then your acquaintances kept popping up around Toronto and we had to make our story look real."

Saying it out loud makes it sound even more ridiculous.

I want the earth to swallow me up. I don't think I can survive this humiliation. How will I face my family again after today?

I seriously consider moving far, far away—even farther than Newfoundland. I doubt I can convince Paige to come with me, so I'll get a cat or two for company.

"Emily?" Mom prompts. "What happened after that?"

I sigh again and continue with my pathetic confession. "I don't know exactly how it happened, but as I got to know Mark, I discovered he wasn't quite who I thought, and I started to fall for him for real."

Allison snorts, and Mom levels her with a sharp gaze.

"I'm not lying," I say. "That's what happened." I hold up my hands.

"See, I knew he was perfect for you," Mom says.

"That's your takeaway from this?" Allison puts her hands on her hips. "I'm still not sure I believe her. After all, she makes up stories for a living."

"Thanks for acknowledging it's a real job," I mutter.

"I'm so confused right now," Dad says. "Are you actually dating Mark, Emily?"

"Yes." I turn to Allison. "You think Mark would be here today if it were still fake? You think he would have come on a four-day vacation with us?"

"I don't know what you offered him so he'd go along with this."

She's trying to get a reaction out of me, but I won't give her what she wants. Instead, I stare her down, trying my best to channel my mother.

Then, to my surprise, Allison bursts into tears.

Despite all the things she's said to me, I feel guilty. I never intended to make my sister—whom I haven't seen cry since she was fifteen and rewatching our VHS of *Titanic*—start sobbing. Something inside me clenches painfully, and I remember how I felt when she had the flu and needed to go to the hospital.

I reach out to touch her, but she slaps me away.

The back door opens. Meghan enters, Timmy in her arms, and May follows.

"What's happening?" Meghan asks. "Allison?"

Allison rejected my hug, but she allows Meghan to hold her. Timmy, however, starts screaming.

I feel like I've ruined my family with my shenanigans.

"He's probably anxious for his cake," Mom says.

I somehow doubt that's the case, but I stay quiet.

She turns to Meghan. "We'll bring out the cake once you're ready, okay?"

Meghan nods.

"And, Emily, we'll speak later, yes?" Mom says to me. "Tell Mark to leave when the party's over. I can drive you home myself."

"Okay," I reply automatically, feeling like I can't say no.

I want to say something to Allison, but I have no idea what. So instead, I go back outside.

"What's going on?" Hannah asks me in a hushed voice.

I tell her the truth, since she'll find out soon anyway, and it hurts more than my other sisters knowing. I can't help recalling when Hannah was a little girl who looked up to me as I made up stories with Trunkit the Elephant.

I can't imagine she looks up to me now.

For the rest of the party, we pretend nothing happened, like we're one big happy family. At one point, I see Auntie Janie exchanging heated whispers with Mom, but then she shuts up.

Meghan helps Timmy blow out a single candle on a cupcake. Then they, along with Meghan's husband, open the presents as the rest of us eat chocolate cake.

I put a bite in my mouth and force myself to chew. I usually love chocolate cake, and I can tell this is a good-quality one, but everything tastes like ash in my mouth. Trying to swallow a tiny bite feels like swallowing a too-large multivitamin.

Mark approaches me. "You okay?"

"I told them what happened . . . Allison cried . . . I don't know."

I look up and see Cilla watching us.

Yep, this just got worse. His parents arrived when I wasn't paying attention, and there's no way they haven't heard about our lie.

I knew it was a mistake to date my parents' friends' son. What must they think of me?

Mark reaches out to touch me, then pulls back, as if thinking better of it. He's right; I wouldn't have reacted well to his touch right now—I might have flinched again—but seeing him pull away breaks something inside me.

I really have come to care for him, despite my initial impressions. Despite my doubts. Sometimes people start relationships all starry-eyed, and they can't see anything that isn't good, but I don't have that problem here.

His brows draw together. "What do you want to do?"

"I want everyone to stop looking at me."

"We can leave—"

"No. I have to stay. My mom insisted I speak to her afterward."

He's still being nice, and I can't stand it. Why can't he act like the judgmental bastard I thought he was? That's what I deserve right now. I shouldn't have involved him in this scheme. I should have been firmer with my mother about my boundaries rather than pretending to be in a relationship.

Except then I never would have gotten to know Mark.

Maybe that would have been for the best, though. I don't know how I can continue after this embarrassment. Everyone in the city will know about this.

Okay, that's a slight exaggeration, but not as much of an exaggeration as it should be. Auntie Janie and Mom do, after all, know an awful lot of people between them.

I wish I didn't care about what others think, but I've never completely mastered that skill. I've made choices despite those feelings, yet I haven't avoided being a little uneasy with my decisions.

"What's happening with us?" Mark asks quietly, carefully.

"I don't know," I say. "I don't know! I can't think about that right now."

His face shutters. It's not a huge change from his usual expression, but I've become so attuned to him in the past several weeks. Even if this wouldn't look like a big difference to most people, I can tell. He's upset, but he doesn't want people to know; when he was young, he was taught that it wasn't safe to show people his feelings, more than I ever was—I felt, for the most part, free to express myself. And if I'd been bullied, my parents would have done everything they could to fix the situation.

My emotions are already a mess, but something further twists in my chest. I want to reach out to him and pull him into my arms. I want to fix whatever is hurting him.

Except that's me, and I *can't* be everything he deserves. I'm the one who caused this fucked-up situation, like something out of a drama.

"I'll talk to you later," I say.

I don't see him leave, but when I glance around the yard five minutes later, he's gone, as are his parents.

"What's wrong?" Scarlett asks. She has a little chocolate buttercream smeared under her mouth. I get a napkin to wipe it off, and I don't say that I'm tired of people asking me questions.

"Nothing's—"

"What's wrong with *you*?"

"Uh . . ."

"Everyone's looking at you weird."

Gee, kid, thanks for confirming it's not all in my imagination.

Allison was right: it did come back to bite me in the ass.

"When are you getting married?" Scarlett asks. "Don't forget I want to be a flower girl."

"When I start planning my wedding, you'll be one of the first to know, don't worry." I plaster on a smile, and I keep it in place as more people start filing out. I'm sure it looks more than a little fake, but whatever.

It's all I have.

Just a few more people left to leave, and then I'll have to face my mother.

34

—♡—

Mark

What should we do now, Ms. Muffins?"

Ms. Muffins regards me with disdain from her perch on the cat tree. The very fine cat tree that I lovingly purchased for her, even though it was more than I meant to spend.

But does she care about that? No.

I take out her favorite toy, but she's not interested in coming down. Hmph.

I feel pathetic, desperate for the attention of a cat who barely tolerates me. Desperate for the affection of a woman who . . . I don't know.

I don't like feeling all mixed up.

After taking off my shirt and treating the chocolate buttercream stain—courtesy of Khloe—I sit heavily on the recliner. I think of Emily and the conversation she must be having with her mom now. I hope it's going well, though I'm annoyed with her for wanting to be done with me just because some people found out the truth—including my parents.

My dad's lips are probably still in a thin line, but he's rarely impressed with anything. I do my best not to let it get to me, though I still struggle with it a little.

My mom is most assuredly still laughing at me, but she'll get over this within a day or two, then go back to being glad I'm dating someone.

If I'm still dating someone.

"Fuck it," I mutter. I go to the kitchen, grab my bottle of red wine from the cupboard—the one I bought for cooking purposes—and pour myself a generous glass. I gulp some wine and shut my eyes.

I could have avoided all this. When we spoke at Lily's Kitchen, I could have said, "No, that's a ridiculous plan."

But there was something about her . . .

I shake my head. Drink some more wine.

I feel a bit out of control, which isn't like me. There's this awful pressure in my chest, and I'm craving some kind of release . . . but I don't know what, and I hate not knowing.

I wish I could have Emily here, laughing at my cat's name, admiring my paintings, filling the silence with her conversation.

At the same time, I want to shout at her, ask her why she's letting this get to her.

Come on. Give us a chance.

35

— ♡ —

Emily

*"She ran her finger over the necklace and wondered
how many other secrets her parents had—and how many
of them she would never, ever know."*
—*All Those Little Secrets* by Emily Hung

Mom and I are finally alone in the kitchen. She insisted on making a pot of tea, even though I told her repeatedly that I'm not in the mood for tea.

After pouring us each a cup, she says, "I'm sorry I made you feel the need to fake a relationship."

She's actually saying she's sorry? Without any prompting?

I'm momentarily too stunned to speak, but then my anger roars back.

"I've never been the daughter you wanted," I say. "Even after you stopped pushing so hard about my job—probably not because you stopped being disappointed, but because you figured it was pointless—we never had *one* conversation where you didn't bring up the fact that I was single. There's nothing wrong with being a single woman in her thirties. It's not—"

"Ah, stop it. I know. You don't have to get married. You can be like Carmen, it's fine—"

"Then why did you act like it wasn't?"

My mom scrubs a hand over her face before sipping her tea. The loud clock in the kitchen counts out the seconds of silence; my heartbeat feels like it's just as loud, but I doubt it is.

At last she says, "I was trying to help you."

"Yes, trying to help me conform to—"

"Emily!" Mom speaks sharply, and her tone gives me pause. It's a little different from the way she usually speaks to me. To any of us. "Let me finish, okay?"

I gesture for her to continue.

"I was trying to help you with *your* dreams," she says.

I don't understand.

"You wish to make a living just from writing books, yes?"

I nod.

"When you first told me, as a child, I thought it was a childhood dream. But over the years, I realized you'd never give up on it. I didn't know how to help you because I didn't know anything about publishing. This is—what would you say—outside my wheelhouse?"

I nod again.

"But I figured, I can learn. We're empty nesters—so much free time now! Even when Hannah was living here, she didn't need much from me. So, I started researching. You told me you were querying, and I learned all about querying and literary agents. You told me you were on submission, so I learned about that. I learned all about how the money works. Wah, publishing is such a mess."

She goes on and on, talking about royalties and earning out and lots of other things, and I just sit there with my mouth open. I never told my mother any of this stuff, but she knows.

"After all this research," Mom says, "and reading that it's difficult for most authors to be full-time, no matter how good they are, I came across a female author who said your best bet is to be independently rich—or have a spouse who makes lots of money and has health insurance. And I thought . . . I can't change the industry, but this is something I can do for Emily."

Understanding dawns.

My mouth drops open farther. I stare at my mother in shock. This explains the title of the matchmaking list I found upstairs. Project Pen.

"Ah, stop looking at me in such a silly way," she says, like she didn't just drop a bombshell. "Drink your tea. It's getting cold."

I'm still not in the mood for tea, but I do as she says.

"When did you decide to do this?" I ask, my voice scratchy.

"I don't know. Two years ago, after you got your contract? But I started considering it years before, making new friends just in case."

I frown. "New friends?"

"Friends with appropriate sons."

"So you befriended Mark's parents because they had a single son with a decent job."

"Yes."

My mother is definitely scary.

"I found your list," I say, "when I was fixing the printer. I can't believe it had sixteen names."

"You weren't supposed to see that. But it was just the short list."

"The *short list*?"

"There were originally twenty-three. I wanted to have more, but so many men over twenty-five are already married or in serious relationships."

"I didn't hear about most of these men. Why did you cross them off the list?"

Mom clucks her tongue. "When I got to know them better—through their parents—most of them weren't appropriate."

"Why not?"

"Some didn't make enough money."

"Were you asking everyone their salaries? Seriously?"

She doesn't answer. "Many had personality flaws. Either I could tell from meeting them, or from how their parents spoke about them. Some men are too spoiled and have no idea how to take care of themselves. You'd have to do all the housework and it would leave no time for writing. Not good. Also, I didn't want you to have a really demanding mother-in-law."

I don't know what to say, so I sip my lukewarm tea.

"One man wanted five kids," she says. "I had five kids. I know if you did that, you wouldn't have time to write, so I crossed him off the list."

"What other flaws did they have?"

"One had a very fragile ego, I could tell. He wouldn't be able to handle having a wife who is a bestselling author."

"I'm not a bestselling—"

"Yet. But once you are, you'd spend far too much time stroking his ego." For some reason, my mom emphasizes this by making petting motions, and I can't help thinking of Ms. Muffins. "Another one worked too much. Not a bad man, but you'd never see him, and you'd probably have to do too many chores."

I'm still simultaneously horrified and in awe of my mother. She put in so much effort to find the right man for *me*. Clearly, this was done with me in mind; she didn't simply pick the guy who'd make the best son-in-law for her, and for that, I'm grateful.

"There were four names left on the list," I say. "What happened to the other guys?"

"One wants to move to Vancouver, so I wasn't as keen on him. Selfish, but I didn't want you to move to the other side of the country. Of the other three, I don't know. I just thought Mark was the best fit, and he speaks Cantonese. Plus, I like his mom."

"What about his dad?"

"Meh. He's okay." Mom makes a dismissive gesture, then sips her tea. "So, I sneakily mentioned Mark in conversations."

"Sneakily? You couldn't shut up about him."

"Maybe I went a bit overboard, and that's why you were fake-dating. But I was right, wasn't I?" She beams. "I have excellent matchmaking skills. He's very nice, yes? Decent job, good manners. He's not the richest one, but his parents are well-off, so they helped him buy a place. I know you want to own a house one day—I hope that isn't just because you're trying to make us proud."

"No. I think it would be nice to own a little house. Have a home office."

"But the market is so bad, I know." She sighs. "I thought Mark would be supportive and respect your work, and possibly in a few years, you can stop working at that coffee shop. I don't want you to wear yourself down and burn out. You'll still be making money from your writing, but if you can't sell a book for a few years, it will be better if you have a partner like him. You'll have the security and time to write more, try new things." She pauses, and a sly look appears on her face. "Based on how many hours you two spent alone in the cabin on our trip—"

"Mom! No. Don't you *dare*."

She just laughs. "What else could I do? Back when you were querying, I thought that I could call up literary agents for you, but apparently that isn't the sort of thing you're supposed to do."

"It isn't." I picture my mother doing it anyway and cringe.

"I also went to lots of bookstores and checked that they had your book. Emphasized that you're a local author and suggested they put a special sticker on your book."

"Oh," I say faintly. Julia mentioned her mother doing things like that at bookstores, but I hadn't imagined mine would, even after she mentioned looking for my book at the library. It's embarrassing, but in a nice way.

"And I figured, if it's part of a book club, more people will buy it; fifteen copies is fifteen copies." She briefly lays a hand on my shoulder. "This wasn't my choice for your career because of the lack of stability, but since you're so intent on it, I'm trying to support you." She frowns. "Instead, you felt like I didn't see you and thought you were a failure. This isn't true. At all."

"Thank you." My voice is hoarse. This conversation has tilted my world on its axis.

"I was so disappointed when you two didn't hit it off at the wedding, but I didn't want to give up. I'd dedicated so much time to this plan. I thought if you gave it one more chance, just the two of you, it would be different. So then I made you think you were meeting me for brunch instead of him."

At which point I became so annoyed with her antics that I suggested the fake relationship.

I rub my temples. After everything that happened today, I have a headache, but I'm also glad that she's my mother.

"There were a few times," she says, "when I was a little suspicious that something was up, but I told myself I was being ridiculous. Maybe I believed what I wanted to be true, so it was easy for you to convince me. If Janie hadn't opened her big mouth, I wouldn't have known."

"She overheard Allison, who was suspicious from the start because I'd never shown any interest in Mark, and then all of a sudden, I was dating him."

"Go easy on Allison."

"She always acts like I have nothing going on in my life, so I should do her bidding."

"I know, I know, but she's having problems." Mom pauses. "Problems in her marriage."

Oh. This is news to me.

"You're surprised?" Mom clucks her tongue. "You aren't paying attention."

"Nothing seemed amiss this weekend or last weekend."

"She loves him, but she has so much resentment built up.

They're both working full-time, but who does all the childcare in the evenings and on weekends? Allison. Your father wasn't perfect, but he was better at this than Duncan. I wouldn't have had five kids with him otherwise. So Allison is stretched very thin. Desperate. When I tried to find a man for you, I had to make sure that wouldn't happen. I don't want that for my girls. If I'd known . . ."

Mom makes a weird gesture, and I think she's miming . . . trying to strangle Duncan?

From everything I know about Mark, he wouldn't be like that if we had kids. I think of how he looked after Khloe and Scarlett when they knocked on our cabin door, and a wave of tenderness washes over me. All the reasons Mom chose him for me—she wasn't wrong.

"So, what happened?" Mom asks. "You and Mark didn't speak much after the truth came out. Is it a problem?"

"How can I date him when everyone knows how it started?"

"Aiyah! Why not?"

"It's too humiliating."

Mom waves this way. "You'll get over it. Why would you throw this away for such a silly reason? I thought dating was very tough—that's what everyone tells me. Are they wrong?"

"No."

"You see? That's why you needed my help."

"You could have told me what you were doing."

"I knew you wouldn't agree, so I had to be sneaky."

It makes me smile, the way my mother thinks she's being sneaky when she's really not, but she did a surprisingly good job of covering up her motives. Or maybe I was just clueless. Mark insisted that my mother was prouder of me than I thought, and he wasn't wrong. I wish I'd listened more to his advice about letting go of some of the pressure, much of which was self-inflicted.

Despite the themes in *All Those Little Secrets*, when it came to my own life, I didn't see my mother as a well-rounded, complex character, and I need to fix that. I'm sure there's an awful lot I still don't know. I thought I understood her, but I don't.

Mom stands up. "Do you want more cake?"

"Didn't Meghan take it home?"

"She insisted it was too much, but I said we didn't need any. Then she put some back in the fridge when I wasn't looking."

I chuckle. "Sure. Why not."

Mom starts cutting a piece that's far too big, but I don't protest.

"I think you should fix things with Mark," she says. "I could see the way he looked at you today. I'm sure it will be no problem to kiss and make up."

It's instinctive to say she's wrong, but I guess I should stop doing that.

She sets a generous plate of cake in front of me and sits down again.

"You're not having any?" I ask.

"I'm full. I'll have it tomorrow. But I could tell you weren't enjoying the cake earlier, so you should have it now." She pauses. "Next time, I'll tell you about my plans—I don't want you to get the wrong impression again—but hopefully you won't need more matchmaking help."

Though I'm a bit overwhelmed with everything, I'm grateful for my mother's support, even if it's not in the most straightforward way.

"I'm sorry I wasn't a doctor," I say.

She waves this off. "No need to apologize. Many mothers brag about their kids being doctors, but I don't know anyone else with a daughter who has a book in bookstores. I did hope to find a doctor for you to date, though."

"How many of the men on the short list are doctors?"

"Four, but they were all unsuitable."

More proof that my mother really was thinking of me, not herself, when trying to find an appropriate boyfriend for me. The chocolate cake feels thick in my mouth and hard to swallow, but for different reasons from earlier.

"When you told me you wanted to be a writer, all those years ago," she says, "I should have known writing wasn't just a childhood dream. It runs in my family, after all."

I freeze, my fork halfway to my mouth. "What are you talking about?"

"Ah, your gung gung, he would make up stories for me before bed. He always talked about writing a book, and he started one, but it was only half-finished when he died." My mom says this casually, as though it's not a big deal, as though it's something I might have heard before. But I'm sure she knows she never told me. "That's part of the reason I had complicated feelings about . . . everything."

I let go of my fork. It clatters onto my plate as I sit there, slack-jawed. I didn't expect to learn any more secrets today, but the grandfather I never met—he died in Hong Kong when I was a baby—was a writer too? Why didn't she tell me until now?

And then she drops another bombshell.

"I have it. The unfinished book. You can read it, if you like— if you remember enough from Chinese school. He also wrote stories for you and Allison. I was supposed to read them to you, since he wasn't in Canada to tell you stories himself. But by the time yours came in the mail . . . it was a few days before he passed, and I only read it to you once." She looks away, and there are tears in her eyes.

"Mom . . ." I put my hand on top of hers, and I don't ask why she never told me any of this until now.

"I think he would have been very impressed that your book is in stores. I wish you two could have met. That's part of the reason I decided I had to make this work for you—it was also for him." She pulls me into a hug that's much tighter than the ones she normally gives. "I'm sorry I made you feel that I hated all your choices. I wanted you to have stability and security, but I know that's hard these days, and it isn't your fault. And I'll get his book—and the story for you—from the attic. But not today."

"Okay," I whisper.

She pulls back. "You want to go?" She sounds like her usual self now, and it's disorienting, after everything she told me. "Should I drive you to Mark's place, or to your apartment?"

I hesitate. "My apartment."

Mom doesn't send cake home with me, but she packs up a small bag of fruit and other things and puts it in the trunk. She still shops like she has multiple kids under her roof, so there's always extra food.

We don't say much in the car; I feel like I've done all the talking I can for the day, and I couldn't deal with any more revelations. I also feel a bit too fragile to see Mark—I'll give it a few days—but as I watch dusk settle over the city, my mind keeps turning back to him.

What if I'd met him in a way that had nothing to do with my mother? Would I have been interested in him? Or would I still have brushed him off as not being my type?

It's hard to wrap my mind around the fact that my mother picked out an appropriate guy for me. That wasn't something I ever expected.

When the car pulls up to my apartment building, I give my mom another hug, then trudge upstairs, looking forward to putting on pajamas and watching TV.

But to my surprise, my apartment is a rather busy place.

36

— ♡ —

Emily

"If I'd known exactly what the publishing industry was like before I started on this journey, I'm not sure I would have tried to become an author. So maybe it's best that I was ignorant because for the most part, I'm happy with where I am today, and there's no better feeling than typing 'The End.'"

—H. A. Kim

Paige is here, of course, because she's my roommate. But I wasn't expecting to see both Andrew and Ashley on a Sunday evening, although Paige and Andrew have been spending a fair bit of time together lately.

I put the food from my mother away, then sit down on the couch next to Ashley. Like me, she looks like she's gone through a roller coaster of emotions today.

"What happened?" I ask. "You okay?"

"I broke down last night because Frank rearranged one of the cupboards. It was just a small thing, but I went to get some crackers, from the place where I always keep them, and grabbed a box of pasta instead. It was the last straw. I told him I needed some space."

"Because he switched the cracker and pasta boxes?" I ask, puzzled.

"I don't know why, but it set me off. I went to my sister's for the night and came here because I'm too embarrassed to go back. He's such a sweetheart, but I'm struggling. Is it unresolved issues from my parents' divorce? Should I start therapy?" She begins to cry, which isn't like her. "I don't want to lose him, but I haven't been feeling like myself these past few weeks. I can barely keep food down."

Paige and I look at each other, and I'm pretty sure we're thinking the same thing.

I go to the washroom and grab a pregnancy test. A while back, we bought a bunch at a discount, just in case. I bring it to Ashley, who shakes her head.

"I couldn't be . . . well, maybe . . ."

"Do you want to do it now?" I ask.

"I can leave, if you want," Andrew offers.

There's a knock on the door, and we immediately stop talking.

"It's Frank," Ashley says. "I know it's him."

"Do you want me to answer it?" I ask.

She nods.

I go to the door, where I greet a large white man with a concerned expression on his face.

"Is she here?" he asks softly, worrying his baseball cap in his hands.

"Yeah, come in." I open the door wider.

As soon as he steps in, Ashley runs to him, tears streaming down her face, and I can tell that Frank is as thrown by her tears as I was. Then she whispers to him, and his eyes widen.

"I'm going to head out," Andrew says.

"No, no." Ashley gestures for him to sit back down. "Don't leave because of me."

"Are you sure? I could step out to get some food."

"If someone else wants something, but I don't think I . . ." Ashley hurries to the washroom and slams the door.

I think we all have pretty strong suspicions about that pregnancy test, but nobody says anything; the four of us in the living room remain quiet.

"Don't listen to me pee!" Ashley shouts from the washroom.

I pull out my phone, scroll to my favorite donkey account, and watch the latest video at a loud volume. Soon the apartment is filled with *hee-haws*.

"I think music would be better," Paige says.

She has a point. I start playing a Green Day album.

"Oh my God," Andrew says, "you guys are so old."

Ashley exits the washroom. "Now we have to wait three minutes." She goes to Frank and nestles against him as I set the timer on my phone.

It's not my pregnancy test, but Ashley is one of my closest friends, and I'm nervous. I want it to be . . . whatever she wants.

"Why did you get home so late from the party?" Paige asks me. "What happened?"

Right. With all the commotion, I haven't had a chance to talk about it yet. "Everyone found out about the fake-dating thing, it was chaos, and I was so embarrassed. Then my mom revealed that she picked Mark out for me because she thought having a good partner was my best bet for being a full-time writer—he has a steady job and would be supportive."

"Wait. She wanted you to go out with him for your writing career?"

"Yes, and she did, admittedly, pick a great guy. But I kinda freaked out on him, now that everyone knows the truth and . . . yeah, I still have to figure that out."

"Did this fake-dating thing start before or after we went out?" Andrew asked.

"Before, but Mark and I weren't going on dates then, just saying we were. Then we went on real fake dates for a while before we started actually dating."

"I'm so confused right now."

I'm not in the mood to explain further, and I'm saved from any questions by the beep of my phone.

"Three minutes," I say.

Ashley doesn't move.

"Do you want someone else to check for you?" Paige asks.

Ashley turns to Frank, who heads to the washroom and looks at the test. I think, under that bushy beard, he's smiling, but it's hard to tell. He comes out and whispers something to Ashley. She bursts into tears again, and he holds her close.

"Are you pregnant?" I ask.

"Yes," she says between sobs.

"Are you happy about it?"

"I think so? It's earlier than we planned, but . . ." She burrows against Frank. "I love you so much. I'm sorry about everything. It's taken me more time than I thought it would to adjust to living with someone—and soon there will be *another* person."

"We'll get a bigger place," Frank says. "I know the market is terrible, but I'll make it happen, don't you worry about anything."

I feel close to crying too. Today has been . . . a lot.

We all gather in a circle around Ashley and hug, and I feel overwhelmed with gratitude that I have so many wonderful people in my life.

And that includes Mark.

Before going to bed, I read over our text messages. I feel guilty that I still haven't said anything to him, but I can't think of the right words. What do you say to someone after your fake relationship is exposed?

Hopefully, I'll figure it out tomorrow.

On Tuesday, I come home from work utterly spent. Some days, I can write after a shift, but this isn't one of them. There were three separate crises today at Coffee on College, and I just want to veg out in front of the TV. I considered stopping for gelato on the way home, but given the quantity of chocolate cake I consumed on Sunday, I figured it was best if I didn't. Also, I need to watch my spending, and gelato isn't a necessary expense.

After I flop onto the couch and lie motionless for a few minutes, my phone buzzes. It's a text from Allison.

Are you free? Can I come over right now?

My older sister is actually asking if I'm free, rather than assuming that whatever I'm doing isn't important.

ME: Sure
ALLISON: Thanks. Be there in half an hour.

With Allison's impending arrival, I'm unable to focus on what I should do about Mark, so I waste time on social media. Paige isn't here; she's at the gym.

When my sister arrives, her hair is a mess and her makeup is a little worse for wear.

"Hey." Somehow in that single syllable, she sounds tired.

"Hi," I say. "What's up?"

She doesn't immediately answer but goes to sit at the dining room table. I sit across from her.

"Sometimes I felt like I had to make up for you," she admits.

I stiffen. "I never asked you to do that. No one did. I—"

"I know, I know, that was on me, but I still resented you at times—and not only because we had to share a bedroom." She sighs. "Now I'm jealous of you."

"You're *what?*" It's hard to believe these words are coming out of Allison's mouth.

"You don't have a whole house to clean," she says. "One kid who thinks bedtime is the cruelest invention ever made, and another who screamed because her apple wasn't round enough.

A husband who only changed, like, twelve diapers ever—which was even worse because Khloe was born during the pandemic and Mom couldn't be there. I'm just *exhausted*, and I know it doesn't excuse everything, but I'm jealous of how you do whatever you want."

"Uh, I still need to make money—"

"But it feels like you have fewer demands on your time, despite your multiple jobs, and you march to . . ." She trails off. "I don't know. I can't think of the phrase. By this time of day, my brain doesn't function anymore."

"March to the beat of my own drum?"

"Yeah. You don't care what other people think."

I chuckle. "I do care. But I don't let it stop me . . . most of the time."

"I love my girls, don't get me wrong, but . . ."

She turns toward the window and looks utterly vacant. I'm not used to seeing her vulnerable. Once again, I recall that bout of the flu, more than twenty years ago now.

I move my chair next to Allison's and put my arms around her.

"I can help you more," I say, "but I can't rearrange my schedule at the last minute and—"

"I know, I know. It's just that sometimes, the thought of having to figure out one more thing is too much for me. I look forward to driving to work, even though traffic sucks. It's often the highlight of my day."

"We need to find you someone in your neighborhood who can babysit on short notice occasionally. I'll see what I can do, okay?"

She nods.

"What's happening with Duncan?" I ask carefully.

She just shakes her head, and I continue to hold her. Eventually, she pats my hand, still looking rather vacant.

My chest squeezes. I don't like seeing my capable older sister like this.

"I'll come over on Thursday," I say, "late in the afternoon. How about that? I'll look after the kids while you get things done. An extra set of hands."

"Thank you. I appreciate it." She manages a watery smile. "I'm sorry I talked about Mark at the party."

"It's okay. You weren't the one who told everyone. That was Auntie Janie."

"Yes. Well. I did consider telling Mom and Dad. I was annoyed that you got to do fun things like fake a relationship while I cleaned vomit out of three pairs of shoes because somebody didn't make it to the toilet in time. Childish of me, I know." She pauses. "What happened with Mark? What did Mom say after we all left?"

I tell her what our mother revealed.

"What? No!" Allison covers her mouth. "She really had a list of men?"

"Yeah, and she'd crossed out *doctors* because she thought they weren't right for me."

We laugh together, and for a minute, it feels like we're kids, rather than adults with the weight of the world pressing down on us. Sure, Allison and I were at each other's throats often when we were growing up, but we still had our moments.

"I haven't read your book," she says. "I've been meaning to, but I don't have the time."

"You don't need to read it to be supportive, I promise. If you bought the book and put it on your shelf, I'll get, like, a buck or two." Well, it'll count against my advance, but I don't think Allison has done as much research on publishing as Mom.

I tell her about our grandfather, and from her expression, it's clear that she didn't know any of this either. I mention that there's a story just for her too, and she says she'll read it to her girls. Gung Gung may have been gone for more than thirty years, but his words . . . they're still here, and that feels miraculous.

"You know," she says, "when he died, Mom hadn't seen him in five years. Not since they'd come to Canada, because it was too difficult to visit—to get time off work, pay for the flights, and travel with babies. I can't imagine not seeing Mom and Dad for so long."

Instinctively, I feel a familiar guilt. Our parents made sacrifices for us, and I didn't do . . .

I shut those thoughts down. I'm okay as I am.

After my sister leaves, I lock the door, then go back to lying on the couch. I make no attempts to be productive by researching murder or generational trauma.

Nope, I just lie here. Sometimes that's all you can do in life, and if I lie here long enough, maybe I'll figure out what to say to Mark.

Wednesday morning, I'm working on updating my website— I need to add the preorder links for my next book—when I receive an email from my agent.

With trepidation, I open it up . . . and grin.

She loves my proposal!

I start to text Mark, then stop, my smile falling. I want to tell him about my good news, but I still haven't resolved everything with him.

It's suddenly clear to me that I desperately want us to be together, despite this complicated situation. I hope he still agrees.

I'll go to him later, but for now I call my mother.

I know she'll be happy for me.

37

—♡—

Mark

Wednesday after work, I'm doing my best to read, but it's a struggle to focus. Although I'm usually pretty good at concentrating, the last few days of work have been excruciating because my mind keeps turning back to Emily.

Half an hour ago, she sent me a text, asking if she could visit. I figured I'd read while I waited for her, but I can't do it.

I think the fact that she's coming to see me is a good thing. I suspect she wants to continue our relationship, even though everyone knows the truth about how it started.

But I'm only 98 percent sure, and that small uncertainty is getting to me. My hands are shaking and my heart is pounding in my chest.

I stand up to organize my kitchen again, even though it doesn't need it, and Ms. Muffins gives me a judgmental look before retreating to her cat tree.

I haven't been sleeping well these past few nights. It's like my brain has gone into overdrive, and I keep replaying things again and again. Obsessing about little details, like the exact pink of Emily's cheeks when she blushes.

My phone rings, but it's not her. It's a video call from my sister.

"Hey," I say. "I can't talk for long."

"Is Meg demanding attention?" Cassie asks.

I mock glare at the phone. "You know she doesn't like being called that."

The last time Cassie visited, she jokingly called Ms. Margaret Muffins "Meg," and Ms. Muffins was even crankier than usual all night. She did not appreciate the diminutive form of her name — or possibly it was just my imagination, though I won't admit that to Cassie.

"But the reason I can't talk," I say, "is because Emily will be here any minute." The last time I spoke with my sister, I told her what happened at the party.

"Oh! I won't keep you. I'm sure she's going to make everything right. Maybe I'll come to Toronto next month so I can meet her."

Before I can tell Cassie about my uncertainties, she ends the call.

A moment later, my phone rings again. This time it's Emily, asking me to buzz her in.

As I wait for her to arrive, my heart pounds faster, and my body feels slightly out of control. I'm usually much more composed, but there's something about this woman . . .

I can't hold myself back from opening the door before I've even heard a knock.

She's hurrying down the hallway. Breathless and flushed and incredibly pretty, in a simple outfit of jeans and a sleeveless pink top.

"I'm so sorry," she says as she rushes into my place. "I'm so sorry I ever doubted our relationship, just because a few people discovered the truth."

"It was more than a few people," I say dryly.

"Yes, yes, basically everyone in my life knows what happened, but I've dealt with lots of awkward questions from my mom over the years, and I can deal with this. You're worth it, and I'm sorry I ever made you feel otherwise. I'm sorry I made so many assumptions about you the first time we met. I'm glad I got to know you better, got to know the real you. Had we not agreed to that fake relationship, I wouldn't have known what I was missing. Which is . . . a lot." She pauses. "I love you and I want to be with you for real. If you can forgive me for ever doubting . . ."

"Yes," I say. "Of course I can."

She smiles at me, and that smile is indescribably beautiful and bright. "I was starting to pull away—I knew you could tell—because I didn't know how we could stay together when the fear of people finding out loomed over my head. But then the worst happened, and I'm still here. If a few people laugh at me, so what? Like I said, you're worth it."

"So are you."

"You'll never believe . . ." She recounts what her mother told her on Sunday after I left. "You said she was proud of my career, and you were right. And she was right about you. And—"

I dip my head and kiss her, unable to hold back any longer. Unlike the first time we kissed, I know exactly where I stand with her, and I know she's not going to run away afterward. I pull her close but step back when I realize that she's not touching me, other than with her lips. It looks like she's trying not to crush a folded piece of paper.

She opens it up and hands it to me.

I read it. "A cake-decorating class?"

"The date we lied about," she says. "We can do it for real. I know I once said that I couldn't imagine you taking a cake-decorating class, but now I imagine you'd be quite good at it."

"Thank you. I look forward to it—and all the other dates in our future."

I start to pull her toward me again, but her phone rings.

She rolls her eyes. "It's my mom. If I don't answer, she might keep calling until I do, but I'll keep it quick." She steps away from me and picks up. "Hi, Mom . . . No, it's not May, it's Emily. You got the wrong daughter again . . . Yes . . . No, you gave me tons of fruit, of course I haven't eaten it all yet . . . Yep, I talked to Allison . . . That's good . . . I gotta go, I'm at Mark's . . . Yes . . . No, you don't need to talk to him right now. We're busy . . . Mom!"

I can't help chuckling.

Finally, Emily tucks her phone back into her purse and wraps her arms around me. I pick her up and carry her into the living room. I settle on the couch with her in my lap, and I slip my hands under the hem of her shirt.

"Before I forget," I say, "what happened with your book proposal? Has your agent gotten back to you yet?"

"She loved it!"

"That's amazing."

"It is, but when I got the email this morning, I couldn't fully enjoy it because I didn't know what was happening with you—and that was the most important thing of all."

"Well, we can celebrate now."

"Yes, we can."

I kiss her again and set about doing just that.

The next day, we go to a place that serves cherry pie milkshakes.

Yes, that's actually a thing. The milkshake literally has a slice of pie on top—and fortunately, Ms. Muffins isn't here to step on it.

Emily explains that she first learned of these milkshakes a few months ago, when she was out with Paige. While I'm not as stuck-up as Emily initially imagined, I'm still appalled by the existence of such an excessive dessert, and she's amused by my reaction. But she insists we get it as further "celebration"—she says it's the perfect treat to share, since it's too big for one person—and afterward, she posts a picture on social media.

When she's sleeping in my arms later, I decide I'll make a

painting based on that photo. I'll frame it and give it to her once I'm done. A gift to commemorate a new phase in our relationship, one in which the truth isn't a secret.

Our lives might get a little messy at times, but I'll be here for her. Always.

Epilogue

—♡—

Emily

"Poisoning someone is harder than I expected."
—*Twenty-Three Lies* by E. H. Shum

I t's a good thing you got married this year," Scarlett says as we're waiting for pictures to commence.

"Why's that?" I ask.

"Next year, I'll be eight, and that's too old to be a flower girl."

"Is that right?"

She nods sagely.

I look up at the photographer, who's reading through the long list of family pictures we want taken.

"Bride and her sisters?" he says.

Allison, Meghan, May, and Hannah—all bridesmaids—follow me into position in the gardens.

There are now five married Hung sisters. At one point, I thought Allison and Duncan would divorce, but Duncan got his act together in the last two years, and after some couples therapy, things are better between them.

The next picture includes the five of us, plus my parents. My mom fusses over me, making tiny adjustments to my hair and bouquet.

"Mom, everything's fine," I say.

She clucks her tongue before smiling for the pictures.

I look over at Ashley, who's trying to prevent her toddler from running into the parking lot. She and Frank got married at city hall while she was six months pregnant.

Paige, my maid of honor, now has a better-paying job, and none of her new colleagues steal her lunch. She's still dating Andrew, and they live together, in an apartment that has in-unit laundry and no leaks in the bathroom. They aren't planning on having kids.

But me and my new husband? We're thinking one or two.

The spouses and kids join us in the next picture, and I smile as Mark comes to stand next to me. I'm almost giddy at the sight of him, so handsome in his tux.

"The first time we met, it was at a wedding," I murmur.

"Yes, and I bet you never envisioned this happening, did you?"

"No, I didn't like you one bit." We can laugh about it now. "But I'm glad that changed."

"Me too."

I moved in with him five months ago. It was a bit of an adjustment, even though we already spent a lot of nights together. I'm still working at Coffee on College, but only two shifts a week, and I'm not tutoring anymore. I have four published books and another coming next year. We did end up selling the film rights for my second book, but unfortunately, nothing ever came of that— though at least I got paid a little. The domestic thriller, published under a pseudonym—and dedicated to my grandfather, whose unfinished manuscript is a mystery novel, of sorts—did better than my first three books. I'm not a huge bestseller, but I'm happy with my modest success. It's a difficult, frustrating business, and in many ways, I'm very, very lucky. Mark and I hope to buy a house in a couple of years, and he promises that when we do, I'll have the little home office of my dreams.

We take pictures with Mark's family next. His mother and I

get along reasonably well. His father, on the other hand, doesn't seem to be my biggest fan. I try not to let it get to me—after all, given the things he's said to Mark in the past, I consider his judgment quite questionable. He seems to tolerate me, and that's all I can hope for.

And Cassie? She already feels like a sister, and she finds it endlessly entertaining that her appendix is part of the reason that Mark made a bad first impression on me.

After a bunch of pictures of both families together, it's time to take some photos of just me and Mark.

"See you soon." Mom waves as she heads to the parking lot. "Have fun. I hope you get some good inspiration today."

"Inspiration?" I say.

"For your next book."

"Um." Given what my next book will be about, I don't want any real-life inspiration for that, thank you very much.

But I know she's just teasing me, and I'm sure she'll do more of that in her speech tonight. I've told her there's a strict five-minute limit, but I'll let her talk for ten if she wants. I love her, and she's the reason I'm now a bride.

I squeeze Mark's hand. "Time to kiss for the camera?"

"I'm ready when you are." His smile is warm and fond and just for me.

I'm happier on my wedding day than I could have imagined— although I do have a pretty solid imagination, as I think I proved with the wedding scene in *Twenty-Three Lies*—and it's thanks to Mark Chan.

Our love story might have had an unusual beginning, but I don't wish I could rewrite it; it's perfectly ridiculous and beautiful as it is.

Acknowledgments

In many ways, Emily's mom isn't at all like my own mom, but I think every mother character I write is, to some extent, inspired by her. Since Emily's mother is an important part of *Love, Lies, and Cherry Pie*, I thought it would be fitting to dedicate it to my mother. She passed away the year I started writing seriously, over a decade ago now, and writing has been a way of keeping her with me. I wish you were still here, Mom.

While in the latter stages of writing this book, I learned that when my maternal grandfather first came to Canada, he'd also written a novel. This was a surprise to me — and many other people. My grandfather passed away a few years after my mother, and I'd never heard anything about it in his lifetime. I couldn't help but weave a little of that into this story and wonder if my interest in writing is in some small way related to him.

Like Emily, I decided I wanted to be a writer when I was fairly young, and I, too, enjoyed reading stories about writers. This isn't the first book I've written with an author as a character, but it's the first one I've written with an author heroine, and I feel like it has long been inevitable.

Publishing is certainly a journey, and it's good to have company. I'd like to thank the many writing friends I've made over the years, including the Berkletes and Toronto Romance Writers.

To my agent, Courtney Miller-Callihan: Thank you for all the ways you've supported me on this journey and for believing in Emily and Mark's story.

Thank you to Lara Jones, my editor, whose insights have been invaluable. I'm so glad this book found a home with you. Thank you to Hydia Scott-Riley, as well as everyone else at Atria who worked on *Love, Lies, and Cherry Pie*. And thank you to Marcos Chin for the incredible cover!

I'd also like to thank the rest of my family, including my father, who's allowed to read my books if he doesn't talk to me about them (too much). I'm lucky to have an incredibly supportive husband, who's the perfect romance hero for me.

Last but not least, thank you to all my readers, new and old. I'm glad I get to share my stories with you.